MICHELLE DE BRUIN

Promise for Tomorrow

Faith Wins!

Michelle
De Bruin

Scrivenings
PRESS
Quench your thirst for story.
www.ScriveningsPress.com

Published by Scrivenings Press LLC
5 Lucky Lane
Morrilton, Arkansas 72110
https://ScriveningsPress.com

Printed in the United States of America

Paperback ISBN 978-1-64917-058-3

eBook ISBN 978-1-64917-059-0

Library of Congress Control Number: 2020940057

Cover by Diane Turpin, www.dianeturpindesigns.com

(Note: This book was previously published by Mantle Rock Publishing LLC and was re-published when MRP was acquired by Scrivenings Press LLC in 2020.)

All characters are fictional, and any resemblance to real people, either factional or historical, is purely coincidental.

All scripture quoted is from the King James Version of the Bible.

To my parents, Arlin and Donna Van Zante
Everything you do prospers.

Psalm 1:3

CHAPTER ONE

"*Y*ou know I'd do anything to help you." Pete's words rang with the brand of loyalty found in friendships that deepened over time and encouraged through the darkest of days.

A grin spread across Logan De Witt's mouth.

"But I can't. Not this time. Sorry, buddy."

"Wh…what?" Logan stifled a groan. Stuttering again. That irritating stutter had left him alone for months. He sure didn't want it returning now. Not when his fiancée needed a place to stay, and fast. He'd barely survived these three days following his Christmas proposal. Gulping, he tried again. "What do you mean?" Much better. He drew in a slow breath.

A smile burst onto Pete's face. "Anna is expecting a baby. Due in July."

"Wow. Congratulations." Pete's news blew air into Logan and sucked it out of him all at the same time. His friend was going to be a father. How terrific for Pete and Anna. And yet Logan still waited for his turn. It would come someday, someday soon now that Karen had agreed to marry him.

"We're making preparations for our extra room to get remodeled."

Logan glanced through the shadowed doorway of the Silver Grove parsonage's spare bedroom. A ladder filled one corner of the room. "The bed and one chair will need to go back to Anna's mother so we can make space for a cradle." Pete's grin threatened to split his face. He turned serious as he refilled his cup with coffee. "Why do you want Karen to move out of your house?"

He should've known Pete would ask. If he hadn't been so distracted caring for a sick cow this morning, he may have come up with a decent answer. "I...uh...well." If he could just lose that ridiculous stutter once and for all. He cleared his throat. "Boarding the teacher hasn't worked out...uh, like I thought."

The statement might sound a little vague, but at least it was true. Boarding the teacher hadn't gone at all as he expected. Miss Karen Millerson lived at the De Witt farm so his grieving sister could have a friend. But what happened instead? Tillie fought with Karen while Logan fell in love with her. The girls had since made up and were pretty good friends, but Logan's heart hadn't improved one bit. And now he had a mammoth problem on his hands.

If he dared to groan he would. But Pete watched him with a twinkle in his eye and a slight lift to the corners of his mouth.

Logan's whole face heated.

"I see." Pete's amused voice said he saw way more than Logan wanted him to.

Logan shifted in his chair. "Look. You answered my question. Karen can't board with you for the second semester. That's what I came here to find out. I guess...well...I guess Mama and I must find another option." Logan stood and forced a grin. "Thanks for the coffee. Tell Anna I said 'hello' when she returns from her shopping."

Pete nodded and opened his mouth to speak.

Logan left the house before he got the chance. The comments were probably more of Pete's not-so-subtle hints at matchmaking. He'd been shameless in the attempt when Karen first came to town. Logan's consistent resistance mellowed him a bit until Pete quit voicing his thoughts. But they were still on his mind. Logan saw it in his eyes whenever Karen's name came up in conversation.

He didn't need Pete's matchmaking attempts anyway. He'd done just fine on his own falling so hard for a young woman he couldn't regain his footing.

Wouldn't Pete love to know. Logan glanced back at the parsonage. A trail of smoke lifted from the chimney. Anna's white curtains graced the windows. A Christmas wreath hung on the door. What a wonderful place to start a family. Maybe the Oswell City parsonage quietly awaiting his return would see a bedroom remade into a nursery. The pattering of little feet in the hall. Childish laughter filling the rooms.

His chest ached. He didn't dare spill the news of his engagement to Pete. Not before he'd told his own family, and that couldn't happen until Karen moved out. Boy, was he in a mess. One of his own making. This was probably the rightful consequence for him proposing while Karen was still a member of his household. He should've thought that one through a little better. Here he was, Reverend Logan De Witt, pastor of Oswell City Community Church and preacher for Meadow Creek's Sunday afternoon services, trapped by his own attempt to live his life in faith.

At the farm, the setting sun cast glowing rays of golden rose across the pure white snow. Logan banged metal pails around with more agitation than necessary as he did the evening milking. He usually hummed a tune, a hymn from the previous Sunday service, as he worked. But no song of praise resonated in his heart tonight.

The apostle Paul knew what he was talking about when he wrote that there should not be any appearance of immorality among believers. Not even a hint. But Logan's failure to remember the wise counsel would soon plunge the community's school teacher, his sister, and his own dear mother into irreparable scandal. If he could just go back in time and try again, he'd make sure and catch on quicker to how much of a gift Karen had always been to him. Then he would have secured other living arrangements for her before he moved forward in giving her the courtship she deserved.

But no, he'd messed it all up. Logan finished his work and headed for the house.

The sight of the petite blonde wearing a floral apron and setting the table brought a wave of reality crashing over him. He must tell her about Pete's answer. How he hated to dash Karen's hopes. She'd devised the perfect plan of discreetly moving from the De Witt farm to the Bettens' home one evening after supper during the Christmas break. Then school would resume. Logan was to call on her Sunday afternoons following the Meadow Creek church service. In a month or two, the engagement ring would abide on her finger. All would be smooth and joyful.

Logan slumped as he sloshed water over his hands at the basin. This very moment, that engagement ring lay in the depths of one of Karen's dresser drawers where she'd stowed it the night Logan gave it to her, nowhere near attaining its respectable place on Karen's hand.

"Everything all right?" Mama peered up at him.

Logan shook himself back to the present. "Uh, yeah. Sure."

Mama patted his arm. "Come to the table, dear. Supper is ready."

He moved to take his chair, trying his best not to notice Karen's furrowed brow as she studied his face. Mama's question must have clued her in that yes, there was something terribly wrong. And he had no way to fix it. He offered her one skittish glance and closed his eyes. "Let's pray."

Karen reached to hold his hand below the tablecloth's hem. This practice, developed over the past three days, brought him assurance of a beautiful future. Tonight, it only made his voice shake until he stuttered his way through the entire prayer.

When he finally spoke "amen," Karen didn't release his hand. Her concern warmed him beginning in his fingers inter-twined with hers. The warmth spread up his arm and across his chest. If Karen would just keep her grasp, he might find enough comfort to believe their world wasn't on the brink of falling apart.

On previous evenings, he'd discovered he didn't need his right hand for polishing off a meal anyway. Not unless the food on his plate required the use of his knife. The meatloaf Mama served tonight made the perfect one-handed kind of meal. Karen let go when she rose from the table to help Mama serve the dessert.

He looked into her eyes as if to say, "I need to talk to you."

Karen gave him a faint nod.

"YOU WERE STUTTERING AGAIN. What's wrong?" Karen faced Logan in the milk parlor. This was the first time since his proposal he'd spent any time alone with her. Karen's heart pounded. Something must be very wrong for Logan to bend his self-imposed rules and request a private chat.

He raked shaky fingers through his hair and then grasped her shoulders. "My talk with Pete didn't go as planned."

A stinging sensation filled her stomach. She swallowed.

Logan looked into her eyes. "They don't have room for you to live with them."

"But they have two bedrooms."

Logan nodded. A dim smile crossed his face. "The empty room is in the process of getting remodeled. Pete and Anna are expecting a baby this summer."

If Logan had thrown an entire bucket of ice water on her, Karen couldn't have been more shocked. "You mean ..."

Logan nodded again. A solemn expression claimed his features. "You'll need to stay here."

"That isn't a good idea." Karen clutched her skirt. "I can't live with you, Logan. Not with the way I feel about you. It's... it's...improper."

Logan grasped the back of his neck. "I feel the same way, but I don't know what else to do."

"Maybe I can move in with one of the neighbors."

"That won't work. You ended up here with us because we're the only ones with any room."

Karen scanned the shelves of shiny pails, the milk cans in the corner, and the pile of straw under the window. If only the simple surroundings could give her a clue.

"Hey, wait a minute. Who said you needed to be the one to leave? I'm the one to blame here. I should move out."

Karen shook her head. "But what about the chores and all of the milking? You can't leave the farm."

"No. Not the farm. Just the house."

"I don't understand."

"The barn, sweetheart. I could move out here."

"You'd live in the barn? In January?" Logan had mentioned to her the night he proposed that he was crazy in love with her. This new scheme actually proved that he was just crazy.

A smile crept over his face. Long and slow, like when he'd told her about his trip to the Oswell City jewelry store to purchase her ring. "I've got it all worked out. I can move the stove out of here and put it in the lean-to."

Logan turned the wick up on the glowing lantern. "Come here." He led the way into the adjacent barn and stopped before a little door near the ladder to the haymow. He tugged on the door. It scraped the rocky barn floor.

Karen stepped into the tiny room. A cupboard of sorts filled one side. Starlight sparkled overhead. "Logan."

He must have caught the disappointment in her voice because he laid his hand on her shoulder. "It'll be fine. I'll move a cot in from the attic. A few new shingles to the roof and it'll be as cozy as the parlor reading by firelight."

Nothing could be as cozy as that. Logan did make a point, though. "Will you do your studying out here?"

Logan looked around. "No room for my desk. I'll try to get more of it done during the day while you are at school. Then I'll come out here after supper to stay."

Karen slumped. She'd miss his company on those long winter evenings reading books from his collection in the glow of the parlor fireplace. "You'll freeze."

Logan sucked in a breath. "I'll make it work."

Her eyes misted. Logan was a man well acquainted with sacrifice. He made another one, this time for her. "I'll bring you some extra blankets."

Logan nodded. "Uh, Karen. Let's hold off on telling Mama and Tillie right now."

"How are we going to do that? You know your mother will ask questions when you drag a cot out of the attic and quit sleeping in your room."

"I know. But I want to wait for the right time to tell her about our engagement. Like both of us, my mother is concerned about decorum. She's also still adjusting to life without Dad. I don't want to cause her alarm with the news of any big changes such as my getting married."

"When do you plan to tell her?"

"I don't know. But not yet."

"How do you plan to explain your move to the barn in the middle of winter?"

Logan pointed at an occupied stanchion. "See that cow? She's been sick and in need of some extra attention. I'll tell Mama that I've moved to the barn to keep an eye on her."

Karen peered at him. His story contained some serious holes, just like the roof overhead.

"It's the truth." Logan's brow raised in a challenge to defy him.

"Would you move to the barn anyway, even if you hadn't talked with Pete?"

Logan's mouth scrunched to one side of his face. "That's a fair question. Maybe not to sleep, but I'll probably end up putting in some late nights."

Karen followed Logan from the lean-to. His yank on the door to close it rattled the barn wall enough to make the rickety lean-to roof creak. She could only imagine what other repairs were required for him to make the tiny apartment livable.

CHAPTER TWO

"*M*iss Millerson, I'd like to have a word with you."

Karen's insides tensed. That raspy voice belonged to none other than Eldon Kent's sister-in-law, Vera. What demands this woman expected to make of her today, Karen could hardly guess. She spun around, leaving Tillie to study bolts of fabric on her own.

Karen pasted on a smile. "Good morning, Mrs. Kent. How lovely to find you here today." She cringed. Last night she'd pressed Logan for truthfulness with his mother, and now she told outright lies to the mother of some of her students.

Mrs. Kent marched over, her brown plaid skirt flapping around her ankles. "What is the meaning of assigning my children homework over the holidays?"

Karen gulped. Not from fear but rather to prevent herself from firing back at Mrs. Kent. "All of my students were assigned homework over Christmas. The superintendent needs final grades turned in the second week of January. I had no choice. I don't want anyone to fall behind."

"Are you saying my children aren't keeping up with the others?"

The heat coming off this woman made Karen's pulse rise. She gulped again. "Your younger children are doing fine. So is Carrie. Sixth grade is a good level for her. I'm most concerned about Joe and Marty. They are in their last year of country school. If they don't apply themselves, then yes, there is a good chance they will fall behind."

"Joe and Marty do not need to study. When they complete the eighth grade, they'll work on the farm like their father." Mrs. Kent pulled on a pair of gloves, carefully sliding them over each of her fingers as if to protect herself from touching something disgusting.

Like this topic of conversation. Clearly the Kents placed no value on education. Karen still must meet the state's standards for her school regardless how Mrs. Kent or any other Kent family member felt about it. "Have the boys done their homework?"

Mrs. Kent glanced up from her gloved hands. "No. Of course not."

The confidence in her answer warned Karen that every last one of Vera's six children would return to school next week with incomplete assignments.

She buttoned her coat. "Good day, Miss Millerson."

"What was that all about?" Tillie held a bolt of gray fabric.

"Just Vera throwing her weight around again." Karen watched Mrs. Kent exit Carter's General store.

"She thinks her word is law just because her husband Evan owns the bank along with his brother and father." Tillie moved to the counter.

Karen sighed. "Families throwing away their opportunities for education. How sad."

Andrew Carter stood behind the counter. "Good morning, Tillie. I see you are wearing your bracelet."

Tillie's face glowed. "I am. It's beautiful."

"Are we on for Friday night?" Andrew cut a piece of fabric for Tillie and rang up the total on the cash register.

"Yes." Tillie handed him her payment.

Karen stood back, happy to let Tillie and Andrew carry the conversation. Her mind spun with ideas for stopping Joe and Marty Kent from causing any more disruption in her classroom.

Logan entered the store, waving at shoppers as he approached.

"Did you get all of your stops made?" Karen looked up at him.

A wide grin spread across his face. "I did. Eldon has the rest of the interest money I owed him by the end of the year a whole two days early, I'm proud to say."

"I feel like celebrating." His grin produced a smile on her face.

"What did you have in mind?" Logan nodded at Andrew and then accompanied Tillie and Karen to the wagon.

"How about one of my specialties? Cherry pie."

"Doesn't get any better than that. I'm looking forward to it already."

Karen smiled as Logan helped her into the wagon. Tonight's supper would see the entire household rejoicing over Logan's hard-won successes.

AFTER THE NOON MEAL, Logan got busy sawing the wood he'd purchased at the lumberyard that morning. On closer inspection by daylight, he'd discovered that the lean-to needed a whole new roof. He faced a much larger and more expensive project than merely nailing down a few shingles here and there.

Through the afternoon hours Logan followed the process of sawing, hammering, and nailing as he worked his way from the lowest eaves of the lean-to up to the place where the roof met the barn's wall. His project came to a halt at that point. The boards in that section of the wall were soft to Logan's touch. Pounding nails into them would do no good. Nothing would fasten to those rotten boards and hold secure.

How fortunate that he'd bought an ample supply of lumber. He should have plenty to make the repairs to the barn wall and also finish the roofing project. Logan climbed down from the lean-to and entered the barn. The best place to work was from the haymow. But first the hay must get moved so he had a cleared area to pile lumber.

Rushing to make time for the extra repairs before he must start the evening milking, Logan scooped up the hay in his path, closing the distance at a rapid pace. When he took his next step, the floor gave way.

The pitch fork thudded. Logan fell through the opening. His whole body floated free.

The rocky barn floor came closer and closer. Logan hit it with a jolt. His left leg cracked, and sharp pain throbbed in his head. His chest heaved, and everything went black.

KAREN TURNED AWAY from the kitchen window where she had been watching the barn. Logan ran late with the milking, but supper was ready. The cherry pie cooled on the counter, its golden crusted top making Karen's mouth water. She could hardly wait to share the special dessert with Logan. But he still hadn't appeared for the evening meal. Maybe he worked so hard on fixing the roof that he lost track of time. Someone should check. "Sandy, do you think Logan has run into trouble?"

Logan's mother glanced at the grandfather clock in the dining room. "It's possible."

Karen had her coat on before Sandy finished the sentence. She rushed out the door.

A wagon rumbled down the lane. The driver called to her. "Miss Millerson!"

It was Roy Jones, a neighbor to the De Witts and the father of two of her students.

He strode across the yard. "Logan mentioned when I saw him at the lumberyard that he had a roofing project. I stopped by to see if he still needed any help."

"That's very kind of you. I'm on my way to the barn now. Come with me." Karen led the way. "Logan," she called once she and Mr. Jones were inside. "Logan? Where are you?"

Mr. Jones opened the door to the milk parlor. Looking over his shoulder, Karen searched for Logan but didn't see him. She moved on.

The stanchions were empty as if milking hadn't yet started. Only the sick cow remained inside. Karen patted her rump. The other cows lowed outside the building, eager to enter. Logan must have kept working on the roof and delayed the milking.

But he never delayed the milking.

Silence surrounded Karen and her visitor. No pounding of a hammer rang in the air. No hummed tune of a hymn floated to her ears. Only dry, dead silence. Karen's throat thickened. "Logan?"

"Over here, Miss Millerson." Mr. Jones beckoned to her from the shadows below the haymow.

Karen rushed to his side. The scene that awaited her made her stomach churn. She covered her mouth while tears filled her eyes. She knelt down.

Logan's crumpled body lay on the packed dirt. Blood oozed from the side of his head. His left leg jutted at a peculiar angle. His chest didn't rise and fall with the steady rhythm of breathing. Karen released a tiny wail.

"Logan? Hey, Logan, can you hear me?" Mr. Jones watched him for a moment. Then he bent over Logan's shirt front and listened for a heartbeat.

"Is he...alive?" Karen choked.

"Barely." Mr. Jones straightened. "I've seen it before. My brother fell off his silo a few years back, but he survived it. I'll go to town and get the doctor. I'll bring him out here and then I'll stay and do Logan's milking." Mr. Jones took off on a run.

Did Logan still breathe? She had to find out for herself. Blond hair fanned his forehead. She brushed it to one side the way he always wore it. Her touch received no response. Logan lay still. Too still. She bent and listened to his chest.

His heart beat steady. Breaths came quick and shallow. Karen straightened as the tears flowed again. She picked up his right hand, the one she held out of anyone's line of vision during evening meals. "Oh, Logan."

She longed to say more. To tell him how much she loved him. To let him know he must recover so they might share a life together. But the words wouldn't come. She pressed his palm to her cheek and prayed for him as she'd done so often in the past months.

His eyes fluttered open. He stared at her for just a moment with deep pain reflected in his gaze. Her name passed over his lips before his eyes closed once more, and his head drooped to the side.

"Logan?" These precious seconds in which he recognized her must not slip away. Surely death hadn't claimed him. She laid her hand on his chest. His heart still beat. Good sign.

Blood still oozed from his head. Karen took her handkerchief from her skirt pocket and pressed it to his temple.

"Karen? Anyone in here?" Sandy's voice floated to Karen's ears.

"Over here." Karen choked on the words. How she wished she could somehow shield Logan's mother from his present condition.

Sandy approached and looked down. "Oh." The syllable

came as a gasp, and she covered her mouth. "What happened?" She turned worried eyes on Karen.

Karen glanced at the pitchfork lying among pieces of broken boards. "He must have fallen out of the haymow. Mr. Jones went to get the doctor."

Sandy knelt down. "We shouldn't try to move him on our own."

"No. That would be too dangerous." Karen kept her focus on Logan's face as she spoke with his mother. If he opened his eyes again, she didn't want to miss out.

"I've left Tillie in charge of the stove. I'll go to the house and tell her. She can help me prepare a place for him on the sofa." Sandy returned to a standing position and left for the house.

The barn's interior darkened with the growing twilight. Mr. Jones and the doctor arrived and carefully arranged Logan on a stretcher. They carried him to the house where a large kettle filled with water steamed on the stove.

Sandy bustled around the kitchen while she gave instructions to Tillie. "Pour some of that water into a basin so that the doctor can clean him up. I'll go upstairs for the blankets."

Karen raced through the parlor moving tables, fluffing pillows, and unfolding the blankets Sandy brought. She stood with Tillie while Mr. Jones and Dr. Bolton carried Logan in. Together the men eased Logan onto the sofa. His limp form sprawled, unable to make any movements of its own.

Tillie whimpered, so Karen wrapped and arm around her.

Sandy worked at removing Logan's shoes, and the doctor shook hands with Mr. Jones.

"Thank you so much for doing the milking this evening." Sandy's words followed Mr. Jones from the room.

He turned and smiled before leaving the house.

She straightened and addressed the doctor. "What do you think is wrong with him? Why won't he move or wake up?"

Dr. Bolton removed his coat. "I'll need to examine him to know for sure, but I'd say he has a concussion. Our most important concern right now is his leg. We need to get it set." He opened his medical bag and proceeded with an examination. The minutes dragged until the stethoscope finally left his ears. "Mrs. De Witt, could you please remove his shirt? I want to check his ribs."

"Certainly." Sandy moved to heed the doctor's request and then went to the kitchen with Logan's soiled clothing.

Dr. Bolton tenderly poked Logan's side, producing a moan from the injured man. The doctor felt along Logan's chest and under his arm. More moans followed.

Karen couldn't decide if she should rejoice in Logan's response to the doctor's pressure or cry over the torment his moans expressed. She'd never heard Logan complain of pain. Not when he injured his hand last fall during harvest or from the smaller wounds that came with the occupation of farming. These groans from deep inside him told her his pain was very great.

"Two broken ribs," Dr. Bolton murmured. He looked at Karen and Tillie. "I'm ready to set the bone in his leg. Could one of you ladies please assist me?"

"I'll do it." Karen heard her voice answer. She didn't know a thing about fixing broken bones. What could she possibly offer the doctor in the way of help? But this was Logan. She'd do anything to bring him back to normal.

"I'll get the water to wash his face." Tillie headed for the kitchen.

The doctor glanced at Karen. "Ready?"

Karen nodded. Her heart leaped into her throat when Logan's leg cracked under the doctor's firm pressure.

Logan's eyes fluttered open again, and he released another groan. His gaze passed over them, and his mouth opened as if he had a message to give them. The fight for alertness lasted only a moment longer than the one in the barn before unconsciousness overtook him.

Tillie and Sandy returned. For the next while, the women assisted Dr. Bolton in various ways while he worked over Logan's broken body, stitching the gash in his head, forming a cast on his leg, and wrapping his torso in a bandage.

Finally, the doctor straightened. "He has a broken bone below the knee. He'll need a cast for six weeks. Make sure and keep the leg elevated. He also has a concussion. There isn't much you can do about it except keep him comfortable. You'll want to monitor him through the night in order to watch for signs of alertness returning. Speak his name, and try to awaken him. That may help him regain consciousness sooner." He scanned their little group. "Any questions?"

Karen had dozens of questions but none the doctor could answer for her. She shook her head.

"All right. I'll return tomorrow and check on you. Good night." He reached for his coat and medical bag and left the house.

"One of us should sit up with him tonight." Sandy scratched the back of her neck.

"Let's take turns. Since there are three of us, we can each take three-hour shifts," Tillie said.

"Yes, I like the sound of that, dear. I'll stay up until midnight and then one of you ladies may take over." Sandy's gaze traveled from Tillie to Karen.

"I'll stay with Logan until three and then Karen can cover the rest of the night." Tillie looked at her. "What do you think of that plan?"

"Fine." Karen nodded in answer to Tillie, but her heart prayed that Logan would wake up very soon.

CHAPTER THREE

*a*t three o'clock in the morning, Karen eased down the stairs so they creaked as little as possible. Sandy needed her rest and shouldn't get disturbed by a series of noisy stairs.

In the parlor, Tillie sat in the rocking chair wide awake with all of her attention on Logan.

"Anything changed?"

Tillie shook her head. "I thought he twitched, but it only happened once. I must be imagining things."

"We'll keep praying." Karen's voice held confidence but inside she wrestled. Maybe God's answer would look different from what any of them expected, or wanted.

"This whole situation feels so much like what happened with Dad. An accident in the barn. No one around to see what happened or to help. Hours of sorrow afterwards. Logan is at least still breathing. But Dad..." Tillie choked on the last word. She looked at Karen. "What happens if he never wakes up? Mama and I will have no one if Logan dies too. All alone in this big house. Out here on the farm. We'd never make it." Tears filled Tillie's eyes.

Karen knelt down next to her. "I doubt if Logan is going to die. But the doctor was pretty concerned about his leg. We need to pray that it was set correctly and will heal so that he has full use of it again."

Tillie nodded. Then she reached to clutch Karen in a hug. "Oh, I'm so glad you are here with us. I don't know what I'd do without Logan or without you."

Karen attempted a smile when Tillie pulled away, but her own heart was full of wondering. Tillie's fears flared Karen's own fears to life.

Tillie stood. "I guess I'll go to bed now." She left and Karen settled into the rocking chair.

Those long-ago days shared with her friend Ella from teacher's college seared her memory as she studied Logan's face for any signs of alertness.

The threshing accident at the farm of Ella's brother had taken his life. The images from that horrible day flashed through Karen's mind leaving her weak and breathless. Just when she'd laid the past to rest, Logan experienced an accident right here on his farm. His fate could follow the same path as Ella's brother. Logan's injury occurred due to a less violent reason, but it might still end up just as final.

She'd fought for so long to keep her heart safe from Logan De Witt, the farming preacher. Now that she'd risked letting him have her heart, she may still lose him to a farm accident. If that really happened, she'd lose her heart too. She and Logan were meant to serve the Lord and to do it together. If Tillie's fear proved true and Logan never came back to them, Karen was destined to live many long, dark years alone.

She stared at the parlor rug. Only the steady tick-tock of the grandfather clock broke the silence. She must get herself under control and believe her own words to Tillie. Logan would not die. But life may look different for all of them if the use of his leg didn't return.

The blanket on the sofa rustled. Karen glanced up. It happened again. The blanket wrinkled across Logan's bandaged chest. He moved his head.

Karen scrambled out of the chair and fell to the floor beside him. She grasped his hand. "Logan."

He mumbled.

Karen's pulse throbbed in her ears. "Logan, can you hear me?"

He squeezed her hand.

"You're waking up. Please try to talk to me."

He moved his head from side to side and mumbled once more.

The interpretation required quite a bit of her imagination, but Logan's murmurs sounded an awfully lot like her name.

One of Logan's eyes popped open. Then he smiled. A large, happy smile. One word whispered across his lips as clear as if he were speaking to a church full of people. "Angel."

Karen's vision blurred. He must think he left his earthly life and had arrived in Heaven. Or maybe he really had seen her and spoke on purpose. She settled back into her chair and waited for the moment when Logan realized he was still very much on earth confined to a body that was sure to give him much pain in the days to come.

He licked his lips. Then he spoke with a deep, slurred voice. "I need you, sweetheart. Don't leave me."

"I'm right here." Perhaps the angelic observation was meant for her after all. Karen scooted forward in her chair.

Both of his eyes opened. "Oh, Karen." His haggard tone belonged to a man who had sojourned all the way to the ends of the earth and back again.

Karen smoothed his hair as her tears flowed.

"What time is it?" His voice grew smoother.

"Three thirty in the morning on Friday."

"Friday?"

"Yes. You fell yesterday afternoon."

With jerky movements, Logan rubbed his forehead.

"Do you have any pain?"

"My chest." He felt around on the side of his head. "What is this bandage for?"

"Stitches. That must be where you hit your head on the barn floor or on a piece of board."

The blanket rustled again. "My leg feels heavy."

"It's broken below the knee. The doctor put a cast on it."

Logan frowned at the ceiling for a moment.

Karen knelt down beside him. "I wish I could find the words to tell you how relieved I am that you are awake. We've all been so worried."

Logan patted her shoulder.

"Your leg will take a long time to heal. Even then, you might be lame or unable to use it again." Karen swallowed the lump in her throat and wiped her eyes. "Can I get you anything? The doctor left some pain medication and told us to give you a dose if you needed it."

"Maybe later."

"Would you like a drink then? Or some food? I can believe you are pretty hungry. You haven't eaten for several hours."

Logan shook his head.

"Then may I get your Bible for you from upstairs?"

He scrunched his eyes shut. "I don't feel much up to reading."

Karen stood. "Are you cold? Your mother left a stack of blankets. I could get one for you." She reached for the blanket on the top of the pile.

"No, Karen. I don't need any of those things."

"Not even the medication?"

He shook his head again. "I just need one thing."

"What's that?"

"You." Logan gestured to the rocking chair at his bedside. "Please come back so you're near enough to kiss me. That's all I ask."

Karen's throat ached. Logan lay helpless flat on his back. He could request so many things that brought him comfort. But he wanted her. She claimed the chair and framed his face. Even in his debilitated state, Logan lacked nothing in his ability to let her know how cherished and deeply loved she really was.

KAREN'S KISS brought Logan back to life. Enough energy surged through his body to power him in running a marathon. But his head throbbed. Each breath seared his chest. His leg felt like one of the stones from the grain mill trapped it.

He heaved in as deep of a breath as he dared while trying to get his mind to absorb the news that he may not walk normally again.

Karen pulled the blanket closer to his chin. "You have broken ribs. But breathing will get easier as your swelling goes down."

That explained the swath of bandage around his middle. And why he was lying around in the parlor wearing no shirt. The thought about who got the job of removing the shirt wavered in his mind. Had the doctor performed the task? Mama? Karen? Logan trembled.

"Do you remember what happened?" Karen adjusted the blanket.

Logan shut his eyes and allowed his mind to spin back, all the way to yesterday. "I bought lumber in town." He took a breath. "I needed the lumber to fix the lean-to. I found some rotten boards in the barn wall. The haymow..." Something about that haymow lingered in his cloudy mind. "I'd been using the pitchfork."

"You fell out of the haymow. Mr. Jones found you. He came to the farm to offer you his help with the shingling. I was on my way to the barn to look for you, so he came too. I'm glad he did. Mr. Jones is the one who fetched the doctor for us. He also did the milking last night. Vern can take it over until you are up and around again. Pete could probably fill in for you on Sunday for the Meadow Creek service."

Logan pressed his temple. "Oh, the Meadow Creek people. I wish I could be there. I have my sermon ready to go. Guess I won't be there next week either."

Karen shook her head.

"That's two Sundays without pay." His chest tightened, but not because of his struggle to breathe.

"Pete can cover it."

"He'll do fine. But that isn't what bothers me."

"What's wrong?"

He glanced at the ceiling. "I love preaching on Sunday after-noons. I'm so thankful to serve them in this way." A tempest brewed inside of him. He looked at Karen. "But if you remem-ber, I'm under a deadline with Eldon at the bank to pay off Dad's debt by April thirty."

"I remember."

"I'm barely keeping up now. If I don't draw a paycheck from Meadow Creek, I'll fall behind. And now that I'm laid up, I won't be able to work the farm."

"The neighbors will help you."

"I'm grateful. But they will need compensation of some sort for their work. Plus, this doctor bill." Logan pressed his temple again. "I don't know how I'm going to make those bank payments."

"One good thing came of all this."

He frowned, unable to follow her train of thought.

"I'm still here. Even though I was uncomfortable with the idea, it's more important that my room and board helps you."

He should smile. Karen declared her staying on the farm a good thing. But he couldn't share her outlook. He'd gladly give up Karen's room and board in exchange for a proper courtship. Eldon's demands weren't worth that much to him after all. He'd much rather fail at saving his family's ground than lose his integrity, or for Karen to lose her impeccable reputation.

"I'd rather have the chance to court you."

"I would too." Karen leaned over him. "But we can't worry about that right now."

She rocked in the chair for a few moments. Tears glistened in her eyes. "These past hours when you lay here unresponsive, I was scared. I thought your accident would ruin our future."

He reached for her hand.

"I'm glad I was here when you fell. If I'd already moved to Pete and Anna's as planned, I wouldn't have known or been here to help your mother and the doctor care for you."

He'd hold Karen right now if his injuries allowed it.

"This will all work out. I don't mind if courtship never takes place."

"You deserve it."

"I'd enjoy it. But courtship might just waste our time."

"What do you mean?"

Karen leaned closer. "Isn't courtship intended to help couples discover if they love each other or not?"

"Usually, yes."

"Logan, we already know this. Why do I need you to take me on picnics and bring me flowers when you've involved me in your Sunday services and given me a place to live while I teach?"

A smile tugged at one corner of his mouth.

"You've rescued me. Encouraged me. Believed in me. No amount of courting is going to tell me what I already know."

His smile grew. Karen spoke the truth. "You're right, sweetheart. Completely right. But I want to protect you. I don't want

25

to risk exposing you to a loss of the respect you enjoy from your students and their families. As soon as I'm able, I'm going to finish that roofing project and move to the barn."

"The weather should be a little warmer by then."

"Yes, it should." Logan closed his eyes. The throbbing on the side of his head grew worse. Maybe from all the thinking about his problems.

"Would you like to sleep?"

He looked at Karen. "No. You offered to get my Bible earlier. If I asked for it now, would you read it to me?"

"Sure." Karen left and soon returned with his Bible. "What should I read?"

"The book of John." The beloved disciple's perspective on Jesus' purpose in the world was the subject of his most recent sermon.

Karen opened the Bible and began to read. Her voice held feeling and understanding. Golden waves of hair flowed over the front of her robe. Lamplight glowed on her fair skin and shone in her eyes.

A fragment of memory returned. "Karen."

She glanced up with a question in her eyes.

"When I woke up a few minutes ago, what did I say to you?"

She blushed. "You called me an angel."

"Then I wasn't seeing things." His hazy mind was finally catching up to his vision. "I said that because of how you look right now."

Karen gave a self-conscious flutter of her lashes and slipped her fingers through a wave of hair.

Logan wrestled with his longing to imitate Karen's movements. Then he could discover for himself if the strands really were as silky as they looked. "Do you know how beautiful you are?"

Karen shook her head.

"Then let me tell you."

Karen leaned in as if she hoped he'd whisper the words.

The shift in her posture brushed his bare shoulder with a curl of her hair.

Logan caught it between his fingers. Smooth. Silky. Satisfying. How he'd managed to share his home with her since last summer and not catch a glimpse of her hair loose and flowing before now stumped him.

He should've paid more attention.

"You are the most gorgeous young woman I've ever met. I'm honored that you have agreed to become my wife. Even without the courtship." He winked. How nice to have his wits returning. Without them Karen had no reason to release that joyful laugh of hers.

Something else he'd miss if she moved to the Bettens'.

They shared one more kiss, and then Karen settled in, reading the Bible once again.

As Logan listened, he did a little praying. Karen truly was the most beautiful, talented, godly young woman he'd ever known. More than Lorraine or any of those other girls Pete thought might be good for him.

The Lord truly knew what he was doing to call Logan to singleness all those years. And now God gave him Karen.

All he wanted to do was sweep her onto his lap and make a full-time career out of landing kisses over her face and neck. If Eldon recognized that sort of occupation as generating the profit he needed at the bank, he'd have that debt paid off by tomorrow.

But Karen lived in his home. She fussed over his comfort and spent long hours in the middle of the night at his bedside. It made a man want to forget the existence of words like decorum or propriety.

In that moment, Logan saw his injuries in a whole new light. The cast, the muddled mind, the ribs in need of recovery were

God's way of helping him preserve honorable living arrangements with his fiancée. As long as his cumbersome leg and dizzy brain kept him confined to the sofa, he was unable to give into the temptations luring him away from all he held as right and true. Logan ended his prayer thanking the Lord in Heaven above from the bottom of his heart for broken bones.

CHAPTER FOUR

*K*aren roused as footsteps creaked on the dining room's hard wood floor.

"Good morning, dear." Sandy pressed her shoulder. "How is he?"

"I'm awake, Mama." Logan murmured in a voice that really said he lay half-asleep. He turned to look at his mother.

"Oh, praise God." Sandy's voice wavered.

Karen gave up her rocking chair.

"When?" Sandy claimed the chair with her full attention on her son.

"About three-thirty this morning, or so Karen tells me." Logan blinked as though the world hadn't quite come into focus.

Sandy turned to look at her. "You should've woken me up."

Karen shrugged. "You and Tillie already lost enough sleep last night. I wanted you to get your rest."

Sandy offered the kind of smile that said she appreciated Karen's gesture but disagreed with it.

"Are you hungry?" Sandy turned back to Logan.

"I believe I could eat something." Logan rubbed his forehead.

Tillie rushed into the room. "I heard talking. Was it Logan?" Without waiting for an answer, she fell to her knees and clasped his hand.

"Yeah." Logan glanced at Tillie.

"He awoke during Karen's shift." Sandy straightened.

Both of them turned to look at her. The expression in Tillie's eyes held a hint of envy.

Karen backed away a step. She hadn't meant to cause discord between herself and Logan's mother and sister. She'd done nothing to force him awake. Logan had just happened to regain his consciousness during the time she was with him. And yet, the timing of the event carried significance. Logan may have been less willing to voice his thoughts with his family around.

Sandy and Tillie may feel a bit put out with her, but she wouldn't trade those moments she spent alone with Logan. Not for anything.

A sigh left Sandy's lips. "Well, how about some breakfast? We still have that cherry pie Karen made for supper last night. I remember how you used to beg me to let you have pie for breakfast in your younger days." Sandy smoothed Logan's hair. "We have so much to be thankful for. I'm willing to indulge you. This once."

Logan and his mother shared a smile before Sandy left for the kitchen.

"Can I help you sit up?" Tillie bent over Logan.

"Careful, Tillie. He might be a little dizzy." Karen rushed to Tillie's side.

"I can't eat lying down." Logan reached his hands in the air. "Help me up."

Karen assisted Tillie in propping Logan to a seated position and then rearranged his pillows to give him extra support.

Sandy returned from the kitchen with a pot of coffee, plates and forks, and the pie. She set everything on a nearby table and cut Logan the first slice. "Do you have any pain?"

"Mostly a headache. My chest hurts too."

"The medication the doctor gave you last night has probably worn off by now. He told us to give you more when the pain grew worse. He'll be coming back this morning to check on you." Sandy finished cutting slices of pie for everyone and then took a seat.

Within the hour, Dr. Bolton arrived. He performed a thorough examination and expressed his relief that Logan had awakened during the night. "With plenty of rest, you should be able to start getting up and around in three or four days." The doctor spoke to Logan before giving instructions to the women about how best to help Logan rest.

No loud noises. A darkened room. Routine dosages of pain medication. Regular meals. Sleep.

Karen listened with complete resolution to keep Logan as comfortable and rested as possible. As much as she longed for Logan to get his rest, the neighbors had other ideas. The doctor barely left the house before Logan's first visitors arrived.

Pete and Anna entered the house and talked with Sandy in hushed tones. After a few moments of conversation, Sandy beckoned to Karen. "Come to the kitchen."

Karen stole another glimpse of Logan's face. His blond hair fanned over his forehead. A fresh bandage covered his stitches. A peaceful expression claimed his features as he rested, giving her hope that the doctor's medication kept his pain under control.

She'd rather not leave the parlor. Even when Logan slept, Karen found comfort in staying near. Tillie and Sandy may come and go in their own need to care for Logan and watch over him, but she intended to stay. Nothing loomed so important as to pull her away from his side.

Tillie came to the parlor. "Pete and Anna are asking to speak with you."

After one more glance at Logan's still form, Karen forced herself to stand and followed Tillie to the kitchen.

"Oh, Karen, we're so sorry about Logan's accident. We found out from Roy Jones when he stopped by on his way home. We knew from his report that Logan needed quite a bit of attention from the doctor or we would've come last night." Anna hugged her.

"The Bettens have asked about those moments when Logan regained consciousness. Since you were sitting up with him at the time, I thought you'd be the best one to answer their questions." Sandy gestured to the visitors.

Her voice carried no trace of the disappointment she'd felt toward Karen upon her discovery of Logan's alertness, so Karen took a breath and ventured an answer.

"Logan awoke this morning at 3:30."

"Did he recognize you right away, or was his recovery gradual?" Anna asked.

If thinking Karen resembled an angel qualified as immediate recognition, then yes, he had gained consciousness quickly. She hardly knew how to answer. "Um, I would say he knew who I was from the beginning."

"That's a good sign," Pete whispered, relief flooding his voice.

"What about his speech?" Anna asked.

Not until she kissed him did Logan start talking without any pauses between his words. She swallowed. "It took longer than his memory, but by morning, talking came much easier."

"How is he now?" Pete asked.

The genuine concern Pete showed for his friend brought tears to Karen's eyes. "He's resting. The doctor said that after three or four days, he may start moving around."

"Would you like to see him?" Sandy moved to the doorway as an indicator for her guests to follow.

"If he isn't sleeping." Anna looked at Karen.

"His eyes are closed, but he hasn't fallen asleep. I'm sure he will be very glad to see you."

The kitchen cleared as everyone left for the parlor. Karen stayed behind preparing Logan's next dose of pain medication. Before she finished, Vern and Wade Patterson arrived. She let them in and encouraged them to join the group in the parlor.

"Were you scared?" Anna asked as she returned to the kitchen and sat at the table.

Karen joined her. "Terrified."

"Tell me what happened."

Karen related yesterday's events to Anna.

"I'm so glad Roy knew what to do and that the doctor was available."

Karen nodded. Anna's words echoed her own gratitude.

So many things could have gone wrong. If he'd fallen on his head, Logan could have sustained permanent paralysis or even death. Or his leg might have been more severely damaged, resulting in an amputation. She would have done her best to move forward in sharing her life with a husband confined to a wheel chair and dependent on her for care. Her love for him would have colored the hardship with pleasure. But the end of Logan's life would have meant the end of their plans, their hopes, and their love. Heaviness weighted Karen's heart until the pain of it blurred her vision.

"Karen?" Anna's gentle voice reached her ears.

She turned while a tear slipped from the corner of her eyes.

"How are you doing through all of this?"

Anna's quiet question invited Karen to share her inner thoughts on more than the tragedy of Logan's accident. Anna's concern seemed to reach deeper, to see farther, into the love and anticipation taking up space in her heart these days.

How she'd love to answer Anna with the full truth. But Logan had asked for a delay in breaking the news of their engagement to his mother and sister. Karen certainly could not confide in his best friend's wife before his own family knew. She must carry the precious secret, along with its struggles, in concealment for many days to come. Nothing would change until Logan moved to the barn, and he must complete the repairs before he moved. His injuries must heal first. Weeks stretched ahead of her until Anna's question received its rightful answer.

Karen bit her lip. "I was worried. So were Sandy and Tillie. The doctor is concerned about his leg. We won't know how much use he will have of it until after the cast is removed. He might still go lame. But Logan is alert and acting like his normal self, and for that I am thankful."

A sympathetic smile pulled at Anna's mouth. "Pete said Logan stopped by earlier this week asking for us to give you a home for the second semester. I'm concerned about you, Karen. Why would Logan feel the need to do that? Haven't you been getting along with the De Witts?"

They were getting along fine, better than Karen ever expected. Never in her wildest dreams did she envision her move from the city and her acceptance of a teaching job leading her to engagement. "Tillie and I got off to a rough start, but we are good friends now." Her answer sounded stiff in her own ears, but at least it was true.

Anna frowned. "If Tillie isn't the reason you wish to move out, then you must have a different one."

Karen did have another reason for a move. It was a big reason, and an urgent one.

"But you can't talk about it." Anna leaned back in her chair as though giving Karen more space. "I won't press you. I'm sorry if I have pried too much already. Please know that you have a friend in me if you ever need someone to talk to."

Karen's insides caved. How she'd love Anna for a friend. Reverend Betten's wife would have so much to teach her about serving a congregation and life in a parsonage. This thought jogged her memory of the news Logan shared with her in the barn. The announcement he'd shared at the time might have ruined Karen's plans, but for the young woman sharing the table with her, the news filled the future with happiness just like engagement did for Karen.

"Thank you, Anna. I would like to have you for a friend. I understand congratulations are in order. Logan tells us that you and Pete are expecting a baby."

Anna smiled. "We are, in July." She continued to talk about her plans for the nursery until Pete, Sandy, and Tillie returned to the kitchen.

"We need to go, Anna," Pete said as he reached for his coat. "I would like to pay a visit to Mrs. Fuller this morning."

Anna stood and gave Karen a hug. "I'm here, if you ever need me."

Karen nodded, the tears once again filling her eyes. She did need Anna. Surely the day would come when she could tell her just how much.

Over the course of the afternoon and all day Saturday, visitors poured into the parlor to see Logan. Vern Patterson or one of his sons stopped in after every milking. Pete came twice on Saturday. The doctor came daily. The Joneses, Hixsons, and the Hinkleys also visited, adding to the generous amounts of attention lavished on their injured neighbor.

Karen appreciated their kindness but struggled with the desire to chase everyone out of the house. Let him take a nap. Leave him alone. If only she could yell those words out from time to time and enforce them with consequences like she did in her classroom. But the tactics she used on her students probably wouldn't produce the same effect on their parents.

Sunday afternoon Evan and Vera came to the farm, accompanied by Bert and Elsie. Karen sat with them in the parlor.

"Did you enjoy your trip? We've hated having your house so dark. The children have had no one to play with this whole Christmas break." Vera sipped from a cup of coffee Sandy poured for her.

"We had a nice time spending the holidays with Bert's

family. His sister's children are the same age as ours. We cut our visit short and arrived home just yesterday, in time, of course, for school to start again, although the children aren't looking forward to it. Not one bit. Bert and I wanted to stay a few days longer. Too bad we had to miss out." Elsie wrinkled her nose.

Apparently, these ladies forgot that their children's teacher shared the parlor with them. Karen's pulse couldn't decide if it should race with indignation over Elsie's eagerness to complain or her lack of concern for her children's attitudes about school. Both of these mothers clearly shared these negative opinions.

Either way, Karen couldn't stop the questions from slipping out. "Did your children take their studies with them, or are they planning to complete their homework today?"

"We do not do homework on Sundays, Miss Millerson. I can't understand why you'd even suggest such a thing." Elsie glared at her.

Karen swallowed and willed her pulse to slow down. "I asked because those assignments are due on Monday when classes resume. These days over Christmas provided plenty of time for students to get their work finished."

Vera sniffed. "My children won't have their assignments finished either. They've had too many better things to do with their Christmas holiday than homework. You'll need to find another way to get schoolwork done. Make better use of your time in the classroom instead of wasting ours."

Karen clenched her teeth. The superintendent's due date loomed over her head. She must get grades turned in. The least these women could do was offer a little cooperation.

Evan and Bert joined the circle, having finished their chat with Logan. Karen glanced over at him. He lay down while Sandy spread a blanket over him. Weariness drooped his features. The poor man needed a nap, but he'd been kept too busy with his visitors. Now that the Kent and Sanders couples were leaving, maybe Logan would finally get the peace and quiet he deserved.

Karen went with the foursome to the door and then watched out the window as they climbed into a sleigh. Her muscles tightened. The six children in Evan and Vera's family plus the four children in Bert and Elsie's family comprised half the school. If they came to class tomorrow with incomplete assignments, Karen faced a situation that would quickly get out of hand. She must devise a punishment before those Kent and Sanders cousins caused any more trouble.

CHAPTER FIVE

"All right, class. Time to hand in your homework assignments. Please pass the work you did over Christmas break to the front." Karen rubbed her hands free of chalk dust. As she made the announcement, she scanned the back rows. Would Joe and Marty have anything to show for their time away from the classroom?

Karen accepted the stacks of papers accumulating in the front row. Then she gave reading assignments appropriate to each grade level. Books thumped. Papers rustled. Eventually the room quieted. Karen sat at her desk with the homework assignments. She flipped through them. The four on top were complete. The next three were not. Followed by two that were finished. Then two that were blank save for the names at the top. The trend continued. Karen counted the completed assignments. Just as she thought. Both families of Kent and Sanders cousins failed to complete their homework.

Something must be done.

"A situation has arisen that I must address." Karen stood. "If you remember, on our last day of class before Christmas, I assigned you work to do on your days at home. I gave you very clear instructions. There is no reason for your assignments to come back to school today incomplete. Some of you did your homework, so thank you for following directions. But some of you did not. To make this fair for everyone, I must give a punishment to those who ignored my instruction. For students who did not complete their homework, you are required to copy out the entire "A" section of your dictionaries during recess until you have it finished to my satisfaction. Understood?"

Groans echoed from the back row.

That sort of response did not meet Karen's standards for respectfulness. She asked again, "Understood?"

"Yes, Miss Millerson." Although half-hearted, that answer worked much better.

"Good. You may read from your books for the next fifteen minutes. Then we will break for lunch."

Later that day, Karen assigned Joe and Marty the task of collecting the water supply for the afternoon. The physical activity should keep them busy and out of trouble. The stream was nearby, so the boys could return before they got too cold.

But the boys delayed their return to their desks. Karen went looking for them, only to discover them in the act of pouring all of the water over the school steps. A glaze of ice coated each one. No one could use the steps without falling. When she dismissed school, Karen had to help the smaller children navigate the slick surface. Even she had trouble staying on her feet. The railing gave her little support in climbing the treacherous steps.

On Tuesday, while doling out punishment to Joe and Marty for Monday's stunt, Emmett and his brother did the stealthy work of stealing lunches from the Hinkley girls. Karen discovered this crime over the noon hour when two of the sisters couldn't find their lunch pails. Of course, Karen drew the conclusion that any trouble of this nature happened because of the Kent or Sanders boys. Sure enough, seated in the usual place in the last row were Emmett and his little brother sharing the blueberry tarts for which Lucy Hinkley was well known.

Karen separated the two of them after that, ordering Emmett to sit with Evie Patterson and for his brother to take a seat with Sarah Hixson. The girls complained. Karen couldn't blame them. Who would want to get stuck with a troublemaker as your desk mate? Not her, and not these close friends who were also two of the best students in the school.

But she had no other choice. In a couple of weeks, she'd change the seating so that the girls might get back together again. Punishing the naughty students shouldn't mean consequences for the good students too.

Tuesday afternoon went better. Karen credited the peace and quiet to the fact that the boys had run out of ideas. As soon as another prank came to mind, though, Karen was sure to see it in her classroom.

She was right. Wednesday morning, in the middle of assisting her three kindergarten students with reading, the stove began to pour out a terrible smoke.

"Ew, Teacher." Evie Patterson wrinkled her nose and whined as she fanned the air before her. Seated near the stove, the black smoke billowed around her desk.

The whine implied that she held Karen personally responsible for this new turn of events. Still not quite over the injustice of her new desk mate, Evie probably felt she had a good reason for blaming her teacher for yet another difficulty.

Karen stood and rushed to the stove. By this time, all the students seated at the desks surrounding the stove were coughing. A peculiar odor permeated the room when Karen yanked the stove's door open. She coughed and fanned the air as the black cloud stung her eyes. Unable to see a thing in the stove's interior, she went for the broom and used the handle to poke around in swift jabs so the broom didn't catch on fire.

Flaming bits of ash leaped from within and smoldered on the floor and on Karen's skirt.

The children scrambled to their feet and left their desks. Some covered their mouths. Others whimpered.

Still, Karen could not see into the stove. "Cal, please open a window. Wade, bring the water bucket." The two eighth graders were responsible enough to be trusted with the tasks.

Karen poked around in the stove until Wade brought the bucket and ladled water over the stove's contents. Gradually, the smoke diminished, leaving behind a gray haze. Karen retrieved the metal basin she used as a sink under the pump in the yard during the warmer months. Then, scooping with the ladle from the water bucket, she cleaned out the stove.

Charred remnants of wood fell into the basin along with some half-burned leaves and a few sticks. These were common items to find in a stove, so Karen kept digging. The next scoop produced a charred sphere, still smoldering black smoke.

She held it up in front of her with the ladle for everyone to see. "Here's the problem."

The students inched closer for a better look.

"Hey, that's our baseball." Marty scowled and looked around at his buddies. "Who pulled such a dirty trick?"

Apparently not Marty. Karen checked one potential prankster from her mental list.

The boys shrugged.

"Which one of you had wood pile duty today?" Karen scanned the group in search of the teen who stocked the stove from the woodpile during his recesses.

Tim Hixson's face turned bright red.

Emmett pointed at him.

"It's Tim. He burned our baseball." Joe's voice dripped with accusation.

Joe, Emmett, and Marty closed in on Tim, backing him into the corner. "You owe us a baseball." Joe rolled up his sleeves.

The traitors. They go and pull Tim in on their stunts so that they have someone to blame but then turn on him when he manages to pull off a prank all by himself. Karen must do something, or she'd soon have a fight on her hands. "Everyone return to your seats. The smoke is gone now."

The students followed directions while Karen stood by her desk facing them. "Tim, can you tell us how this happened?"

"I...I don't...don't know."

Karen clenched her teeth against a laugh. Tim reminded her of Logan when he got flustered about something. If Logan ever got into trouble during his country school days, he probably would've sounded a lot like Tim.

Karen cleared her throat. "You didn't do it on purpose."

Tim shook his head with enough vigor to toss his red hair into complete disarray. "No, Teacher. Honest I didn't."

Karen rounded the corner of her desk. "That will ease your punishment."

Tim almost smiled.

"Shall we just say the last time someone played with the baseball it landed in a place where no one could find it?"

"Sure, yeah." The smile worked across Tim's face.

"But I gave you boys clear instructions to bring the sport supplies indoors after every recess. That baseball was on the shelf by the door. I remember seeing it there. You haven't played baseball since November."

The room grew quiet while all the students watched their teacher.

"For that baseball to get lost in the wood pile, someone would've had to take it out and then lose it at some time other than recess." She peered at the back row. "Am I right?"

Joe and Marty exchanged furtive glances.

"Do you boys know anything about this?" Karen focused on the Kent brothers.

In his usual insolent way, Joe made eye contact and shrugged.

"Maybe we need to punish the person who lost the baseball instead of Tim." Karen crossed her arms.

The room stayed silent.

Joe glared at Tim.

"Let's get back to work." Karen sat. "I'll think this over and decide how to discipline you for not following directions, Joe." She glanced over at Cal Jones. "Cal, could you please close the window?"

"Yes, Miss Millerson." He moved to fulfill her request.

"Tim, I'd like you to refuel the stove. Could you take care of that now, please?"

He stood on his lanky legs.

Joe jutted a foot into the aisle and succeeded in tripping him.

KAREN ENTERED the farmhouse in late afternoon. She'd stayed after school to prepare exams for the next morning. The superintendent's deadline loomed only days away. If she didn't administer those tests on time, she'd have no scores to turn in. That would reflect on the students' records as failure to complete the first semester. Then they wouldn't pass their current grade level. If those boys would just stop cutting up, she could spend all that valuable time on teaching instead of on discipline.

With a wave to Sandy and Tillie busy with meal preparation, Karen breezed through the kitchen. She needed to talk, to vent, and find a measure of solace. The best place to look for it was in the parlor with her fiancé who, still confined to the sofa, would have plenty of time to listen.

Logan's full attention lay on the piece of paper propped on his knee with the help of a book. He wrote on it with the pen in his left hand. "Hi, sweetheart," he said without looking up.

"Hi." Karen dropped into the nearby rocking chair with a sigh. "You'll never believe what those boys are up to now. They keep coming up with more ways to cause trouble. And at a time when I need them to behave."

"Hmm mmm." Logan kept writing.

"Today, Tim Hixson threw the baseball in the stove along with a load of wood. The baseball." She leaned forward and emphasized the words.

But Logan only nodded.

"He made Marty so mad, I sent Wade Patterson to the Hinkleys to fetch Tom so that he could referee the noon recess. Good thing I did. The boys got in a fight. I wouldn't have been strong enough to break it up."

"I'm sorry." Still, Logan wrote on his paper.

Did the man dare to write a sermon instead of listening to her? He had no need of one yet. His injuries required more healing before he might return to the pulpit. He really should pay more attention.

Karen stood. "What are you writing?"

Logan grunted when she snatched the paper out of his hand. He reached for it, but his pain-dulled movements were no match for her anger infused ones.

She studied the page. A long, jagged line of ink trailed from the last letter. Her stomach pricked. That impulsive reach for his paper meant he'd need to redo his work. At the top of the page, Logan had written the date and Uncle Henry's address.

She read the salutation. "Dear Mrs. Millerson." A frown held her forehead captive. "You're writing to my mother?"

Logan scratched his jaw. "Yes."

"But why?" Surely Logan wouldn't rehearse in detail every last trial of the past few days. Mother would think she couldn't teach. That she'd failed. Never would she want Uncle Henry to think his investment in her education had been wasted.

Logan puffed out his cheeks. "I'm asking for her permission to marry you."

Karen released a shaky breath. "You are?"

"Your father is gone. I've never met any of your family, so it made sense to me to use this time while I'm laid up to contact your mother and let her know of my intentions."

Karen's mouth dropped open.

A glint of humor twinkled in Logan's eyes. "Our engagement may appear improper, but that doesn't mean I can't act as a gentleman and ask for your hand in marriage."

Karen wrestled with her desire to plant a kiss on his mouth and yet strangle him at the same time. "Mother may not give her blessing since you are a preacher."

Logan didn't reply. Instead, he reclaimed his letter from her grasp, and, ignoring the trail of ink, continued writing.

"I don't know what to do." Karen dropped into the nearby chair once more.

"Not much you can do. Just wait for her to respond." His pen scratched the paper at a rapid pace as though he had much to say to Mother.

"I'm not talking about your letter. I can guess her reaction anyway. You're a minister, just like the man who ruined her life. She won't be too eager to run the risk of the same thing happening to her daughter." Karen's own words shot all through her heart. If Mother really didn't approve of Logan, Karen might get forced into choosing between him and her family.

Logan paused and looked at her. "Don't borrow trouble, Karen. We believe the Lord wants us together. He'll find a way."

If he wasn't bandaged and casted, Karen would hurl herself into his arms and stay there until she'd absorbed a degree of his optimism. Or was it faith? Logan had a way of viewing all of life through a lens colored with a quiet assurance of God's sovereign care for him. Nothing went awry without God's explicit permission. Not burned baseballs, or skeptical family members, or even Logan's health.

The picture he made propped on pillows and patiently awaiting healing comforted her heart. In His time, God would provide all she needed.

She leaned to kiss his cheek. "You're right."

He only glanced up, offered her a quick grin, and kept writing.

CHAPTER SIX

he superintendent's deadline arrived. Karen got her
scores turned in to him with no time to spare. The
boys had settled down to a degree of cooperation, but they still
acted ornery and then turned surly when Karen corrected them.
If the weather would warm up, she might be able to give them
more time to run off some energy outside, but snow still covered
the ground and ice still coated the steps.

Tim did not end up owing anyone for a baseball. Karen
coached him on his tendencies toward forgetfulness. Maybe he'd
develop a little more responsibility if he stayed better focused.
Mr. Hinkley promised the boys a new ball from the school's
budget when the weather warmed. Much to Joe's disappointment, he was told by the school board chairman and his teacher
that he could not play baseball with the rest of the boys because
of his treatment of Tim.

Karen kept watch over Joe and his buddies. It was only a
matter of time until Joe retaliated or one of the others dreamed
up a new prank. She tried not to hold her breath and turned her
attentions instead to the students who deserved just as much of

her attention for their good behavior as some of the others did for their naughtiness.

"How are your piano lessons going?" Karen asked fifth grader Alice Hinkley, who studied under her mother's tutelage.

"Fine. Mama wants me to play for church sometime. Do you think Reverend Betten would like that?" Alice looked up at Karen as they sauntered through the snowy school yard during the noon recess.

"I'm sure he would. And if Reverend Betten decides not to use you, then maybe I can persuade Reverend De Witt to call on your help for the afternoon service." Karen bit her lip. She may have spoken too soon. Just because Logan was back on his feet again didn't mean he saw the need for Karen's assistance. She probably wouldn't have much sway with a man intent on working alone.

Alice shrugged.

Karen's idea met with as much enthusiasm as her suggestion that she go with Logan and lead the singing when he returned to preaching later this week.

But he'd done more than just shrug. He'd shaken his head and told her to stay home. Now that they were engaged, Logan should welcome her help. Maybe his refusal was another attempt at making their present living arrangements as honorable as possible. He certainly would not need to spend time with her if she stayed behind at home with Sandy and Tillie. But couldn't he see their efforts were for the Lord? Surely that would ease Logan's conscience.

A cracking sound split through Karen's thoughts. She glanced up. Children of all sizes rushed to the fort made of snow bricks where Joe and Marty, along with cousins Emmett and Wally, hunkered down beside Tim.

Joe's snickers alerted Karen that trouble brewed.

She marched to the fort. "What happened?"

All four cousins looked up at her. Amusement and defiance lit their eyes, but no guilt.

Typical.

"Come out here and tell me what happened." Karen pointed to the packed snow in front of her.

Tim Hixson stood, his cheeks red from cold and his eyes bright. "We were shootin' rocks."

Karen frowned at him. "I told you boys not to shoot rocks. Only throw snowballs. Why didn't you listen?"

No answer.

"What did you hit?" Karen's gaze danced over her students. No one cried out in pain or wiped blood from their faces.

"The...the...school." Tim stuttered, which was a good sign that she could at least conjure up a little guilt in one of them.

Karen shifted her attention to the outside wall of the school. A jagged crack ran diagonal across one of the windows. "How did you shoot so far?" She turned back to the boys.

A wooden handle to something peeked out of Marty's coat pocket.

"Give it to me."

Marty shook his head. "I don't have nothin'."

Karen pointed. "That. In your pocket. Right now."

Marty slipped his hands from his pockets, palms to the sky.

Karen took advantage of the cleared pocket, reached in, and held the offending toy out for all to see. "A slingshot. I warned you boys not to bring these to school. Whose is it?"

Everyone pointed at Tim.

"This is yours, Tim?"

"Uh huh." His head bobbed, and his voice wavered.

"You know to leave it at home. What is it doing here?"

"Joe told me to bring it so's we could shoot the girls." Tim must've agreed in order to get back into Joe's good graces. Silly boy.

The boys laughed. For a moment, Tim was the hero.

For a short moment.

Shattering sounded behind Karen. She swiveled. The bottom half of the window crashed to the icy ridges of snow on the ground. Sharp edges peaked on the glass that remained ready to slice the hands and fingers of curious children. A frigid breeze swayed the white curtains as it passed into the classroom. The stove would never keep up.

Only one thing remained for Karen to do. "Well, children. It looks like we can't have class any more today."

The fort occupants cheered as if that had been their goal all along.

Karen quieted them down. "Go inside and collect your math books. Take them home and complete the assignment I gave you this morning." She really should discipline the culprits by assigning more cleaning duties, but those shards of glass were too dangerous. Consequences must wait for another day.

The children moved to the stairs, but Karen remained where she was and stared at the broken window so recently repaired after the hail damage at the beginning of the school year. Now it needed repair again. Not because of natural causes like a storm but because of unruly boys she as the teacher should have the skill to manage. Karen's stomach sank. Whatever would she tell Mr. Hinkley?

THE DOOR of the farmhouse banged shut as Karen entered, rattling the icy windows of the kitchen where Sandy washed dishes. Logan sat at the table. His casted leg rested on a stool. Books lay open and stacked one on top of another surrounding the fanned pages of notes before him. He glanced up. "Karen! What are you doing home?"

Sandy turned around, the dish cloth sagging from her grasp.

"You'll never believe what happened." She unwound her

scarf and draped it over a chair. "Those Kent boys are causing trouble again."

Logan dropped his pencil. His eyes rolled.

"They shot a rock through a window. Cracked and shattered half of it. I cancelled class and sent the students home. I've told those boys to leave their sling shots at home, but Tim brought his anyway. Joe provoked him." She sank into a chair. "The window they broke was one the school board replaced after the storm damage. Wish I didn't have to tell Tom Hinkley that the school board has to spend the money to replace another window."

Even worse, the news of a broken window admitted her failure to maintain control of her classroom. Ever since the older boys returned to school in November after harvest, she'd had nothing but trouble. One of these days she was going to keep order, but in the meantime the school board chairman would think her incompetent. The very word grated on Karen's sense of worth.

"How do I know those boys weren't trying to find a way to get out of staying in school today and doing their work? Vera won't make them complete their homework, so every one of those cousins will come to school tomorrow with incomplete assignments. Only when I supervise their work during school hours does anything get done." Karen lifted her chin.

Logan hefted himself onto his one good leg. "Hand me my crutches please, Mama."

"Where are you going?" Sandy asked after fulfilling his request.

"To the barn to hitch up the sleigh."

"But you aren't ready."

"Karen needs to talk to Tom." He said the words through gritted teeth as though the shift to a standing position caused pain. Or maybe he was just as frustrated over the situation at the school as she was.

"Andrew can take her the next time he stops by. Dr. Bolton

gave orders for you not to go outdoors in the snow except to do the milking. You need to stay here."

Logan ignored his mother, leaned against the wall, and worked at putting on his coat. "I'll drive you, swee—" he bit his lip "—Karen. Just give me a minute to get outside."

Karen's face heated. Logan nearly slipped calling her by his own special endearment for her. That would've been almost as treacherous for him as a slip on the ice and snow with a pair of crutches. Karen glanced at Sandy to see if she noticed. But Sandy's attention stayed on Logan's casted leg, her eyes full of concern.

After a quick flash of a grin at Karen, he was gone.

Twenty minutes later, Logan pulled the sleigh into the lane. Karen got in for the two-mile ride to the Hinkley farm. If the biting wind in her face would cool her insides, Karen might enjoy the ride with Logan. But her pulse raced right along with the speeding runners on the snow.

"I wish I could just make them mind me." Karen glared at the road. "Tim goes along with whatever Joe and Marty Kent say. He listens to them before listening to me, even if it means getting in trouble. I don't understand why Tim would take that risk. He knows the rules."

Logan didn't say anything, but he didn't need to. His willingness to listen was enough.

She continued to complain until they drove into the Hinkleys' lane. Logan slid from his seat and leaned against the sleigh.

"Let me help you." Karen reached for his crutches that had been riding at their feet. She held them upright so that Logan could maneuver them under his arms. "Don't move until I come around to your side."

Karen left the sleigh and held onto Logan while he tied the reins to the fence. Then she walked at his side while Logan inched his way across the snowy yard.

The door swung open. Tom Hinkley stood on the porch,

smoke swirling around his head from the pipe in his hand. "Afternoon, Miss Millerson. I bet I know why you're here. The girls told me all about it when they came home."

"I'm awfully sorry, Mr. Hinkley. The school board already spent so much money on repairs after the storm and now one of those same windows is broken." Karen followed Logan into the house.

"Let me take your coats." Tom's wife, Lucy, helped Logan slide his coat from his arms while Tom situated a chair for him. Then she took Karen's coat and disappeared into another part of the house.

"Good to see ya out, Logan." Tom leaned the crutches against one end of the table when Logan sat down.

"Thanks. This is the first I hitched up the sleigh and drove anywhere since my fall." Logan accepted a cup of coffee from Lucy.

Mr. Hinkley joined him at the table. "The girls are in the parlor studyin' if you want to say 'hi.'"

Karen left in search of Faye, Alice, and Mary Ellen. The three of them were so engrossed in their math homework that they failed to notice their teacher in the room. Using a quiet voice so she wouldn't frighten them, she called their names.

"Hi, Miss Millerson," Alice said. "We're almost finished. Mama promised us sugared donuts when we got this done. Would you like one too?"

"I would." Karen's heart constricted. What a lovely sight, these sisters working with diligence to prepare for class. Teachers really shouldn't play favorites, but if Karen ended up falling to the temptation, she'd lavish special attention on these young ladies. She left them alone and returned to the kitchen.

"Faye tells us the older boys shot off a sling shot. That right, Miss Millerson?" Mr. Hinkley stirred some sugar into his cup.

"Yes." Oh, the humiliation of confessing her failures. "I've told them repeatedly not to bring those toys to school, but they don't remember."

"I think I've got an idea that may help."

Karen could only guess what was going on in Mr. Hinkley's mind.

He took a sip of coffee. "Marty, Joe, Wally, Emmett, and Tim should all share the cost for purchasing the new window."

"That sounds fair."

"I'll go to the school and nail some wood over that window until the glass arrives. Then I'll head to the Kent farm and have a talk with Evan."

"Thank you."

"You should be able to have school tomorrow."

Tom's daughters entered the kitchen and were served doughnuts. Karen's pulse finally settled down. She still had a few students who wanted to learn. For their sake, she'd figure out how to maintain order once and for all.

CHAPTER SEVEN

$\mathcal{L}$ ogan wiped the fine flour dust from the cover of his commentary.

Mama stood at the table kneading dough. "Sorry, dear." She slid his stack of books away from her work area. "I'll be finished in a minute."

He flipped a page in his Bible. How he'd love the peace and quiet of his room right now. But the doctor hadn't given him permission yet to climb stairs. Yesterday's run with Karen to the Hinkleys' had taxed his endurance anyway. He'd better take it easy today which meant sermons must get written at the kitchen table, even on Mama's baking day.

In addition to tiring him, the trip to the Hinkleys' had also stolen some of his study time, putting him behind schedule in the routine he followed to develop a sermon. Sunday loomed only two days into the future, marking his first day back in the pulpit for the Meadow Creek congregation. They deserved nothing less than his best.

Mama thumped dough into a tin loaf pan. She covered it with a cloth and moved it over to the stove top. "Let me wipe off the flour and then I'll move out of your way."

The tabletop clean, Logan spread his books out and set to work taking notes.

Tillie entered the kitchen. "Can I help you get dinner fixed, Mama?"

Mama nodded and gave Tillie a few instructions.

The women banged cupboard doors, clanked pans, and stomped back and forth to the pantry. All the noise and commotion made the minutes stretch into what might as well have been an entire hour.

If Logan could just escape upstairs to the quiet of his own room. Maybe he could secure the use of the dining room table for next week's study if Tillie finished sewing the dress laid out in pieces and taking up every inch of space the larger table afforded. He sighed and ducked his head to reread a paragraph.

A horse whinnied in the lane.

Logan glanced up. "Oh, no." Not only did he have yet another interruption, but that interruption was his most dreaded visitor.

Eldon Kent hadn't been to the De Witt farm since his last attempt to court Karen. As far as Logan cared, Eldon could stay in town, minding his own business, and leave everyone in Logan's household alone.

He clenched his teeth and asked the Lord to replenish his patience.

"Looks like you have company, Logan. I'll let him in." Tillie hastened to the door and opened it for Eldon.

"Good afternoon." Eldon's greeting was as stiff as his sharply creased clothing. He looked as though he belonged on a city street and not standing here in the kitchen amidst the mess of open books and clanging pans.

"What can I do for you?" Logan congratulated himself on producing such an accommodating tone of voice.

"I've been concerned about you lately." Eldon's words held a spark of compassion. Logan might fall for the façade if his past experience hadn't already proven how cold and uncaring Eldon really was.

"I appreciate that." He meant it. Maybe a little kindness would thaw Eldon out a bit.

Eldon took a seat at the table. "The injuries from your fall have probably created difficulties for you. I hear the Pattersons have been doing your milking."

"Yes, that's right." Logan laid his pencil down. Mama and Tillie clattering around in the background and Eldon pressing him for information crowded out his opportunity for sermon writing.

"I assume you've still been supplying milk to the creamery in Bridgewater Springs."

"I should receive payment from them any day." Most of that money would compensate Vern for doing the work. The remainder would pay the doctor. No money would end up in the bank's possession this time around, but Eldon didn't need to know all that.

"Good. I'm glad to hear it. Your first payment for the new year is overdue so I've come to check up on you but also to collect." Eldon's eyes narrowed, and he folded his hands in front of him.

The gesture transported Logan back to Eldon's office at the bank once again. He cleared his throat. "I told you the check from the creamery hasn't arrived yet. As soon as it does, I'll find a way to pay you."

"I don't tolerate late payments. I'm leaving here with cash."

Logan leaned back in his chair with a sigh. Mama had slipped into the pantry at some point during the exchange, so the only person in the room capable of climbing the stairs was his sister. "Tillie, could you come here, please?"

She paused in pouring cake batter into a pan.

"Go upstairs and get the money Karen paid me at supper last night. You remember where you put it?"

"In your top desk drawer on the left." She took the stairs and soon returned.

"Thank you." Logan accepted the bills she handed him. Then he turned them over to Eldon. "This is all I have."

"What about your income from preaching?"

The man was relentless. He needed to experience a fall out of a haymow, a hit to his head, and broken bones. Then he'd understand why Logan fell behind. But for someone as demanding and uncaring as Eldon, a much larger crisis would be required before he'd understand anything about someone else's struggles.

"I start up again this Sunday."

Eldon counted the money in his hand. "You won't get that debt paid off at this rate."

"I'm trying my best."

Eldon scanned the kitchen as if he searched for articles of value to confiscate. He'd find nothing. The De Witts lived too simple of a life to spend extra money on valuables. Even if they had the funds to indulge in pretty artwork or other extravagance, Logan's parents would've invested it in the Lord's work or secured it in the bank.

With a frown tugging on his mouth, Eldon stuffed the money in his pocket. He stood and shook his finger at Logan. "Bring that payment from the creamery to the bank immediately."

There would be no money left over for the bank, but Logan nodded anyway. Letting Eldon think his word was law worked most of the time as an effective way to keep the peace.

Eldon turned and marched out of the house.

"Good riddance," Tillie muttered. "Didn't realize he was such a crank."

Eldon had actually acted pretty civil today. If Tillie would've accompanied Logan to the bank on the day Eldon informed him of how close his family came to losing their home, she could've seen what Eldon's true colors really were.

Logan shook his head, trying to deal with his disgust. "Tillie, I need your help again."

She came to stand at his side. "Sure. What is it?"

"Please get my account book. It's in the same drawer where I kept the money."

Tillie nodded and left the room.

Logan flipped his Bible shut. No use trying to formulate any more profound theological concepts. Eldon had completely sabotaged any headway Logan had managed to accomplish before his visit.

Tillie returned with the book.

"Thanks." Logan took it and opened it. Just as he expected. No entry had been made since the December day when he paid the last of the interest. Most of January had passed without any change to his account. No wonder Eldon confronted him. Logan would get nervous, too, if he was in Eldon's shoes.

And yet Logan could do nothing about his situation except sit around and wait for his leg to heal. He'd gone out to the barn a few times on his own but still relied on his neighbor's help.

Perhaps Karen staying under his roof was a good thing after all. If she'd moved out as first planned, Logan wouldn't have had even one cent to hand over to Eldon today.

Logan stared at the numbers on the page. If he focused solely on the monetary value of their living arrangements, maybe he could forget he was engaged to the most beautiful woman in the whole world. Then he wouldn't bear this constant ache to hold her in his arms and share kisses like they did the night he proposed.

But a lapse of memory would never last. One glimpse of Karen was all his heart needed to fall prey to the desire that stalked him night and day. He'd have to run away from home and take up residence under a rock to make it stop. Even then, desire would still follow him.

Three more weeks and the cast would come off. Then he'd

move out so fast the women would forget about him. He'd also take over the milking and his other work in enough time to get a payment to the bank before another month passed.

FRIDAY AFTERNOON, Karen swept the school floor as her last task before leaving. The door thumped. She turned around. Vera Kent and Elsie Sanders frowned at her.

Forcing a smile, Karen set her broom aside. "Good afternoon, ladies. Is there anything I can do for you?"

"Tell us why our sons must pay for this window." Vera pointed at the board covering the gap in the wall awaiting a new pane of glass.

"They broke it, Mrs. Kent. The school board chairman and I felt the fairest way to handle the situation was to split the cost evenly between all of the boys who contributed to the damage." Karen stood a little taller. With the truth of the matter on her side, she'd manage to keep this conversation headed in a positive direction.

"You think our children are to blame." Elsie settled her hands on her hips.

"I have proof that Joe, Marty, and Emmett were involved in the incident. I found a sling shot in Marty's pocket at the time the window broke."

"That doesn't mean the boys are guilty of anything requiring payment." Vera scoffed.

"That's right." Elsie nodded. "The kids play with their slingshots around the farm all the time. Even the girls. They don't hurt a thing."

"The fact is, we have a broken window now, and it needs replaced."

Vera's eyes narrowed. "We will not be paying for any broken windows. Not my children. Not Bert and Elsie's. No one. You will need to find a different way to cover the cost of the new glass."

Karen's insides heated. Vera had no right to speak to her in this fashion. Karen was the teacher here, and she had the backing of the school board chairman. Just because Vera was a Kent didn't mean she could get out of taking responsibility for damage done by her own children.

"The glass is already ordered. Mr. Hinkley took care of that yesterday."

"He may regret responding in such a rush." Vera peered at her. "Tom shouldn't listen to the complaints of an inexperienced city girl over the opinions of his own neighbors. We're people he's done business with for years."

Vera's words punched Karen where she'd hurt the most. She most certainly did have experience, even if it came from time spent in a high school classroom. And she'd made strides to fit in with the De Witts. This qualified her as a member of the same community where Vera claimed to have influence.

Elsie's brow rose as if she defied the young outsider to challenge her sister-in-law.

Karen gulped to keep her emotions under control. "Mrs. Kent. Mrs. Sanders. I apologize that I am unable to accommodate your wishes. If there was any other way to repair the school, I would do my best to make sure it happened. But the truth is, your sons damaged school property. Now they must pay."

Vera frowned. Few people in Silver Grove probably stood up to her as Karen had just now. But as the teacher, Karen must develop the character of her students as well as helping them learn. She'd committed to nothing less when she decided to become a teacher. Uncooperative people, even if they did happen to be mothers of her students, would not stand in her way.

"Well." Vera's cheeks reddened. "You may believe what you wish, Miss Millerson, but our sons will not be held responsible for an accident that you as the teacher should've stopped from happening. Not only are you inexperienced in the classroom, but you obviously do not know how to handle teenage boys. Come along, Elsie." The women turned and strode out of the school.

Karen's insides withered, but she stood tall and straight as the women made their exit. No way would she let Vera Kent see that her words mimicked Karen's own. She'd said the very same thing to herself several times since the incident. As the teacher, Karen should've been able to manage those boys so that the damage hadn't occurred.

Still, the information didn't need to get used against her in such an unreasonable way. What parent wouldn't want to see their children act responsibly and cover the cost of their own damages? Karen shook her head. Eldon may have decided to leave her alone after the Christmas season had passed, but the rest of his family more than made up for his aggravations.

"DO YOU FEEL READY FOR SUNDAY?" Karen sat with Logan in the parlor after supper while Sandy and Tillie worked on assembling a dress from the pieces of fabric spread over the dining room table. He read from one of the books Karen had given him for Christmas. She checked Tim Hixson's math paper. The boy had made some progress in math by the time Christmas came. But the days off following the holiday put him behind again.

"I think so." Logan looked at her over the edge of his book.

"Are you sure you don't need any help?" Karen swallowed. Maybe she shouldn't bring up the touchy subject again.

Logan lowered his book far enough for Karen to catch a glimpse of the grin pulling at his mouth. "Thank you, but no."

"We'd be doing it for the Lord, Logan."

Logan leaned forward and whispered. "It doesn't change the fact that you're beautiful."

Karen frowned at him.

"If you really knew how hard I must work to keep our living situation honorable, you'd be glad I turned you down." His features turned serious. If he hadn't already asked her to marry him and then kissed her in a way that revealed his love for her, she'd expect both of those gestures now.

Karen's stomach tingled as the truth of Logan's confession saturated her brain. "I didn't know this was so hard for you."

His jaw twitched. "Some days it's nearly impossible."

Maybe today had been one of those days. She wrestled with her longing to know the answer, but pressing Logan further may make his struggle worse. A change of subject was in order.

"Vera Kent and Elsie Sanders visited me at the school this afternoon."

"What did they want?"

"They're upset that Mr. Hinkley and I are requiring their children to pay for the new window."

Logan gave a cynical laugh. "All those Kents are the same. What did you say?"

"I didn't back down. I told them the glass is ordered and the boys must pay for it."

"Good for you. Vera isn't accustomed to giving in. She may cause you more trouble."

Karen crossed her arms. "I wouldn't be surprised. She blamed me for the incident, saying I wasn't experienced enough to manage a classroom."

"Sweetheart, you are the best teacher those kids could ask for. Don't listen to the Kent family's complaints about you. If Vera saw you for who you really are, she'd change."

Karen's cheeks heated. "Thanks, Logan. Let's pray that something happens to give her a new outlook."

CHAPTER EIGHT

"*L*ogan dear, let me help you with your suit." Mama's voice carried from the hall.

He looked at his reflection in his bedroom mirror. His shirt had slipped into place just fine, and the buttons gave him no problems. But his trousers were another story. One of his legs fit properly into the length of black fabric. The other one stretched straight out in front of him, too wide in its plaster encasing to cooperate with his efforts.

As a grown man, he shouldn't need his mother to help him. Neither could he stand before a congregation half dressed.

Logan opened the door.

"Oh, my." Mama's eyes grew round at the sight of his empty pant leg dragging along between his legs. She entered the room and set to work coaxing Logan's cast into his trousers.

The pants fit tight but covered his cast. If he didn't still hobble around on crutches, no one would even know about the broken leg.

Mama tucked his shirt in and reached for his suit coat. After easing it onto his shoulders, she lifted his tie off the hanger.

Logan snatched it out of her hand. He might not succeed with the other pieces of his attire, but he could at least tie his own tie. Wrapping the blue strip around his collar, he made quick work of tying it at his neck.

His shoes provided the next challenge. Mama eased his good foot into the black dress shoe and tied it. The other shoe couldn't swallow his foot plus the wide cast, so Mama covered the cast with a black sock.

"You look nice." She handed him the crutches.

He bent to kiss her cheek. "Thanks, Mama."

"Be careful," she said as he hobbled to the stairs.

The climb to his room to wrestle into his suit had been his first use of the stairs since his fall. The strategy he'd relied on to go up would not help him on the way down. He handed the crutches off to Mama and eased into a seated position. Sliding over each step with his casted leg stretched out in front of him, Logan made his way to the kitchen.

Tillie and Karen stood around with worried looks on their faces.

"Are you sure you should do this? There's snow on the ground." Tillie glanced out the window.

"I'll make it." Logan leaned against the wall and let Mama help him with his coat.

Karen settled his red scarf into place and tucked the ends between the coat's lapels. "Take care."

He gazed into her eyes for a moment to assure her he'd do his best. Claiming his crutches, he gathered his Bible off the table and hobbled out the door.

The snow made everything slippery. He inched along to avoid another fall. Hitching the horse to the sleigh and climbing in took extra time. He finally left the barn, on his way to conduct his first service of the new year for the small but faithful congregation from Meadow Creek.

While he drove, his thoughts returned to the summer day when Pete offered him the job as Meadow Creek's preacher after a windstorm demolished their church. Even in winter, the congregation made the drive to Silver Grove to use the church for services. A new building meant much to them, and he would do everything he could to help them meet that goal.

When he arrived, Pete met him in the yard. "Good to see you out again. Let me take care of your horse. The church is unlocked. Go on in."

Logan climbed from the sleigh and crossed the snowy church yard with the help of his crutches. Once inside, he used the few remaining minutes to prepare for worship.

The church filled, and Logan began with the story of his fall from the hay loft. Then he moved into the call to worship and the first hymn. Boy, would he enjoy having Karen here. She could lead the singing, giving him a break to sit down. Leaving her at home was best. If she lived anywhere except with him, he could pick her up and return her to her home, giving the time they'd need to spend together an honorable place in a proper courtship.

The pleasure of bringing Karen with him and taking her back home again belonged to a couple who was already married. The most prudent course of action for his situation was to deny himself any reasons to spend extra time with her. That meant ministering alone on Sunday afternoons. He might as well get used to it. Not even a move to the barn provided a sufficient enough reason for Karen to start helping him again. He'd still have the same problem. His move to the barn only eased the burden he'd created for his household. It did nothing to restore Karen's role in their shared ministry.

He may not see Karen returned to her rightful place until the day he took her as his wife. That glorious moment lay months into the future. He'd do well to accustom himself to functioning like the bachelor he knew how to be for a while longer.

Logan glanced away from the hymnbook, his thoughts returning to the congregation as he finished singing and began the sermon. The Harper family sat on the right side, half-way to the back. Both boys and Agnes sat to one side of their mother. Mr. Harper sat near the aisle. His eyes looked glassy and his movements were clumsy. Something was wrong with the man. Maybe he felt sick. Logan tensed. Surely he hadn't come to church drunk. But considering Mr. Harper's past struggles, the possibility was more likely than Logan wanted to admit.

His attention returned again and again to the Harper row as he preached. "And so we see from Mark's writings in chapter two that Jesus is the one with the power to forgive sin. When he does, healing takes place in your life. All you need to—"

A groan and a thump cut off Logan's words. The entire assembly gasped as Mr. Harper fell into the aisle.

The man lay so still that several people seated nearby left their pews and bent over him. Logan rushed to the scene with as much ease as his cast allowed and bent down. He checked Mr. Harper's eyes and felt for his pulse. Both indicated that Mr. Harper didn't happen to choose the middle of the church service as a good time to take a nap. He'd passed out and needed more help than Logan could give him.

"Lester, could you please go to the parsonage and get Peter Betten? Mr. Harper can rest there until he feels well enough to drive home."

Within minutes, Pete arrived. Lester assisted Pete in hauling Mr. Harper's slumped form from the building. Mrs. Harper and her children followed.

Logan returned to the pulpit and cleared his throat. "Let's finish the service the best we can. I'll cut it a little shorter since we're all concerned about the Harpers. Please join me in praying for them."

Choosing his words carefully, he kept many of his thoughts to himself. Mr. Harper had come to church drunk. Logan couldn't imagine why. The man had been doing so well since his conversion last fall.

As he said "amen," Logan pushed his wonderings from his

mind and concentrated instead on finishing his sermon. After the last hymn, Logan went to the back of the church and prepared to greet everyone who'd come to church today.

When the building emptied, Logan made his way to Pete's house. Anna answered the door and led him to the place where Mr. Harper lay. The man's eyelids drooped, but he recognized Logan.

He reached for Logan's hand and spoke with slurred speech. "Rev, I'm awful sorry. I feel so dumb for passin' out like that."

Logan eased into a nearby chair. "What happened?"

"My old friend, Chet, stopped by the cabin last night. Said he wanted my help celebratin'. With Chet, celebratin' means drinkin'. Always has. I told him I'd quit livin' that life. I'm sober now, and I've been doin' a good job bringin' Amelia all my pay." He paused and looked at his wife.

"Chet wouldn't listen. His wife left him before Christmas, and he's been awful lonely. I sorta felt sorry for the guy. I figured a couple of hours sittin' around keeping him company wouldn't hurt nothin', so I went home with him."

He shook his head. "Big mistake. Turns out Chet had a whole houseful of our old drinkin' buddies already gathered. Now, Rev, I've got the strength to stay away from the bottle when I'm by myself. But in the company of all those guys livin' it up and havin' a good time, I caved. I wandered home again around one this morning. Amelia insisted on goin' to church. I wanted to be there. I really did. I figured I'd pull through even if I still didn't feel the best. Never dreamed I'd faint right there in front of everybody."

"How are you feeling now?" Logan asked.

"Better. I should be able to drive us all home."

"Mr. Harper."

"Call me Jack."

"All right. Jack, I'm concerned about you. Will you continue staying sober, or was last night's exposure enough to pull you back into drinking again?"

"I've thought that through myself. I'm gonna try real hard to stay out of trouble."

"Trying may not be enough. Do you have anyone in Meadow Creek to support you?"

"My wife. And my boss at the mill. He does pretty good tellin' me I'm doin' the right thing."

"What about taking time to read your Bible? Does anyone help you with that?"

"Yeah. Amelia does some, but the kids are always askin' her for stuff."

"How would you like to meet with me? I'm a bit confined to home right now, but maybe when my cast comes off and the weather warms, we can study together. Learning more about God's word will give you the strength you need to say 'no' to drinking in any situation."

Jack rubbed his forehead. "I'd like that. Thanks, Rev." He worked at sitting up. Once he achieved an upright position, he held his head. "Feelin' a little dizzy, but I'll manage. Help me so we can go home."

Mrs. Harper got him standing and walking. Agnes paused to give Logan a hug. "Share that with Miss Millerson. I miss her. When is she coming back?"

"I'm not sure, but I'll let her know you asked." Logan released Agnes and looked into her eyes.

Sadness dimmed them, but she nodded in quiet acceptance of Logan's answer.

"Come, Agnes. It's time to go." Mrs. Harper gathered the boys from the table where Pete entertained them with a game.

"Bye, Reverend De Witt." The little girl turned to look at him over her shoulder and waved.

Logan followed them to the door and leaned against it as he

watched them climb into their sleigh. Even with Logan's help, Jack Harper had a long road ahead of him.

He prayed for the Harpers all week. When they came to church the next Sunday, Jack was with them. His eyes looked a little clearer, and he did better staying alert. He even attended the meeting held after the service. Five others joined him.

Logan stood before them to begin the discussion. "Thanks for taking this extra time to meet. Your church board asked me to help your congregation make plans for rebuilding the church you lost in last summer's storm. I have some questions we need to get answered before moving forward. First, how much money do you have to buy lumber?"

Lester, the man who'd helped Jack the previous Sunday, was also the one who sent Logan his monthly payments. He spoke up. "We have thirty-two dollars."

The amount wouldn't go very far in constructing an entire building. "Do you have any ideas for raising more money?"

The men looked at each other. Lester spoke up again. "We've been talking it over with our wives. They'd like to host a bake sale. One sale won't generate all the funds we need, so we should come up with more projects."

"Discuss that some more and bring your ideas to our next meeting."

Some of the men nodded.

"The second question I want to ask is if you have a date in mind for when you'd like to have the building completed."

"We were hoping to start by the end of March. The snow should be gone by then. We'd like to have the church completed and ready by the time school gets out in May," a man in the back row said.

Logan nodded his agreement. They'd need to spend the month of February raising funds so that they could purchase lumber and windows in March. "Anything else you want to talk about?"

"That about covers it, "Lester said.

The men left to find their families while Logan put on his coat. The cozy parlor lured him where he'd have just enough time before the evening milking to talk with Karen and tell her all about the plans for Meadow Creek's new church. She may not be included in the services, but that didn't mean she'd stopped caring about the people in his little congregation. She might even have ideas for fundraisers she wouldn't mind sharing with him.

Now he just needed his leg to heal. Meadow Creek had large amounts of work ahead of them, and he wanted to be right in the middle of all of it.

CHAPTER NINE

*B*oy, did Logan long for a good scratch. The skin under his cast was getting tired of the confinement. The summer haying season with its bits of straw dropped down the back of his neck was a bubble bath compared to the consistent irritation of the cast.

One more week. Just one more, and Logan would be free to walk on his own again. He dragged his leg out from under the Holstein and crept to a standing position. He was so slow, milking took longer than usual. At each cow, Logan knelt down, leaning on the stanchion for support. Then he wedged his casted leg under the cow while he bent the knee of his other leg and leaned in to reach the udders.

That didn't go so bad, but the return to a standing posture was the worst. The cast weighed as much as a millstone and possessed about as much flexibility as one. By the time Logan finished with the last cow, he was ready for a nap. He made his best attempt to mask his fatigue in the evenings and on week-ends. Neither Mama, Tillie, nor Karen knew how tired he really was.

Tired of lugging around a cast and leaning on crutches.

Weary of the confinement to the house due to cold temperatures and his weakened condition. But most of all, Logan was exhausted from keeping himself under control. Engagement had to be the toughest assignment he'd ever been given. If he had to do it again, he'd make sure Pete stood by at the church, wedding liturgy at the ready so that the minute Karen said "yes," Logan could drive her straight to the ceremony and marry her on the spot.

Then he could share everything with her. Sunday afternoon ministry, his last name, even his room.

Logan sloshed milk out of the pails as he maneuvered through the barn on crutches. This afternoon, he planned to set up housekeeping in the barn. Mr. Jones had returned to the farm and finished the shingling job for him. Now the lean-to sat ready for a new occupant, complete with the cot and small stove he'd set up before beginning work on the roof. Tonight, he'd take up his new residence far, far removed from the comforts of the house before the longing and the waiting tore him apart.

The milking finished, Logan worked in the milk parlor filling cans. This job also took much longer than it had before his injury. At his delayed pace, Logan labored right up to the noon hour. He finally swept the floor and then made his way to the house, inching the crutches along, careful to avoid uneven patches of snow.

In the house, he removed the shoe from his good leg, washed his hands, and sat down in his chair at the table.

Mama ladled chicken noodle soup into bowls. The steaming broth smelled wonderfully of onions and herbs, making Logan's stomach rumble. The move out of the house would be unbearable without the simple comfort of Mama's cooking.

She brought the bowls to the table and took her seat. "Tillie is in town with the Carters today. Andrew picked her up, so it's just you and me for dinner."

Andrew sure was getting serious if he allowed time during a

busy work day to spend with the girl he courted. Logan's little sister might get married before he did. He brushed the thought aside. Tillie was much too young. She needed to stay here under his care for a while yet. Besides, chances were slim that Tillie had a ring buried in one of her drawers like Karen did. Logan smothered a grin and offered a prayer to start the meal.

Mama broke the silence. "When Andrew came for Tillie this morning, he shared his plans with me. He'll be speaking with you soon to ask permission to marry her."

Logan's heart thumped. He sure was glad Mama gave him this advanced warning. If Andrew sprang the question on him cold, Logan would surely answer with a decisive "no." "I don't know, Mama. This seems so sudden. Tillie is too young."

"I thought you might feel that way, but wait until you hear the rest of the plan. Andrew mentioned that he and Tillie would like for me to live in town with them after they are married."

Since when had Mama learned how to fire cannons? She'd just landed a fiery blast square in his lap. "You can't be serious." Like Tillie, Mama belonged here with him. Under his care as she'd been with Dad. Not removed from the farm and living in town where Logan couldn't provide for her.

"I am, dear. Tillie's eighteenth birthday is only a couple of weeks away. She'll be the age of most girls when she gets married." Mama paused to eat her soup. "What do you think? I told them I wanted to talk with you before making a decision."

Words escaped him. Even the stuttering, bumbling kind that seemed to dribble from his mouth in those moments of anxiety when he should have one hundred better things to say.

But here he sat. Quiet. Stunned.

Mama threw another blast. "If I moved to town, you could return to preaching."

Words came this time. "Don't make such a big change because of how it might affect me. You do what you want." Tillie's new marriage should start strong, free from extra burdens her big brother should carry. He kept that thought to himself. Mama might think that he saw her as a burden and get her feelings hurt.

"Don't you want to return?"

"Of course I do. But I can't until I see you provided for."

"I will be if I move to town with Tillie and her new husband."

"Only if you are sure, Mama."

"I'm sure. Someday, when Tillie has a family, I'll be right there to help her out." Mama laughed. "We've shared a kitchen for Tillie's whole life. I doubt that either one of us could accomplish anything alone."

Logan forced a smile.

Mama grew serious. "I appreciate everything you do, dear. I don't know how to tell you what it means to me that you were here during those days following your father's death. You've given more than I ever expected." She reached across the table and squeezed Logan's hand. "Still, if I move to town, you'd be free to pursue your own life wherever or with whomever you choose."

Heat spread up Logan's neck and over his cheeks. He didn't dare entertain the thoughts rushing into his mind. Mama's words offered him marvelous hopes for marriage, for family, for ministry. He moved his hand away from Mama's grasp and shifted all his concentration onto stirring the soup around and around in his bowl.

"I thought so." Mama's voice was quiet and reflective like she could see straight through him. "You've been acting differently lately."

"Any man with a cast hobbling around on crutches is going to act a little odd." Amazing he hadn't put on more of a show. Those crutches possessed a knack for exaggerating even the slightest lack of coordination. Logan never would understand how he managed to stay on his feet at all.

"I'm not talking about that." Mama smirked. "You've got all the symptoms of a young man who's sweet on someone."

In spite of the rising temperature in his cheeks, Logan shook his head and reached for a slice of bread.

"Did you leave a special young lady behind in Oswell City?"

Another shake of his head.

"Do you care for any of the young women at church?"

Not a large selection to choose from. The Silver Grove congregation included all of three young ladies unattached at the moment. Logan hadn't even given them a thought until Mama asked. "No. Of course not."

Mama leaned on the table. Mirth twinkled in her eyes. She was having entirely too much fun poking around in her son's heart. "Is there anyone in town?"

Logan never paid attention to any of the young women when he went to town. His goals were strictly business. What a silly question for Mama to ask. "No, Mama."

She cocked her head and studied him. "Maybe I'm mistaken after all." She picked up her spoon and continued eating.

Logan drew in a slow breath as he buttered his bread. He'd just survived the most scouring interrogation of his life. He prayed Mama would lose interest and change the subject. Or maybe he could eat faster so he could leave the table sooner. He bit off large bites of bread, not swallowing before he took the next one.

Didn't work. Mama still stalked him. "No. I'm not mistaken. You're in love with someone." She searched his face. "So, if you don't have a girl in Oswell City or in Silver Grove then who?" Mama's gaze shifted to the window. After a few moments she murmured, "Oh, my goodness." Her gaze returned to him. Joy radiated on her face. "You've gone and fallen in love with our own dear, sweet Karen, haven't you?"

Logan bit his lip. Never in his wildest dreams did he see

things coming to this. Mama really should mind her own business more often.

"This is tremendous!"

Apparently no answer from him meant a "yes" in his household.

"How long have you known?"

Mama always did have a way of pressing him into honesty. Boy, he wasn't ready to expose the depths of his love for Karen. Not here. Not yet. Mama deserved to know, but not over a mundane meal of soup. And not while he was still in a cast. And certainly not while he still slept in the house. Couldn't Mama at least wait to get curious until he and Karen had a few more details worked out?

Logan puffed out his cheeks with the breath he'd been holding. "Too long." That about summed up all his struggles.

"Does Karen know?"

Oh, yes. Karen knew. He'd kissed her passionately enough the night he proposed to leave no question. He nodded.

Mama smiled wide. "Does anyone else know?"

"I hope not."

Mama's happiness faded. "You aren't excited. Is something wrong?"

Logan paused. His hand trembled as he held his spoonful of soup midair. A bit of soup spilled over the edge and splashed into the bowl below like a trapeze artist from a circus he'd seen one summer while in seminary. The poor man had failed to maintain his precarious posture on the tight rope. Like Logan right now with Mama. He dropped the entire spoon and remaining helping of soup into his bowl with a clang. Impatience threatened to hijack his voice. "Mama. Karen shares my address, my kitchen table, even my...my..." As much as it convicted him, Logan must spit it out. "Even my...my...up...upstairs."

The Lord may not have spared Logan from stuttering, but he'd sure saved Logan in other ways. Praise God for the small graces of the heavy cast that prevented his occupancy of the room directly across the hall from Karen's. Wow. This must be how the person in First Corinthians chapter three felt after barely surviving the flames of refining fire.

Logan's mind spun with all the potential hazards available to him if he'd remained uninjured and whole. In those places where Logan would've been unable to hang on to his honor, the Lord had protected him in the form of that itchy, clumsy cast. But the battle still wasn't completely won. As long as Logan resided in the house, temptation lurked.

"Oh, I see." Mama sounded a bit contrite. "I'm sorry, dear. Karen is just so much like family that I didn't think about what was at stake for you." She took a drink. "You've been struggling with this for a while."

Logan couldn't deny it, so he didn't try. If Mama followed her pattern of no answer from him meaning "yes," she'd interpret correctly.

She shot to her feet and headed for the stairs. "Stay right where you are. I'll return in a moment." After completing her errand, Mama stood in front of him. "Hold out your hand."

He followed directions.

Mama dropped a cool, smooth object onto his palm and curled his fingers around it. Then she went to her chair.

Logan opened his hand. His stomach lurched. He held the wedding band Mama had worn through all of her years of marriage to Dad.

He choked. "I can't take this."

"Yes, you can. I don't need it anymore."

"But, Mama…"

Mama curled his fingers back around the ring. "When your father died, I'd made up my mind this ring belonged to you someday. I've been waiting for just the right time to give it to you. I believe that time has come."

Mama was actually telling him to propose to Karen. Not just

propose, but marry her. This must mean she'd approve of the choices Logan had already made. God sure had creative ways of giving his blessing. Logan must try to put some of this into words. "You think I should marry Karen."

"I do. She's the one who will stand by your side through a lifetime of ministry."

Mama spoke truth. But ministry didn't receive all of Logan's energy right now. He still farmed. That meant as much to him as anything Mama might be telling him. "But what about the farm? This is our land. It's everything Dad wanted. Everything he spent his whole life working for. It's what...it's what he died doing." Logan's voice trembled.

Moisture gathered in Mama's eyes. "Logan, dear. That may be true, but do you know what made your father prouder than anything else in the world?"

Logan shook his head.

"You."

"What?" He'd deserted Dad to carry the work and financial demands alone. That would hardly make a father proud.

"Not a day went by when your father wasn't praying for you or thanking the Lord for your dedication to ministry."

The tears streamed from his eyes.

"He'd also be pleased with Karen as your choice for a bride." She blinked back tears, probably bittersweet ones mixed with joy for Logan's future and sorrow from her loss of Dad. "Sell the farm if you have to."

Mama fired yet another flaming cannon ball, making Logan's gut collapse as if he'd been hit with ammunition.

"Do what you love, what made your father proud. That's what would've made him truly happy." Mama pulled a scallop-edged handkerchief from her apron pocket.

She openly wept now.

Logan should go to her and offer the reverent phrases he found helpful in these times when people needed comfort. But he couldn't. His insides turned cold, and his tongue tensed into complete stiffness. In the space of one meal, Mama had announced her contemplated move to town, unveiled his heart, and suggested he sell their farm. Mama really ought to be a preacher. She'd managed to create more sensation than he ever could. And she hadn't even pelted him with any Scripture passages. She would've been a menacing force for sure if she'd tried it.

Rising from her chair, Mama slipped the handkerchief back into her pocket. The simple movement roused Logan. He shifted in his seat. If only he could find somewhere to go for a second opinion. Mama didn't have all the answers, did she? Dad was the one who would steer Logan right in this talk about selling the farm and getting married.

But Dad was gone. Only the tombstone with his name on it remained behind.

Better than nothing.

Logan hefted out of his seat and reached for the ever-present crutches propped against the wall nearby. "I need to leave for a little while."

Mama turned to glance at him, worry lines creasing her forehead.

But Logan didn't look back. He had an appointment to keep. Dad may not be able to talk, but he'd sure have plenty of quiet in which to listen.

CHAPTER TEN

A chilly, east wind blew as Logan negotiated a trail around tombstones on the slippery snow. Low, gray clouds hung close to the horizon, promising another round of snowfall. Logan angled toward the fence where John De Witt's stone protruded from the pure white snow.

Logan bent and traced the engraved letters spelling out his own name: De Witt. They were the only De Witts in the county that he knew of. Logan's father immigrated from Holland in 1875 at the young age of twenty-two. He'd saved enough guilders from his work as a blacksmith to travel to Iowa and purchase his farm.

Mama's family had been here longer. He'd visited the cemetery in Bridgewater Springs as a teen, where Grandpa Dielis and Grandma Trintje Overkamp rested in their graves. Mama had married Dad at quite a young age and helped him establish his dairy farm.

Now Dad was gone. Did Logan, as his son, have the right to sell off everything Dad had planned and saved for? But Mama said Logan's call to ministry made Dad proud. Mama's words helped him make a connection. Logan's grandfather, Jacob De

Witt, had been a pastor too. A *dominee* in the Dutch Reformed Church.

"Come with me to America," John had said to his father.

But *Opa* Jacob refused. "The Dutch people need to hear the gospel." So John had sailed alone, his parents staying behind in the home and country they loved.

Logan recalled the entire story as he studied Dad's grave. As a boy, he'd seen the letter in Dad's handwriting, reporting to his parents on his farm and his son Logan. That letter had also included the invitation for his brother to join John in Silver Grove, but no reply ever came.

Dad knew much loneliness in his life. Maybe Logan's choice to go into ministry comforted Dad by bringing his own father a little closer to the new home he'd established. If Logan could've met Opa Jacob even once, he'd have a lot more peace right now.

Did Logan resemble his dominee grandpa in any way? Logan's looks resembled his father, so did the family traits belong to his grandmother or his grandfather?

Logan brushed away the snow at the base of the stone as if the newly exposed portion might provide him with a clue.

More engraved letters filled the bottom of the stone. Logan worked swiftly until the complete message emerged. *All things work together for the good of those who love God, who have been called according to his purpose.* Romans 8:28. Mama had mentioned Dad wanting a Bible verse on his tombstone, but Logan had forgotten until now. Mama had taken care of that detail herself. Logan read again, savoring the words. All things work together. The Reverend Grandfather left behind in Holland. Logan's father buying land and dying before he saw it become a success. Logan as his son following in his grandfather's footsteps, proclaiming the gospel and preaching Christ's message. Not in Holland but in a new land. People needed to hear the gospel in America too.

A rush of energy filled Logan. He worked in partnership with the grandfather he'd never met. Maybe he did resemble Jacob De Witt in some way. Not so much in appearance but in the Holy Spirit's call in both of their lives.

All things work together for good. If Logan sold the farm, he wouldn't betray Dad. Instead, he'd be standing for what the De Witt men believed in. Salvation. Eternity. Evangelism. Logan breathed in the February air that stung his cheeks and chilled his nose. "Dad, I think I'll do what Mama says and sell. I trust that is the decision you would make." Logan wiped his eyes. If he could just hear Dad's voice, he'd feel a little better about making such a large decision on his own.

A voice called to him, but it didn't belong to Dad. Logan turned in the direction of the feminine call. Anna Betten stood on the back porch of the parsonage waving to him.

"Come in out of the cold. I'm concerned about you standing in the wind with no cap on."

He touched the top of his head. Sure enough, the warm hat stayed home. His big decision distracted him more than he thought. "Be right there," Logan called out before taking one last look at the tombstone.

Many conversations awaited him with Mama and with the bank. Logan's heart thudded. Eldon would probably welcome the sale of the De Witt farm. Then he'd have lots of money instantly. He should write Paul Ellenbroek and let his church in Oswell City know what was brewing. Depending on how quickly Logan could finalize his plans, he might return sooner than expected.

Thoughts of the church building housing his cozy study and the sanctuary where many dear people gathered each week to worship put a spring in his step, the steps taken with his right leg anyway. The left leg still dragged along in its plaster cocoon.

As soon as his leg healed, Logan's whole life would change. Like a butterfly after a season of metamorphosis. His spirit and his left leg would both enjoy their own releases into a new freedom. Logan shivered. Whether from the cold wind or the enormity of what awaited him, he couldn't say.

Anna met him at the door. "You must be frozen."

Pete joined them. "Do you have time for a hot cup of coffee?"

"I do." If Dad couldn't share in his decision, his good friend was the next best thing.

"Come over to the table." Pete led the way. "What brings you out to the cemetery on such a raw day? Most people wait for milder weather to visit a grave."

Logan dropped into a chair while Anna leaned his crutches on the wall. "Mama."

"Something the matter with Sandy?" Concern edged Pete's voice.

"No. She's fine. I...I had to get away...and think." Logan accepted the cup Pete poured for him.

"What's on your mind these days, my friend?"

Logan hardly knew where to begin. Mama had spun his world into such topsy-turviness that everything swirled together. He cleared his throat. "At dinner she encouraged me to sell the farm. Said that she'd have a place to live with Tillie and Andrew in town since they're talking about getting married. She wants me to go back to Oswell City."

"That's a lot to take in all at once. What are you going to do?"

"I don't know. I'd love more than anything to return to Oswell City and my life as their pastor." Logan shook his head. His brain housed as many clouds as it did the night he regained consciousness.

"Would you return to Oswell City alone?"

Logan shrugged. "I guess. If Tillie gets married, she will want to stay here. Mama will, too, since she knows she'll have a place to live."

"That's not what I'm talking about."

Pete's quiet voice pricked Logan in a deep place. He raised a questioning gaze to Pete's face.

"What about Karen?" The earnest expression on Pete's face looked innocent enough, absent of any teasing or matchmaking nonsense. The only deserving response Logan could really offer was one of openness. Especially with a wedding band searing him through his shirt pocket.

He pulled it out and laid it on the table.

Anna's eyes grew round. "Sandy's wedding band."

"She wants me to give it to Karen."

"What for, safekeeping?" The teasing hadn't stayed away from Pete's voice for long.

But Logan couldn't laugh. The ring had come from Dad after all. "No. So that Karen might be the next Mrs. De Witt." Boy did he like the sound of that.

Pete leaned back in his chair. "Well done, Sandy," he murmured to himself. Then he chuckled.

Anna leaned forward. "What do you think of that, Logan?"

"What, of my mother and best friend ganging up on me?" He snatched the ring and dropped it back in his pocket before it invited any more taunting.

Anna shook her head. "No, of marrying Karen."

"I'd do it in a minute." The words flew out of his mouth.

Pete and Anna shared one long, intent gaze. A message must have passed between them because Anna nodded.

Pete cleared his throat. "We're still working on remodeling our extra bedroom. It should be finished in a month or so. Even then, we'll still have a bit of a mess, but if Karen wouldn't mind, she's welcome to move in here. We'll find a way to accommodate her the best we can until the two of you set the date." Pete winked at him. A studious and devout friend, Pete had picked up his buddy's ornery habits.

Logan exhaled and shook his head. He could hang on another

month. He had to. His small apartment in the barn would help him.

KAREN CAUGHT a glimpse of Logan standing in the doorway of the dairy barn when she returned to the farm at the end of the school day.

He called out to her. "I need to talk to you."

She adjusted her course and went to the barn instead of the house. "What is it?" she asked as soon as she stepped inside.

Logan closed the door and kissed her. One of his long, lingering kisses that swept away all concern for anything except how his arms felt around her.

"Hmm. I needed that first thing this morning." She smiled the kind of smile only a girl caught in a dream would know how to produce.

"What happened?"

"Lacy Jones is sick again. Running a high fever. I hope it isn't the measles. More of the students might come down with it."

"Sorry to hear that. I'll pray that she doesn't have anything contagious and that she feels better soon."

"I'd like to visit her as soon as the doctor has had a chance to examine her and give an official diagnosis. Could you please drive me to the Jones' farm sometime?"

"Of course I can." Logan released her from his embrace. "I need to tell you about some things that have happened."

Karen's stomach clenched. Logan's warm voice held weight. Whatever he had to say deserved her full attention.

"Come, sit down." He led her to the pile of straw in the corner. "Mama and I had a long discussion over the noon meal today. Change is coming."

"What kind of changes?" Karen held his hand.

He sighed. "Tillie and Andrew are talking of getting married."

"Really? That's wonderful news."

"I guess. Mama thinks it is. She said Andrew has offered for her to live with them in town." Logan grasped the back of his neck.

Karen sat still. The sorrow in Logan's voice drowned her joy. Questions about the farm rested on the tip of her tongue, but Karen bit them off. Logan needed space to tell her in his own way and at his own pace how this new development affected him.

He cleared his throat and then coughed. "Mama said I should sell the farm. No one will live here anymore. She and Tillie will be in town. I'll go back to Oswell City. Dad is gone..." Fine lines creased the corners of Logan's mouth.

Tears sprang to Karen's eyes. If only she could think of something to do or say to ease Logan's anguish.

"These changes affect you, too, sweetheart." He pulled a shiny gold band from his shirt pocket and laid it in her hand.

The afternoon light glinted on the ring.

"It's Mama's wedding ring. Like the farm, she said she wouldn't need it anymore."

"Oh, Logan." Karen's heart squeezed. With the sale of the farm, Logan probably felt as though his mother no longer needed him either.

"She gave it to me today with the hopes that I would give it to you. Said she's been saving it for the day when I met the right woman." Logan turned his gaze on her. Love shone in his moist eyes. "She's right."

Karen heaved in a breath. "Your mother wants me to have her ring?"

Logan nodded. "What would you think of melding it to your engagement ring in time for the wedding?"

"I love that idea. Your mother is very kind."

He put the ring away. "After Mama and I talked, I visited with Pete and Anna for a while. They've changed their minds about letting you live with them."

"You mean, they'll give me their spare room?"

"They hope to have it finished a month from now. Pete said you may use it even though they will still have some cleaning up to do."

Karen's heart swelled. "I'd put up with anything."

Logan didn't respond. His sadness still hung on.

"What's wrong? You don't want me to wear your mother's ring. Is that it?"

"No, of course not." Logan shook his head and ran his hand through his hair. "I just…Mama and Tillie shouldn't have to lose my care for them so that I can move on with my life and be happy."

"The sale of the farm is your mother's idea."

Logan nodded, but his gaze remained fixed on the packed dirt at his feet.

"She wouldn't tell you to do something that wasn't in everyone's best interest."

A single chuckle escaped his lips. "All things work together for good. I read that on Dad's tombstone this afternoon."

"Maybe that is what your mother is trying to tell you." Karen stood. "The sale of the farm. Both of her children getting married. She sees them as God's provision for her family. You can't make a bad decision here, Logan. God already has it all planned out. You only need to follow Him."

For the first time since her arrival home from school, light flickered in Logan's eyes. He stood and grasped both of her hands. "You're the best thing that ever happened to me. Thanks, Karen."

A smile pushed at her mouth, but she held back. "I only see one complication to the plan."

Logan's brow furrowed.

"How much does Tillie know?"

"Not sure. Mama didn't say. But I'd make a guess Tillie hasn't caught on to our engagement. Come to think of it, I never told Mama about it either."

Karen reached up and patted his cheek. "Sounds to me, Reverend De Witt, like you have some explaining to do."

KAREN LAID down her fork after finishing a modest slice of apple pie. Logan had been rather silent during the meal, probably preoccupied with finding the right words for the upcoming conversation. Karen didn't envy him one bit. She could only imagine what Tillie's response might be to his announcement. But Karen couldn't blame her. Any younger sister who'd struggled with grief as much as Tillie had may express confusion or even anger to what he planned to say. Tillie clung to her older brother and relied on him in so many ways. The news that Logan already made plans to leave her and marry soon may prove to be too much.

The plates around Karen quickly emptied of dessert. Logan released her hand and settled both of his on the table's surface.

In the moment Sandy stood to clear the table, Logan cleared his throat. "Mama. Tillie. I have something I must tell you."

The gravity in his voice caught their immediate attention. Sandy sat down.

"Thank you, Mama, for the gift you gave me for Karen today. I showed it to her when she came home from school. She liked it very much."

Sandy's attentive expression relaxed into a slight smile.

"What did you give him?" Tillie searched her mother's face.

"Something very special to me." Sandy's voice quieted, and her eyes turned watery. "My wedding band."

"Why?" Tillie's question came with a sharp inhale of air.

"I want to pass it on to Logan so that his wife may wear it just like I did when his father gave it to me."

"His wife?" Tillie turned her attention on her brother.

Logan slid in his chair, casted leg and all, to Karen's side of the table. Then he wrapped his arm around her shoulders. "Mama, the truth is Karen and I are already engaged."

The air got sucked out of the room while Sandy and Tillie stared.

"I gave Karen an engagement ring for Christmas." Logan spoke in the low tone of a reverend who must break the news to a family that someone died. "I proposed that night after both of you went to bed."

"So you have been in love with her," Sandy whispered.

Logan nodded. A smile tugged at one corner of his mouth.

Tillie continued to stare.

Logan cleared his throat. "Now, look, Tillie. I know this is sudden news. I didn't intend for you to have to find out in this way. I never expected to get married before you did, but it looks like that is what will happen."

Tillie's eyes widened. "Did Mama tell you about me and Andrew?"

"Yes. She said you've offered her a place to live after you and Andrew marry. I'm sorry. I should be the one caring for Mama." Logan's words rushed, one right after the other. "But the farm will get sold."

Tillie nodded her head. "I knew that was probably coming. If Mama moves to town with me, then keeping the house here in the country wouldn't make any sense."

"You also understand that I'll be leaving?"

"I do."

Logan's voice turned scratchy. "I need to return to preaching this spring. That's been the arrangement all along. But, if Karen and I move away before your wedding date, we'll come back to see you get married. I promise."

Karen nodded her agreement when Logan glanced at her.

"So much is happening so fast." Tillie shook her head. "I don't know if I should feel happy or sad."

Karen fiddled with the edge of the tablecloth as the silence grew.

Tillie left her seat and bent down to hug Logan. "One thing will always bring me much joy."

"What is that?" Logan studied his sister's face.

"Karen is staying in our family as my sister." A smile engulfed her entire face.

Logan grinned at her. "Yes, she is. Our family has many decisions that still need to be made, but that one is a guarantee."

Karen smiled, and Sandy laughed.

Logan stood on his good leg and leaned on the table for support. He looked at Tillie with concern in his eyes. "You really don't mind that I'll be getting married and moving away?"

Tillie settled her hands on his shoulders. "Of course I mind. I've always wished you lived closer. Now that you'll take Karen, too, I feel like I'm losing both of you. But, I want to see you as happy as I am with Andrew. The change will take some getting used to, but I wouldn't want it any other way."

Karen's smile wobbled. Tillie had grown so much over the winter months.

"I can't believe I didn't see your true feelings for each other. Karen is perfect for you." Tillie embraced her big brother.

Mama stood and squeezed Tillie's shoulder. "To think that all the time we were teaching Karen how to cook, we were actually training Logan's future wife."

"I'll miss them both so much, but at least I can count on Karen fixing food I like whenever we go to visit them." Tillie's eyes twinkled.

Karen struggled with her longing to break into dancing and twirl about the room. Logan's family had come so far. Each day brought them more healing from their grief. Sandy had given her a most generous gift as affirmation that she welcomed Karen so completely into her family. Tillie could rejoice in the happiness of others. Logan grew more comfortable with the changes a new season would bring.

She looked forward to a future filled with promise as her own heart prepared to share her life once again with a man in ministry.

CHAPTER ELEVEN

*F*riday morning, the doctor bent over Logan with a saw in his hand. Logan's casted leg lay propped up on a kitchen chair.

"This shouldn't cause you any pain. Hold still." The doctor glanced at Logan. "Ready?"

Logan nodded, but his stomach twisted. The teeth on that saw looked awfully jagged. What if the doctor cut too deep?

He scrunched his eyes closed as the saw made contact with the cast. He really shouldn't let this procedure bother him. He'd looked forward to the removal of this cast for weeks. As a grown man, he could handle a saw blade within inches of his leg. He need not cower like a little kid or allow the whimpers at the back of his throat to escape. Especially with Mama and Tillie in the room, attentive to every move Logan or the doctor made. He could handle this. Logan kept his eyes closed and gripped the sides of his chair.

"Done," the doctor announced in a firm voice.

Logan peeked an eye open. The discarded cast lay on the kitchen table. He opened his other eye and glanced at his freed leg. The sight that greeted him made him sick.

His skin was all shriveled and pale. This leg did not make a good match to his other one. He wiggled his toes.

"Your leg will feel weak from not being used for so long, but give it a few days and hopefully your muscles will strengthen." The doctor put his saw away. "Stand up and try to walk. Let's see if that bone healed properly."

Logan allowed the doctor to help him from his chair. With wobbly steps, he made a trip around the kitchen. Dr. Bolton was right. His muscles were weak and would need time to recover, but he could walk. That was all that mattered. How good it felt to get around on his own. He shook the doctor's hand.

Taking the crutches with him, the doctor left the farm. Only a slip of paper remained behind. Logan studied it. A bill for the doctor visit. He'd add it to the stack of other expenses needing attention.

For the first time since the beginning of the new year, Logan climbed the stairs on his own to his unused room. The lean-to on the barn's backside had been his new sleeping quarters for the past week. It was a little on the chilly side, so Logan had stolen the quilt from his bed and moved it to the barn. With snow still on the ground, his trip outside in the dark would go so much better now.

Logan pulled his desk drawer open and retrieved his other bills. Flipping through them, he prayed a prayer of thanks that he and Mama had a meeting set up with Eldon. The farm sale would provide him with the necessary money to get caught up on all these expenses.

The following Monday, he dressed in his suit and tie and ushered Mama into the bank. He asked for Eldon and then waited for the banker to meet with him. Mama removed her coat and hung it near the door. She looked nice, having traded her usual house dress for the gray woolen dress she wore to church in the winter. A black hat sat at an angle on her head, comple-menting her black gloves.

Eldon appeared. He shook hands with Logan and Mama. Then he led them down the hallway to his office.

"I understand you've decided to sell." Eldon retrieved Logan's account book from a stack on the shelf behind him and sat down.

Logan cleared his throat. "Mama and I were talking earlier this month about the future. She wants to move to town. I'll be returning to my career, so we believe the time has come to sell."

Mama smiled at him when he glanced her way.

Eldon opened the account book and read the column of numbers. "The cash I collected from you is the only payment you've made in this new year. Do you plan to make another payment soon?"

"The doctor removed my cast, so I'm able to do all my own work again. As soon as I repay my neighbors for their help, I'll pay you."

"Hmm." Eldon's attention stayed on the numbers. "The balance of your debt is due April 30. This is already the middle of February. Two months doesn't give you very much time."

Eldon was right. Logan nodded his recognition of this truth.

"What should we do?" Mama leaned forward.

Eldon picked up a pen. "I'd suggest that you schedule the sale early in April so that you have time to collect payments and get them turned into the bank before your deadline."

"Sounds fair." Logan consulted his mental calendar. Paul had sent a letter recently announcing that Dan's plans had changed and now he could stay in Oswell City until May. That would give Logan plenty of time to sell the farm and get Mama settled in town. He liked that idea.

If he heard back from Karen's mother soon, he and Karen could move forward with their plans for a summer wedding. Then he'd have some time to replenish his own account before his marriage to Karen.

Logan smiled. He liked that plan too.

"Why don't you and your mother think it over and let me know in the next few days." Eldon was the most helpful and cooperative Logan had ever seen him. Probably because he knew that if he worked with Logan in planning this sale, the sooner he'd acquire Logan's money.

"Sure. We'll be in touch." Logan led Mama from the bank and over to the hotel.

A waiter showed them to a table in the dining room. Logan held Mama's chair for her while she sat down.

"What do you think about all this, dear?" Mama removed her gloves and laid them on the white linen tablecloth.

"Wish we didn't have to sell."

"I know. But it's the right decision, don't you think?"

"Given the fact that you and Tillie will live in town and Karen and I will be moving away, I don't see that we have any other choice." Logan opened a menu.

"The only way we could keep it is if you farmed it."

"Even then, we owe too much money. We'd need to start selling off portions of the land anyway to satisfy the bank."

"You're right, dear. I just wish you felt better about it."

"Maybe in time. I'll miss the farm. I enjoy the milking and working in the hayfield. Sure be nice if I could do both. Farm and keep up with the chores while also preaching and caring for my Oswell City congregation. But that would be too much responsibility for any one man. And to add a new marriage on top of it wouldn't be fair to Karen."

The waiter arrived and took their orders.

"You've changed," Mama said when the waiter left.

"Have I?"

Mama nodded, a smile playing about her lips. "You protested your stay on the farm at first."

"I did. But it's important to me to see you well taken care of, Mama. Besides, the people I love most needed me here."

Mama smiled. "You'll get to take one of us with you."

"I'm not too far away to look after the ones I've left behind."

Their meals arrived. Logan offered a quick prayer and then started eating. In between bites, he voiced an idea forming in his mind. "What would you think about opening up your own account?"

"What for?" She glanced up from her plate.

"I'd like to see you have your own funds to live on. When the farm sells, we can take a portion of that money and put it in the bank for you."

"I suppose, but you should wait. See how much you have left over after paying Eldon. Then we can decide. I'll be a member of Andrew and Tillie's family, so I can't think of too many expenses I would accumulate on my own that Andrew couldn't cover. Town living is much different than the farm."

How true. Living in town, Mama wouldn't need to worry about barn repairs or stocking groceries. Logan ate his meal and pondered the best way to care for her after he moved away.

LOGAN ENTERED the house after the Saturday morning milking, ready to enjoy a breakfast of bacon and pancakes.

"You look like a whole new man without those crutches." Karen smiled at him from her place at the stove. She flipped pancakes. The breakfast food had been more difficult for her to master than the baked goods Mama had taught her how to make.

He glanced at the griddle and inhaled the delicious scent of golden pancakes, perfect for a winter morning. The absence of smoke in the air clued him in to the fact that Karen had finally gotten the hang of cooking pancakes.

"I feel like a whole new man. Never realized how slippery snow was until I had to use crutches on it." Logan handed the pail of milk he brought from the barn to Tillie.

"How did you sleep, dear?" Mama paused in setting the table and looked at him.

"As well as expected for a drafty barn on a winter night. But, the experience will all be worthwhile in the end." He kissed Karen's temple on his way to the washstand.

How nice to possess the freedom to express his affection for her in the company of his family. If any more days had passed in which he'd needed to keep it inside, he would've exploded.

"Karen, I have an invitation for you," he said as she set a platter of pancakes on the table. "I plan to start meeting with Jack Harper today at his home in Meadow Creek. How would you like to come with me and spend time with Agnes and her mother?"

"I'd love to. I haven't seen them since Christmas." Her words held no accusation, but they stung anyway.

Maybe he'd been too firm in his standards by not allowing her assistance on Sunday afternoons. He shook his head. He'd expect the same from any other young fellow in his predicament. His good mood shouldn't dictate a bend in the rules.

After breakfast, they started out and drove to the Harper cabin. A stream of wood smoke curled from the chimney. A lamp glowed in a window as a welcome to visitors on this cloudy morning.

As he assisted Karen's climb from the sleigh, he shared a smile with her. It was a smile that rejoiced in his restored health. He was once again the provider of strength and safety, no longer dependent on others to take care of him. And boy, did it feel good. Logan followed Karen to the door, thankful for the complete absence of pain that had weakened him for so many days.

"Good morning, Amelia. Is Jack home?" Logan asked when the door opened.

"He is. Come right in. He'll be glad to see you." Amelia

Harper opened the door wider and gave Karen a hug. "We've missed you. Why don't you come to church anymore?"

Logan moved into another room so that he didn't have to suffer through hearing Karen's answer. She smiled, and her words held a light tone, but Logan was all too aware of the longing deep in her heart.

Jack turned away from his collection of tools spread over the floor and shook Logan's hand. "Amelia's got me fixin' cupboard doors this morning. I sure didn't realize how run-down a place got when I spent all my money on whiskey. I'm so glad I caught on before it ruined my family."

Logan nodded. "I thought we might start meeting today. I brought my Bible. Do you have one?"

"Over here. It was Amelia's mother's." He retrieved it from the stand near the window and joined Logan at the table.

Logan flipped his Bible open.

"You know, I'd like for Chet to start comin' to church. He needs to hear what you've been tellin' us about salvation and redemption. The message might make him change his ways. If Chet quit drinkin', he'd influence my other friends. They'd quit too. I'm sure of it."

"Let's pray about that."

"Maybe he'd even be willing to meet with you and talk about the Bible like I'm doin'. He might even get his wife to come back if he took religion a little more serious."

Logan gave Jack directions on where to find the Scripture he intended to study and began to read. The next hour passed in solemn discussion as Jack asked questions and shared past hurts.

From the occasional laughter and children's voices that accompanied the women's, Logan believed their conversation focused on a lighter subject. He smiled. Karen most likely provided Amelia Harper with a nice reprieve.

The men prayed. Jack spoke the "amen" just as the front door slammed. Crying followed.

Jack and Logan glanced at one another before rushing to the kitchen.

A distraught woman heaved in air as though she'd been running.

"Esther Murray, my goodness! What has happened?" Amelia sprang from her chair.

Jack leaned in and whispered, "She's Chet's wife I told you about. She's been living with her parents on their farm."

Esther heaved another breath. "It's Chet. He's demanding I come back home, but I won't go. Not until he straightens out. I came to tell you before he got here. He's on his way now. He thinks you might side with him, Jack, but you can't. Please don't. Tell him to change like you did. I can't take it anymore."

Jack trembled. His mouth set in a straight line and he scowled. "You're safe here, Esther. Stay as long as you want. I've been talkin' with Reverend De Witt. Chet's drinking days are numbered."

CHAPTER TWELVE

*K*aren stood before her class, the empty desk in the second row weighing on her mind. Lacy Jones should be sitting there. Mr. Jones had informed Karen in church on Sunday that the doctor declared Lacy no longer contagious, but the cough still lingered severe enough to keep the girl at home.

Lacy had caught this whooping cough from the Sanders family. Karen was sure of it. Wally and five-year-old Lizzie had missed two days of school when Lacy began running a fever. The two of them still had not returned.

"Any word on your brother and sister, Emmett?" Karen made a check by his name as she took attendance.

Emmett shrugged. "They're still coughin' pretty bad. I shoulda been the one to get sick, not Wally. Then I'd be the one stayin' home instead of goin' off to dumb ol' school."

Yes, that's how Karen would want it too. The good students staying well and the ornery ones suffering with fevers and coughs.

"How about Lacy, Cal? Any word on her?" Karen turned her attention to the responsible young man who helped put out fights, not start them. He worked hard too. He really should go on to high school next year, but Mr. Jones relied on him too much to allow it.

"Her cough is still really bad. She can't sleep at night since she has so much trouble breathing. Ma has to keep her home another week. Maybe even two."

Karen nodded and put the attendance book away. "Thank you, Cal."

She led the children through the pledge of allegiance and then the Lord's Prayer. As the children settled into their history assignment, an idea took form in Karen's mind. She should tutor Lacy. Then the girl could stay caught up on her studies. If she was no longer contagious, Karen could spend time with her. After school two or three days a week, she'd have plenty of time to give to tutoring. She scribbled a note and sent it home with Cal at the end of the day so his mother would know of her plans.

"I need your help." Karen said when she arrived home. She glanced over at Logan as she sat in the parlor checking writing assignments.

Logan shifted his attention from the fat commentary in his lap and onto her.

"Lacy still hasn't returned to school. Cal said today she may be out for two more weeks. She'll fall behind. Reading is already so difficult for her. If any more work piles up, I fear she won't pass this grade and will get held back."

"What do you need me to do?" Logan's brow wrinkled.

"If you could drive me over to the Joneses' farm two or three times each week, I'll tutor her." Karen pressed her hands together. Not until the words were out of her mouth did she realize how her plan might affect others. Maybe she asked too much.

"We'd need to work around the milking."

"If you pick me up from school, that would give me an hour with Lacy before you needed to come home."

PROMISE FOR TOMORROW

Logan smiled. "When would you like to start?"

"As soon as possible. I sent a note home with Cal, so when Mrs. Jones responds, I'll decide."

"You can plan on me."

Karen's chest expanded. "Thank you, Logan."

During the next two weeks, Logan drove her to the Joneses' farm after school. On their last night of study, Lacy's mother met them at the door and took their coats. Logan stayed in the kitchen, chatting with Cal as he'd done on previous visits.

Karen moved on to the family's simple sitting room. Lacy appeared much improved since the last time Karen had seen her. The weekend had passed, inserting five days between tutoring sessions. She still coughed, but the wheeze was nearly gone. Lacy had every reason to return to school by the end of the week.

Karen smiled at her. "Hi, Lacy. You're looking better."

"I feel better. I'm sleeping at night again. Having you come is the best. That helps me more than anything."

Karen's eyes grew moist as she reached for Lacy's reader. "Thank you, Lacy. I'm glad it helps you. I want you to stay caught up on your lessons."

"It's working. Ma thinks I'll have the best grades ever when report cards come out."

Karen opened the reader. If Lacy hoped to compete with the likes of Becky Hixson and Evie Patterson, then she needed to get busy.

Two days later, Lacy came to school. The girls welcomed her back with warm displays of friendship. Lacy was the guest of honor at the noon recess tea party. She went home at the end of the day with pages of artwork from each girl.

Karen was sweeping the floor when a visitor arrived and stomped across the newly cleaned floor. Karen straightened and forced a smile. "Good day, Mrs. Sanders."

Elsie sniffed.

107

"Is there something I can do to help you?" Karen leaned the broom against the wall.

"You can stop playing favorites." Elsie's curt words made Karen's jaw drop.

"Excuse me?" She'd been so careful not to give special privileges to her model students, girls like the Hinkley sisters, Becky, and Evie.

"Lacy Jones." Elsie spat out the name with a high degree of irritation.

"How have I been favoring Lacy?" Karen frowned

"Two of my children have been sick, but did you spend any extra time helping them catch up on their school work? Oh, no. All of your attention went to Lacy." Elsie settled her hands on her hips.

Karen's blood heated. This woman, who viewed homework as a waste of time, confronted the teacher for ignoring her children during their absence from the classroom. What nerve.

She took a deep breath and assumed the same pert dignity she'd used on this woman's brother when he forced her into attending the Christmas gala. "Mrs. Sanders, your children have absolutely no trouble with reading and comprehension. Lacy struggles in those areas. Without additional coaching, she may not pass her grade."

Elsie's eyes bulged. "You are giving her an unfair advantage over my children. Lacy has always been slow. No one can help her. It would be a better use of your efforts to pour them into the intelligent kids than wasting them on Lacy."

Karen's heart raced until it felt ready to burst. Patience and professionalism clearly had no effect on this woman. She needed to be taught a little compassion, and Karen was ready to go to any length to get that lesson across. "You know what's the matter with you, Mrs. Sanders? You can't think about anyone but yourself. There are people in this world with far greater struggles than yours. For once, why don't you stop complaining about costs and look around? This world doesn't need another grumpy wet hen like you." Karen pushed passed the woman and slammed the door.

Her walk home with no coat and a nice venting session in the barn with Logan should cool her down. That is, if she knew for a fact she'd never have to see or hear of Elsie Sanders ever again.

After supper, Karen sat on the love seat checking papers when Logan arrived in the parlor with his Bible. The fire glowed with warmth overcoming the chill from the gusty winds outside. Sandy and Tillie pieced a quilt on the kitchen table. All felt cozy and comforting on this winter night.

Logan stopped before her and held out an envelope.

"What's this?" Karen asked.

"I think it's from your mother. I found it at the post office today but waited for you to share the parlor with me this evening so we could read it together." Logan claimed the nearby rocking chair.

Karen's heart pounded. This could very well be the moment when she learned if her family agreed to join her in the future. Her hand trembling, Karen ripped open the fateful piece of mail and read in silence.

Dear Reverend De Witt,

Please do allow me to call you "Reverend." Even though you signed your letter simply as "Logan," Karen has kept me informed of the sacrifices you have made, one of which is your choice to leave the church you served so you might care for your mother and sister.

I know all about you, thanks to Karen's frequent letters, so it comes as no surprise that you are asking for my permission to marry her.

I would prefer to give you my answer in person. Since Karen was unable to come to the city for Christmas, I would like to come to Silver Grove and pay her a visit. You may plan

*on meeting myself, my other daughter, Julia, and her two
children. We will arrive on Monday, March 6, on the 10:00
train. Karen will probably have class at that time, so could
you please plan to meet us at the train station? We've
arranged to stay at the hotel in Silver Grove, so we will only
need your assistance getting our trunks moved. Thank you so
much.*

Say "hello" to Karen for me.
Looking forward to meeting you.
Margaret Millerson

"Oh, my!" The shout of joy leaped from her throat. Karen
covered her mouth with her hand.

"What is it? Did she approve?" Logan leaned forward and
searched her face with an intent gaze.

"She didn't say."

"What do you mean?"

"She's coming here for a visit. Julia and her children are
coming too. I'll finally get to see her baby." Karen stood and
waved the letter around.

"What?" Logan also stood. He ripped the page out of her
hand so fast a corner of it remained in her grasp.

He mumbled the words of the letter. "I know all about you,
thanks to Karen's frequent letters." He paused and frowned
at her.

Karen blushed.

In silence, he read the remainder of the letter. Time stood still
when he looked up. He rubbed his forehead, and his speech came
out so broken it hardly sounded like English. The frequent "z"
sounding syllables and scraping sounds from his throat
convinced Karen he indeed spoke in another language. Perhaps
he'd picked his vocabulary up from his father, a new immigrant
wishing to share his heritage with his son.

The tutelage certainly served Logan well right now. Karen

hardly knew if she should wait for his agitation to run its course or if she should go to him and try to calm him down.

Logan solved her problem. He came to a halt before her, the words flowing fast but broken from his lips. "Your *moeder*... she...she can't. I mean, your mother. She can't come right now. Not...not...until, why, I still in the *schuur slapen*. Oh..." He ran a shaky hand through his hair.

The time had come to exert a bit of her no-nonsense demeanor reserved for those days when Tim Hixson couldn't pull himself together after acting as accomplice to a stunt. Karen grasped Logan's upper arms and looked him square in the eye. "Logan. Sweetheart. You aren't making any sense. Whatever is the matter? Start over, and tell me what's wrong."

He exhaled and looked at her as though seeing her for the first time. A few silent moments passed while he scanned the letter once more and folded it up. He dropped it as if any response he might give qualified as a lost cause.

"Karen, your mother is a respectable woman, and she arrives in four days. She'll come out here and discover you living in the house of the man who wrote asking to marry you." A flush crept up Logan's neck and into his cheeks. "From what you tell me of your family's mistrust of preachers, I stood a slim chance of securing your mother's approval. After she sees your living arrangements for what they really are, winning your mother's blessing will be impossible."

Her throat went dry. Logan's admonishment from the day she'd expressed her own fears raced through her mind. Don't borrow trouble. She released her hold on him and forced out as many words as would come. "We believe the Lord wants us together. He'll find a way."

Logan attempted a smile.

"Remember those words?"

"I just hope they're true." He broke eye contact and looked at the floor.

"We'll make them true."

"What do you mean?" His attention returned to her face.

"I choose you, Logan. Even if Mother disapproves of you, I'll still marry you."

"Not sure I should let you do that. Marriages rarely thrive at the beginning without support from both families. I wouldn't want to set you up for unnecessary heartache later on." He returned to the rocking chair and opened his Bible.

More papers waited for her to check. She stifled a sigh and turned her attention to the assignments. Only four days remained until she would learn if her mother had put their past behind them forever.

CHAPTER THIRTEEN

"*K*aren, tell us your news. Logan said earlier that you have some." Anna passed the platter of meat to her husband.

Along with Logan and his mother, Karen accepted the invitation to share the noon meal with Pete and Anna at their home. She glanced at Logan for a clue of how much she should say. One bit of information may only lead to their wish to hear more.

Logan appeared unconcerned. He winked at her as he accepted the meat platter from Pete.

She took a deep breath. "My mother and sister, along with my two nephews, are coming for a visit. They arrive tomorrow."

"How exciting. What made them decide to come?" Anna asked.

"Since I'm not allowed to leave during the school year, I couldn't go home for Christmas. But their biggest reason is to meet Logan."

Pete turned to him. "Do they know about, well…your relationship?"

Logan grinned. "You mean that I've proposed?"

Anna glanced at Karen through wide eyes.

Pete stared.

"Don't look so shocked," Sandy said, waving her spoon at Pete and then at Anna. "We all know. Our family had a big discussion and got several issues out in the open."

Pete relaxed and began to eat his meal.

"Karen's family knows because I wrote to her mother asking permission to marry her."

"What did she say?" Pete asked around a bite of bread.

"I don't know yet. She wants to give her answer in person." Logan's voice quieted, and fine lines appeared at the corners of his mouth.

Karen shared his tension. If Mother had written her decision in the letter, this weekend would've passed with much less strain. Karen made her best effort to stay focused on conversations or assist with meal preparation, but so many little thoughts intruded, dragging her back to the question of Mother's response.

"And now she's decided to make the trip to Silver Grove to determine if you're the right man for her daughter." Mischief hung in Pete's words as though he meant the comment as a joke on his friend, but he'd spoken the truth more than he may realize.

"That about sums it up." Logan pushed the food around on his plate. If he felt like she did, the looming arrival of tomorrow's train had wrecked his appetite.

Karen cleared her throat. "Pete, I wonder if I might ask a favor of you."

"What can I do?"

"Mother and Julia arrive at ten in the morning. Would you have time to fill in for me at the school until the students go out for their noon recess?"

"I can. In fact, I'll relieve you for the entire day."

"Oh, but I..."

"How about if I give them an early dismissal and send them home by two o'clock?"

Karen thought over his words for a moment. "That should

work fine. Dismissing at two will give you enough time to read to them after recess and then go over the homework assignments I'll have ready."

"Then it's settled." Pete smiled.

"Thank you."

"Enjoy the day with your mother and sister. You'll want to spend time with them."

Pete was right. Now that she had the whole day off from school, she could hardly wait to see Mother again and Julia, Ben, and baby Sam. She'd finally get to hold him in her arms. If only she could lose the uneasiness that pressed on her heart. Mother had to approve of Logan. She just had to.

"How is your remodeling coming along?" Logan asked Anna.

"Slow. We discovered water damage to one wall and the floor from a leak in the roof. Now we must repair it."

"You mean..." Logan's face went white.

"I know we promised you Karen could move in with us the first of March, but we aren't ready. Here, I'll show you." Pete led Karen and Logan from the table.

Her heart nearly stopped at the sight of the room intended as her new residence. It looked worse than the last time she'd seen it. Tears stung Karen's eyes.

"Oh." Disappointment weighted Logan's voice. "We'd hoped Karen might move in with you before her mother arrived. Today, if possible, but that obviously won't work."

She and Logan had talked the matter over and had settled on Logan reminding Pete of his offer. A month had passed. Even if the project wasn't completely finished, surely Pete and Anna could accommodate Karen in some way. Then the courtship would be proper. She could wear Logan's ring and announce a wedding date to friends and neighbors, and with plenty of time to make the change before Mother arrived.

But none of that would happen now. Karen could almost sense Mother's disapproval all the way from Chicago.

"Come to the kitchen with me. I need help with the dessert." Anna beckoned to her.

Karen followed, but no amount of a yummy dessert could lift her spirits.

Anna took her hand. "Congratulations, Karen. Logan stopped by earlier this week and told us about Sandy's wish for you to have her ring."

Karen nodded, but even that simple movement felt heavy.

"How long have you and Logan cared for each other?"

Karen shrugged. "I don't know. It came on so gradually. He proposed Christmas night and gave me an engagement ring as my gift."

Anna tapped her chin. "So that's why Logan came over asking for you to live with us during the second semester."

Karen nodded again.

"Is this the matter you couldn't talk about when Pete and I came for a visit the morning after Logan's fall?"

"It is."

Anna gathered her in a hug. "Oh, Karen. You've had to carry this wonderful secret around inside, unable to say a word or openly express your love for him, haven't you?"

A sob erupted from her throat. She buried her face in Anna's shoulder and wept.

Anna stroked her back. "Let's see. Maybe you can move into Pete's study or one of the closets at the church. But the closets aren't heated. If we didn't have guests in so often, you could use our sofa in the parlor as your bed."

"Logan and I already considered those options." Anna's white blouse muffled Karen's voice.

"The two of you are in a predicament. I don't know what I would do if this was Pete and me." Anna handed Karen a hankie and then went to work cutting slices of cake. "You'll get it worked out. In the meantime, you're welcome to stop in if you need to talk. As soon as we get the wall and floor fixed up, the room is yours."

Karen couldn't keep her laughter and tears from happening at the same time. Even though they couldn't help her yet, Pete and Anna were on her side. She'd need her friends if Mother's visit didn't go as she and Logan hoped.

OF ALL THE challenges Logan had to deal with at the moment, this was his worst. Pete's future nursery should be fixed up enough for his fiancée to use. He'd promised it. Now the woman who he may have the pleasure of someday calling his mother-in-law, would come to town and see for herself the utter tragedy of her daughter's circumstances.

Logan sank into a chair in Pete's parlor and raked his fingers through his hair. His life was over. The end with all its unforgiving doom already hung over him.

Pete claimed the chair nearby. "I'm sorry, Logan. We honestly thought this project would be done by now."

"It's not your fault," Logan said in a voice full of disgust. "It's mine. I didn't plan very well. I should've waited to ask her to marry me. Making sure Karen had a meaningful Christmas gift from me was the only thought I had at the time. I should've been more concerned about her reputation."

"But you're staying in the barn, right?"

"Oh, yes." The barn, his haven. It was the only place where he removed himself far enough from her to think about anything other than getting married.

Pete clutched Logan's arms. "I've been where you are, engaged and making plans. It passes quickly. Doesn't feel that way at the time, though. I was still away at seminary, and Anna lived at home with her parents. Those were the longest days of my life, but we survived. You will too."

Logan exhaled and managed a smile. "Thanks, Pete. Appreciate it."

"Staying for dessert?" Pete asked when Logan stood up.

Logan glanced at the table where Mama poured coffee and Karen and Anna set plates of cake at each place. "Better not. I still have some preparation to do for this afternoon's service. Mind if I use your study?"

"Be my guest."

"Thanks. I'll come back for Mama and Karen in a couple of hours." He left the house and made his way to the church. The Harpers would probably attend today. He'd check in with Jack to discover how his week had gone. A conversation about God's abilities to handle the impossible might do them both some good.

"WE MISS Miss Millerson's singing. She does a nice job. When will she return?" Lester's wife asked Logan when she shook his hand in the line after the service.

"Uh...I'm not sure." He'd stuttered through all the Scripture reading and most of the sermon. He had nothing to lose from stuttering through the shaking of hands too. He should've known people would start asking about Karen, but he could think of nothing to say that would fully explain her absence. Now that the holidays had passed and weekly worship services had settled into a steady routine, the congregation deserved a continued relationship with her. But that would require him to lower his standards. What a mess.

He clenched his teeth. Pete's spare room should've been ready long ago. The conversation with Pete after Christmas had resulted in Logan's move to the barn. Now visitors were arriving. Whenever they came to the farm, Logan would stay outdoors as much as possible, just as if he really did live elsewhere. He'd lay in an extra supply of wood for his little stove and raid Mama's pantry for food he could store in the one cupboard of the lean-to that looked mouse-proof. He'd gotten lax in his use of the parlor in the evenings when he knew Karen would share it with him. That had to stop. The women could have the house and the parlor. He'd stay in the barn.

Logan suffered through the rest of the hand shaking, facing two more questions about the talented Karen Millerson. Again, he stuttered out a vague reply. It must have satisfied his inter-rogators because they moved on and didn't expect him to clarify. When the last family passed through the line, Logan rushed into the church, ready to get his mind on something else.

The same six men gathered at the front of the sanctuary for another meeting about their new building.

"Our wives hosted two bake sales. Now the total of our funds is forty dollars," Lester informed him.

"That's a start. Have you decided on any other ways to make money?"

"We're thinkin' of asking businesses in Meadow Creek to help us out, either with gifts of cash or donations of supplies. What do you think of that idea?" Jack asked.

"Talk to the businessmen who are a part of the congregation. You have several. See what they are willing to do."

The men agreed. They talked for a few minutes longer about the best places to order supplies and when to start. Logan ended the meeting, connected with Jack, and then went to get Mama and Karen.

Here they were, driving home together. Again. The idea of Karen's mother coming to town still rattled him. He must get himself under control. A good place to start was by doing a little accepting of his own. Whatever tomorrow brought his way, he'd welcome it. Acceptance or disapproval, anger or favor, it didn't matter. He couldn't change Karen's mother, her past, or her response to him. He could only do anything about himself, and he was still the provider of strength and safety for Mama, for Tillie, and even for Karen.

Margaret Millerson's arrival didn't change the fact that he still had sermons to preach, cows to milk, and a household and congregation to care for. His life must still go on regardless if Karen's mother came to town or not.

Plus, he did sleep in the barn, after all. He did his best to honor Karen and their relationship. His efforts were good enough for him, for Mama, for Karen, and for Pete and Anna. They'd just have to be good enough for Karen's mother too.

CHAPTER FOURTEEN

$\mathcal{T}$he train from Chicago pulled into the Silver Grove station behind a monstrous locomotive that hissed out steam as the smell of burning coal and hot metal filled the air. Iron wheels screeched as the train crept to a halt. Doors on the passenger cars opened.

Karen's heart pounded. They were here. Mother and Julia had arrived. "Come on." She pulled on the sleeve of Logan's suit coat.

He gave a serious nod. Logan had been quiet all morning. His smile had not yet appeared for the day, and his responses were measured. This reserved side of him Karen had not seen before. At least he didn't stutter an incomprehensible mix of Dutch and English. He'd calmed down a bit in preparation for Mother's visit, but something still bothered him. Mother had better not keep him waiting long for her response to his request for her blessing.

They moved farther down the platform as people emerged from the cars. One stylish woman in a wide brim hat with an ostrich feather swaying in the wind caught Karen's attention.

"There they are." She jogged over to the cluster of women and children. "Mother!" Karen waved.

"Oh, Karen." Mother caught her in an embrace, their hats bumping. "How lovely to see you. We've all missed you so."

"And I've missed you."

Julia loosened Karen's hat more when she took her turn with a hug.

"This must be Sam," Karen said to the baby on Julia's hip while adjusting her hat pin.

"Say 'hello' to your Auntie Karen." Julia brushed the baby's cheek.

He stayed silent, but a little boy nearby tugged on Karen's skirt. "Hi, Auntie Karen. I like trains."

Karen bent down to look Ben in the eye. "It's a long ride all the way out here, isn't it?"

He gave an exaggerated nod. "Sure is. I never been on a train before."

Karen smiled at him and straightened.

Logan had caught up with her and shook Mother's hand. "Welcome to Silver Grove, Mrs. Millerson."

"Thank you, Reverend De Witt. It's a pleasure to be here." Mother motioned to Julia. "Please meet my daughter, Julia, her baby, Sam, and her three-year-old son, Ben."

Logan's eyes twinkled even though his features remained sober. "And how did the young men enjoy train travel?"

"Better than I expected. I'm still waiting for the moment when Sam realizes his father stayed home. He's such a Daddy's boy." Julia shifted Sam to the other side.

Her comment brought out Logan's smile. He flashed the same one he'd given Karen in the kitchen all those months ago when they met for the first time. The sun had nothing on Logan where warmth was concerned. "We'll see if we can't make him feel at home."

"The hotel serves lunch. Would you like to eat there after you've found your rooms?" Karen asked.

"That sounds wonderful." Mother held out her hand to Ben. "Come with Grandma."

Logan picked up the two satchels sitting at their feet. Karen in the lead, the group crossed the platform and headed in the direction of the hotel.

Mother and Julia received their key at the front desk while an assistant from the train station brought in their belongings. They left for their room, and Logan and Karen took the children to the dining room.

"Karen, I'm surprised you aren't in school," Mother said moments later, claiming a chair at the table.

"Why, Mother. You know I wouldn't miss your arrival. Logan's friend, Reverend Betten, is filling in for me, so I have the whole day to spend with you."

"I'd hoped you might be free, but I didn't want to intrude on your schedule. How nice of Reverend Betten to help you." Mother removed her gloves and laid them in her lap.

"Logan and I thought you might like to come to the farm this afternoon and meet Sandy and Tillie." Karen reached for a menu.

"I can't wait. You've written about them so much in your letters, I feel as though I already know them." Mother shifted her attention to the waiter who had arrived and stood ready to take orders.

"Tell us about the farm," Mother said to Logan after the waiter left with their list of choices.

"It belonged to my father. He died last summer, as Karen has probably already told you."

Mother nodded.

"We have seventeen dairy cows. I sell the milk to the creamery in Bridgewater Springs."

"What do you enjoy most about farming?" Julia asked while attempting to interest Sam in her shiny spoon.

"Can you believe I enjoy the quiet of the barn the most? The early morning hours spent milking are the times when I think through ideas I've studied and organize my thoughts for my next sermon."

Karen's mouth dropped open. Logan shared yet another trait she must learn about him. She should've asked him the same question months ago. He truly was a preacher. Through and through. Mother may find fascination with Logan's farmer side, but his more dominant preacher side may take her some getting used to.

Their food arrived, and the meal passed with pleasant conversation about Chicago. Mother shared news about Uncle Henry's successful steel business. Julia talked of society events she and Mother had attended. Karen listened, expecting homesickness to settle in. But it never did. The people Julia mentioned, their cares and their associations, belonged in the city. Karen belonged here, with Logan, in his wide and open spaces where the direction of the wind and the changing of the seasons held sway over people's lives.

The baby fussed. Since Karen had already finished eating, she offered to take him.

"He's ready for a nap." Julia handed Sam to Karen. "Arthur woke him early this morning so we could catch the train. Now he's tired."

Karen bounced him on her arm and managed to get him settled enough so that the others could finish their meal.

Once they returned to the hotel room, Karen paced with the baby while Julia and Mother unpacked. Still the baby remained awake. She laid him on the bed. Maybe he needed a comfortable location to fall asleep. His crying only grew worse. Karen patted his back, but her attention made no difference in his wailing.

Julia looked over her shoulder. "Sam is missing his father. Arthur settles the baby down for a nap while he's home for his noon meal."

Logan left his task of piling hat boxes on a high closet shelf and joined Karen. "Let me take him."

Karen stood and watched as Logan lifted the baby into his arms. Logan's black suit coat made his shoulders appear so broad while Sam's white gown made him look so small. They were a rather unmatched pair.

"This little man and I will search out a quiet corner of the hotel." Logan grinned at the women and left the room.

"You're next." Julia led Ben to the bed and offered him a picture book. "Even if you don't sleep, I'd like you to rest here while Grandma and I unpack."

Ben settled in with his book and held a conversation with himself about the animals on the pages.

Karen set to work removing Mother's dresses from a trunk. Mother took them and put them on hangers. Julia did the same with her wardrobe.

"We brought new dresses for you, Karen. I thought you might like wearing the new spring styles. You may wait to unpack those until we go to the farm. Your new clothes are in the bottom of Julia's trunk. Be sure and ask Reverend De Witt to load it for us."

"Thank you, Mother. That is very thoughtful." Karen hugged her and returned to her task.

An hour later, Mother and Julia felt settled in. Ben lay sleeping on the bed, his picture book opened at his side. Logan had not returned with the baby. Maybe one of the women should find him and offer to take Sam off his hands. The image of a screaming, writhing infant entered Karen's mind. Logan might appreciate a little help.

"I'm going to find Logan and ask when he wants to leave for the farm," Karen said and left the room.

She wandered down the hall in the direction of the dining room. The sounds of clattering dishes and conversations rang in the air. If Logan wanted a quiet spot, he would not have come here. She turned around. At the other end of the hall she discovered a sitting room, decorated like an inviting parlor in a city home. Logan lounged on a burgundy sofa reading the paper.

Sam lay fast asleep on Logan's chest, a thin line of drool dampening one of his lapels.

"Shh." Logan held a finger to his lips when he saw her.

"How did you get him to sleep?" Karen whispered.

"He wanted to lie against me like he is now, so I let him. Eventually he fell asleep," Logan whispered back.

Karen could think of no response to give but to shake her head.

"Is your mother ready to go to the farm?"

"She is, but now Ben is napping too. We can wait until the boys are awake. Julia would appreciate the delay if it means naps for the children."

Logan and the baby looked so at home on their cozy sofa, Karen didn't want to leave. She claimed a chair and watched the baby sleep. After missing his birth and then waiting six months to meet him, she was in no hurry to rush away.

AT THE FARM, Logan brought the team of horses and the wagon to a halt in the lane. He jumped down. A slight ache in his left leg from the movement reminded him of his recent accident. He tethered the reins to a post of the picket fence and assisted first Margaret, then Julia, Sam and Ben, and finally Karen. They followed his lead to the kitchen where Mama stood at a window watching them.

Karen took care of the introductions. Mama offered their guests cups of coffee and took them to the parlor. Logan stayed behind in the kitchen. He removed his suit coat and draped it over the back of a chair so Mama could cleanse baby drool from it. He also removed his tie. It needed a little cleaning too. The part he'd left out of the story he told Karen involved his tie. Sam had found chewing on it a soothing activity. Logan couldn't deny the little guy the simple comfort, even if his indulgence meant extra work for Mama later.

What baby wouldn't need some tie chewing to relieve his anxiety after being cooped up on a train and then landing in a strange place? It was the least Logan could do.

He climbed the stairs to change so that he could get a start on the milking. In the parlor, he interrupted the women's conversation. "Would anyone care for a tour of the barn?"

"Yeah!" Ben came to life, abandoning his pile of blocks.

"Count me in," Julia said.

"I'm afraid we didn't bring any other shoes." Margaret set her cup down.

"Logan keeps the barn very clean, Mother. If you stay on the main path, you won't get dirty." Karen stood.

"While you are all outdoors, Tillie and I will finish supper. We can eat as soon as Logan finishes the milking." Mama gathered the cups and left for the kitchen.

In the yard, Logan turned to Karen. "Could you please take them to the barn? I'll go round up the cows from the pasture and meet you there."

Karen nodded while Logan veered off in the direction of the pasture. In the barn, he herded the cows into their stanchions and retrieved the three-legged stool. He showed the group around the milk parlor, explaining the process of preparing the milk for sale.

"Cows, Mom. Cows." Ben pointed at the swishing tails while Julia kept a firm hold of his other hand.

"Yes, Ben. Don't get in the way. The cows may not see you and hurt you."

"They're in my picture book. Remember?" Ben looked up at Julia.

"I remember. You like animals."

Ben nodded, a smile lighting his face.

Logan worked while the women looked around. From time to time they'd ask questions, and he'd answer them. By the fifth cow, he had his own three-year-old equivalent of a shadow. Ben stood as close as Julia allowed. His eyes took in everything. He chattered to Logan about the hay, about the cows' spots, and about the sound the milk made when it hit the pail. Everything Logan did, Ben noticed.

Each time Logan stood to move to the next cow, Ben jumped and skipped in little circles, like a puppy frolicking in spring grass. Happiness and adventure prompted his repeated dance. With a whoop and a clap of his hands, he'd rejoin Logan. Every time, all the way to the last cow.

"All done." Logan stood and smiled down at him. "Will you help me carry this milk to the house?"

Ben's face, downcast at Logan's announcement, lit up at his question. He reached his pudgy hand out to grasp the handle next to Logan's. Together, they managed to get the milk across the yard without spilling. Ben's shorter legs, coupled with uneven ground, jerked against Logan's stride. But the excitement on Ben's face made the awkward tote worthwhile.

Logan chuckled as he entered the kitchen. "All right. Come wash up."

Karen pushed a chair over to the wash stand. Ben stood on it while Logan poured water over the little boy's hands and Karen dried them.

Mama had the dining room table decked out with her fanciest dishes. She directed everyone where to sit while Tillie brought in the food. Logan took his place at the head of the table and prayed. The meal passed with conversation about Mama's garden. Margaret asked her all about it, what sorts of vegetables she raised, and which varieties of flowers she grew. Karen served cherry pie for dessert. Her mother and Julia raved over it, bringing a happy flush to Karen's cheeks.

In the busyness of clearing the table and dish washing, Logan slipped away to the barn. He'd already stocked his small apartment with study materials. He'd have no problem occupying himself through the long evening hours. A glowing lamp and a set of commentaries, and he'd stay quite content.

The evening passed as a sermon took shape in his mind. Engrossed in his notetaking, Logan almost missed the creak of his door. Not until a throat cleared did he shift his attention away from his books.

Margaret Millerson stood before him.

He scrambled to his feet. Books flopped to the ground and papers scattered. "M...M...Margaret. Good evening." He thrust out his hand for a mannerly shake.

She took it. "Reverend."

Karen's mother really should quit using his title all the time. The formality put him on edge, as if she expected him to have all the right answers. He'd prefer for her to accept his search for wisdom instead of assuming he'd already attained it and view him as the family member he wanted to become.

"It's time you and I had a talk." She looked around for a place to sit.

Logan shoved books off the cot and offered it to her while he dragged a stool out of the corner.

Margaret scanned their surroundings. The light of the lamp warmed the rustic boards of the barn wall and gleamed on the golden straw at their feet. "Karen said I'd find you out here. She said you've been calling the barn home these past weeks."

Logan nodded. Surely she wouldn't ask to hear his reasons. He hardly knew where to begin with an explanation anyway. Whatever he might say would only lower this woman's view of him. He stayed silent.

"I suppose you've been wondering why I would travel all this way instead of simply writing my response in a letter." Margaret picked a bit of straw from her skirt.

The question had crossed his mind.

"When Karen wrote confessing to me she'd fallen in love with a minister, I was disappointed. I don't want the same life for Karen marriage brought me. I came to Silver Grove with the goal of breaking the two of you up. I even have an offer from an acquaintance for a teaching job Karen may take in the city."

Margaret's words soaked in deep. She would never agree to a union between him and her daughter. He should've fought his attraction and stayed on the hard yet narrow road of apostle Paul's example for singleness.

He sucked in a deep breath and bent to retrieve a page of notes. "I can't blame you, I suppose. Arriving here at my farm and seeing Karen's living arrangements would convince any mother their daughter could do better."

More pages of notes lay on the floor. He picked up another one. Maybe the activity would distract him from the sorrow ripping his heart to pieces.

"Reverend."

She needed to quit calling him that. Especially now that she'd shared her thoughts with him. Her use of his title gave her one more way to keep him and Karen apart. To Margaret, it served as a reminder of who he was and what he represented, all of which had brought her pain in the past. Her formal address of him helped her put him in his place and keep him there.

He'd better get busy cleaning up his books before he fell to the temptation to throw her out of his lean-to.

"Logan." His name carried from her lips with a softness and a bit of pleading.

He ventured a look at her face.

"Sit down. Let me tell you about Karen's father."

Logan placed his commentary on the cupboard and did as she requested.

"My husband was a good man. Even after he fell into trouble and lost his ministry, he still retained his good qualities. But he did a better job looking after the cares of others than he did his own daughters. This morning, I got off the train in a tiny town where I met a young man who cared enough to help my infant grandson take a nap. I watched you with Ben in the barn at milking time. This place and Karen's living arrangements, I know what it means."

Oh, boy. Here it comes. Logan held his breath.

"Karen coming here to live with you last fall, becoming part of your family, and receiving your provision and protection was exactly what she needed."

The air rushed out of his lungs.

"You've been good for her. I would be a foolish woman to deny her, to deny us, a relationship with you."

"Y…you…mean." He searched her face.

Margaret stood. "You have my blessing. Please marry my daughter."

Logan also stood. His knees shook. He wanted to whoop, to find Karen and swing her around in the air. But all he could do was stare.

Margaret patted his cheek and one of her brows rose. "You've won me over to the point that I've fallen a little in love with you too."

"Does this mean you'll quit calling me 'Reverend'?" His heart held so many meaningful expressions longing to get said. He stifled a groan. He could have chosen a better response than that one.

"Only if you'll agree to call me 'Mother.'"

He nodded. "I'd be honored."

A smile broke out on Margaret's face.

One gesture suggested itself as the best conclusion to this conversation. Logan took the risk. He opened his arms. Margaret stepped into his embrace and rested against him for several moments as if she found healing there.

"Let's go to the house. I want to tell them. Everyone knew I'd come out here to find you." Margaret pulled away.

The lamp in hand, Logan accompanied her to the parlor. Conversation halted. Karen's mouth fell open.

Margaret rubbed her hands together. "Logan and I reached an understanding. I gave him my blessing."

Karen rushed from her chair. "Oh, Mother."

Margaret hugged her. "Keep your summer wedding date on the calendar. You'll be needing it."

CHAPTER FIFTEEN

"Oh, Logan, am I glad to see you," Julia said when he arrived at the hotel after breakfast. "Sam didn't sleep a wink last night. Too many strange noises in a hotel for him to settle down. Maybe the farm will be a quieter place for a baby to take a nap."

"Can we go to the farm, Grandma? I want to see the cows again," Ben said as he entered the room with Margaret.

"Just as soon as we get your shoes on." Margaret bent to place a shoe on Ben's foot.

"Yay!" He clapped his hands and kicked his legs.

"Hold still. You will get to the farm faster if you help Grandma." Margaret attempted once more to place shoes on active little feet.

Julia handed Logan a bag and within minutes, everyone was loaded in the wagon and headed to the school to see Karen's classroom.

She dismissed her students for a recess break when the group entered. Ben watched the older children race out the door. The expression on his face said he wanted to join in their play.

Sam fussed, so Julia bounced him on her arm. He quieted for a moment and then wailed louder than before.

"I'll take Sam outside. He might like to watch the children." Logan stepped forward and reached for the baby. Karen would want her sister to continue the tour of the classroom.

Julia relinquished him with the simple instruction to keep him clean.

Logan nodded. "Ben, why don't you come too?"

The little boy trotted along at Logan's side. His complete interest lay in the baseball game in the back yard. Ben pointed and cheered whenever someone hit the ball, but Sam continued to fuss.

The children scrambled to the steps when Karen rang the bell calling them back inside.

"I'll see you this afternoon," Karen said as she hugged her mother and Julia.

In the wagon, Margaret took a turn with Sam, but he remained wide awake and fretful.

"Go on upstairs and use Karen's room to take a nap," Mama said to Julia when she heard about the difficult night at the hotel.

"We'll take care of the baby." Tillie reached for him and headed for the rocking chair in the parlor.

"Thank you. That's very kind." Julia went upstairs.

Logan hung around the kitchen with his attention on Tillie. She may turn out to be the one in the house with the right touch to help Sam find rest. Mama and Margaret tip-toed into the kitchen and carefully poured themselves cups of coffee. They sat at the table and murmured through a conversation.

Ready to go outside and get some work done, Logan looked out the window. He needed to wash out some milk cans, but he didn't dare leave the house. Opening and closing doors might undo Tillie's calming effects on Sam.

He poured himself a cup of coffee and took his seat at the table.

Tillie came to the kitchen. "Sam is asleep. I put him on the love seat surrounded by pillows."

Margaret smiled at Tillie. "Thank you. Julia will be so relieved to know he took a morning nap. We'd hoped he'd do better at your house. Looks like he finally found a quiet place."

Logan left the kitchen and slipped into his boots. As he reached for his coat, a bold chime rang out from the grandfather clock in the parlor. By the third chime, Sam was screaming. Logan tugged off his boots and followed the women to the parlor.

Mama picked up the flailing baby.

"I didn't think about the clock. What should we do now? It makes noise every half-hour." Tillie settled her hands on her hips.

"We could take him upstairs to one of our rooms." Mama sat in the rocking chair.

"But they're both directly above the parlor. He could still hear the clock." Tillie pointed to the ceiling.

"I've got an idea. What if the baby slept on my cot in the barn? It's quiet out there this time of day since the cows aren't in the barn for milking." Logan's face lit up as he spoke.

"Worth a try. You were successful yesterday getting Sam to sleep. I don't see why you couldn't do it again." Margaret straightened the pillows on the love seat.

Logan took the baby from Mama and held him against his shoulder. "I've got the perfect place for you, Little Sam. Come with me."

Mama draped a blanket around the baby while Logan put his boots on and found his coat. The poor baby fussed all the way to the barn. Logan lounged on his cot in the same way he'd done on the sofa in the hotel parlor the day before. Sam snuggled into his chest and within minutes, he fell asleep.

Logan reached for the commentary that had so ungraciously tumbled to the floor during Margaret's visit. He opened it and found the place where he'd been interrupted. A preacher with the next Sunday right around the corner could never get too much study time.

KAREN SHARED the large dining room table with the De Witts and her own family. This was how she wanted life to stay forever. The people she cared about most enjoying a delicious meal and spending time together. Her gaze traveled from one shining face to the next. Julia looked much more rested than she did that morning at the school. Ben built a dyke with his mashed potatoes. Sam lay on a quilt nearby, gurgling and reaching for his toes. Mother and Sandy talked about recipes. Logan and Tillie asked Julia about her husband and the life they lived in Chicago. In only a few months, Karen had missed so much of the happenings of Julia's family. She welcomed this chance to catch up.

"Logan dear, weren't you saying something about Meadow Creek hosting a bake sale? I would love to get Amelia Harper's recipe for cinnamon rolls." Sandy turned her attention to him.

"They've actually hosted two sales in their effort to raise money for a new church building."

"Is this the church that blew down last fall?" Julia asked.

"It is."

"Logan preaches for them on Sunday afternoons here in Silver Grove," Karen said.

"How are they coming along in their fund raising?" Mother joined the new topic of conversation.

"Slow." Logan laid down his fork and reached for his water glass. "They still need to find a large amount of money to get started with the construction."

"I wish there was a way we could help them." Julia flattened Ben's mashed potato dyke with her spoon, causing him to whimper.

"We have so many resources in the city, but I don't know how to get them here." Mother used her napkin to wipe Ben's face.

"Hey, I know what we should do." Tillie gained the attention of every person in the room. Even Ben, who protested Grandma's efforts to remove gravy from around his mouth.

"Host a style show." Tillie radiated with enthusiasm.

"A style show?" Karen couldn't follow Tillie's train of thought.

"Sure. Use the hotel dining room. Charge for tickets. Maybe give away prizes. Find women to model the beautiful gowns you brought with you from Chicago. The proceeds can go to Meadow Creek to help out their building fund."

A smile grew over Mother's face. "I like it. You are full of good ideas."

"You should be one of the models, Tillie. You've worn my dresses before, so I'm sure the new ones Mother brought along will fit you." The idea took root in Karen's heart. How fun if her wardrobe would help families like Agnes's. It would help Logan too. Concern for Meadow Creek dominated their recent conversations. Now that spring was approaching, Logan wanted to get moving on the project.

"You should be the master of ceremonies." Tillie nudged Logan with her elbow.

He laughed. "I don't think so. I could tell you a fact or two about the Gospels, but women's fashion is where my expertise runs out."

"It's easier than you think. We'll tell you what to say. One of us will write all the descriptions. You will only have to read them." Tillie's gaze held pleading.

"Come on, Logan. You'd do a great job," Julia joined in.

"Yes, my dear. Say you'll agree to helping out." Mother gave Logan a warm smile.

"The people from Meadow Creek would love to see you there." Karen grasped his arm.

"When do you want this event to take place?" Logan hadn't exactly agreed, but he didn't say "no" either. Karen read what encouragement she could find in the response.

"How about next week? That will give us time to get the word out." Julia looked at everyone.

"Will you do it?" Karen gazed up into Logan's face.

The sober expression stayed in his eyes for a moment before he swooped a kiss onto her forehead. "For you, sweetheart."

The room erupted in cheers. They spent the rest of the meal making plans with excitement and deciding which dresses to use in the show. Tillie had two friends from town she would ask to help. Along with Julia and Karen, she'd also serve as a model.

They worked together to clear the table. When the job was completed, the time had come for Julia to gather her family and return with Mother to the hotel.

"I dread the thought of another sleepless night. Logan, I wish we had room for you to stay with us. You seem to be the only one with any success in getting Sam to settle down." Julia looked weary just talking about it.

"What if Sam spends the night here on the farm with me? We can move the crib out to the barn. He'll have all the peace and quiet he could ever want."

Julia's mouth fell open. "That's very kind of you. I wouldn't want to impose. He might keep you awake. Besides, if the baby stays on the farm, I'll need to stay too."

Karen stepped forward. "You may wear one of my nightgowns."

"Take Logan's room at the top of the stairs." Sandy gestured in that direction.

"Me too, Mama. Me too." Ben tugged on Julia's skirt.

"No. You should go with Grandma back to town."

Ben began to cry. "If Sam gets to stay in the barn, I want to stay too."

Julia looked at Karen with the expression of a mother who truly had her hands full.

"I could fix up a bed for him. There's room for him to stay with me." Logan's eyes twinkled.

"Are you sure you want them both spending the night with you?" Julia smoothed Ben's hair to help him stop crying.

Logan squatted down to Ben's level. "It'll be fun. Ben, what do you say to camping out in the barn?"

Ben didn't say anything. Instead, he squealed and hurled himself into Logan's arms.

Karen's eyes filled with tears. Not only Mother and Julia gave their full acceptance of him, but now both of her nephews, even the tiny Sam, welcomed Logan into their lives. Her blessings continued to multiply.

Logan drove Mother back to town while Karen helped everyone prepare for bed. When he returned, Karen worked with Sandy in carrying the crib to Logan's lean-to in the barn. She stayed behind and made up a small bed for Ben from a bench Logan moved in from the milk parlor.

His apartment was cramped with the cot, the crib, Ben's bed, and the cupboard in one corner. He'd have no room to take a step without bumping into a little boy. Once again, Logan made sacrifices for her and now for her family.

"Thank you."

He glanced up from trimming the lamp.

"I've been thinking about this situation of Mother coming for a visit and getting to know you."

Logan straightened and gave her his full attention.

"She's seen you for who you really are, for who I've always known you to be."

He glanced away in a moment of self-consciousness.

"Logan, do you realize Mother wouldn't have learned of your piety and your integrity if I didn't still live here?"

Red stained his cheeks.

"She's seen where your heart really is, and she loves you for it."

His focus returned to her face. In his eyes, she read his heart. It belonged to a man who had already decided to love and cherish her until death parted them.

She walked back to the house with the image imprinted in her mind of Logan standing in his crowded apartment. She could believe he never dreamed his emergency move to the barn could turn out so fine.

CHAPTER SIXTEEN

*W*hen Logan arrived at the hotel to take Margaret to the farm for the day, satchels and hat boxes were stacked in the hall. His stomach clenched. Surely Margaret didn't intend to leave so soon. Nothing about the conversation in the barn struck him as offensive. Unless Margaret had changed her mind. She had every right to. Just because he found satisfaction with his impromptu living arrangements didn't mean they were good enough for Karen's mother. He fought the slump claiming his shoulders and knocked on the door.

It opened immediately. Margaret stepped into the hall. "Good morning. Could you please help me with our trunks? They are too heavy for me to move on my own."

She really did intend to leave. And she wanted him to help her do it. The whole notion threw his mind into confusion. "W... where...uh...do you want them?" He rubbed his forehead. His tongue had graced him with eloquence as long as Margaret Millerson had known him. Now it bumbled around at just the moment he must rely on it to somehow convince her to stay.

Margaret paused and studied him. "Why, in your wagon, of course."

"To…uh…haul them to the station? Would you like for me to…uh…to bring Julia and…and the children from the farm?" His face heated. No way would this woman worthy of a good impression ever believe he could preach a sermon.

Her mouth dropped open. "Oh. Sure. Yes. We can leave today, if that is what you wish. Karen will be disappointed. We have all these plans made for a style show."

Logan's heart thumped. "No. I didn't mean…your bags…the hat boxes. I thought you were…well, leaving."

Margaret's hand fluttered to a rest on her chest. "Oh my. We do have a way of misunderstanding one another. I should start over."

She led Logan into the room and sat on the plush wingback chair near the window. "The hotel is so lonely without Julia and the children here. I cancelled our reservations for the remainder of the week. You were so welcoming of the boys, allowing them to stay with you in the barn that I hoped you might be able to make a little room for me too."

Logan's eyes widened. She couldn't be asking what he thought she was asking. "You mean, you want to stay in the barn?"

She laughed, an easy, trickling sound that reminded him of water flowing over the smooth stones of the creek in the summertime. "Not in the barn, but maybe in the house. I could share your room with Julia or even sleep in the parlor."

Logan relaxed. He even managed a smile.

Margaret stood and looked him in the eye. "I want to be with my family, with my daughters, my grandchildren, and with you. But I should have asked you first. I'm sorry."

"We'd be honored to have you." Logan bent to pick up a trunk.

"There's more to you than meets the eye, Reverend De Witt, and I want to get to know you better." She patted his cheek on her way out the door.

There she went with the "reverend" thing again. He suppressed the desire to give his eyes a good roll. "I thought we agreed you would call me Logan."

"Don't forget to call me Mother." She lifted two hat boxes and preceded him down the hall.

At the farm, Mama converted the sewing room into a bedroom for Margaret. Ben was thrilled with the news that Grandma would stay on the farm with him, but Margaret's presence couldn't pull him away from Logan's side. He went everywhere with Logan.

With Julia's careful schooling on family relationships and Logan's proper place in them, Ben started to call him Uncle Logan. The "l" consonant gave Ben some difficulty, so "Uncle Logan" came out sounding more like "Unca Wogan." Logan didn't mind. The acceptance that came with the status of uncle to Julia's children more than made up for any minor mispronunciation of his name. Karen found it adorable and, like him, rejoiced in the deeper meaning it represented.

The household adjusted quickly. Sam still took his afternoon naps in the barn but transitioned into sleeping in the house at night. Ben still stayed with Logan in the barn in spite of his mother's coaxing to move to the house.

"No way," he said. For Ben, the barn was the place where he learned from "Unca Wogan" how a man did an honest day's work spending time with animals and getting gloriously dirty in the process.

Mama and Margaret became fast friends, talking over recipes and patterns. They had in common the loss of their husbands so spent the evenings sharing mutual encouragement and comfort. Mama's eyes grew brighter and her step lighter from Margaret's companionship.

Margaret was a cheery, no-nonsense kind of woman. Logan could see where Karen got her refinement and kindness. She resembled her mother in her taste for fashion, her proper, reserved demeanor, and her elegant manners. Both of them held the highest of standards, but these were balanced with just as much grace.

Tillie found fascination in Julia. Karen's sister exemplified the life Tillie hoped to one day live, married to an upstanding town leader, raising a family, and living in a comfortable house in town. Tillie was learning from Julia in much the same way Ben learned from Logan.

Friday night, when Pete and Anna came for supper, Julia found a lifelong friend in Anna Betten. After recently giving birth, Julia offered Anna all kinds of advice and answers to questions. The two laughed and talked right up until Mama and Margaret served the meal.

Logan prayed, and then the group focused on Logan's and Karen's upcoming wedding.

"Mother and I decided on the style of my wedding gown," Karen said in answer to a question from Anna.

"It's beautiful. A lovely train with lace." Tillie gestured in the air to indicate ample amounts of flowing material.

"Shh." Julia glanced at Logan. "Don't let him hear."

He probably wouldn't understand anyway. Besides, he had a style show to survive. The thought of describing in satisfactory detail the dresses Julia and Margaret brought with them still made him break out in a cold sweat.

"I assume the wedding will be in Chicago," Pete said.

"We haven't actually discussed that yet." Karen looked Logan's way.

"What's there to discuss? Our church in Chicago will make the perfect setting for your wedding." Margaret resumed eating as if the subject needed no further conversation.

"I had something quite different in mind, Mother." Karen's simple statement captured everyone's attention. "I'd like to get married at Logan's church in Oswell City."

"Not in Silver Grove?" Tillie asked.

"No. A wedding in either Chicago or Silver Grove wouldn't be fair to the other side of the family. If the wedding is in Oswell City, everyone must travel. Plus, Logan's congregation is there. I'm sure it would be important to them to attend his wedding. Maybe the bakery in Oswell City could make our cake. We could ask someone else to supply our flowers. Oswell City is where I'll be living as Logan's wife, so I'd like to get married there, among those we'll be serving."

"This is news. I thought you would choose to get married here." Mama's comment broke the silence that followed Karen's words.

This conversation should have happened in another place at another time with no audience. He and Karen needed privacy to work out decisions like this one. Their wedding in Oswell City? The thought never entered his head. He wanted a simple, quiet ceremony with only family and closest friends present. No end existed to the amount of grandiosity that would get assigned to the affair if the women of his Oswell City congregation became involved. Fewer occasions went down in a town's history than the wedding of their pastor after his years of self-imposed bachelorhood. He'd never enjoyed making a sensation, and he didn't want to start now.

He cleared his throat. "I need to think about it."

"I do wish you'd choose to get married in Chicago. Your Uncle Henry will be disappointed. He'll be the one walking you down the aisle and giving you away, after all." Margaret frowned.

"He can give me away in Oswell City just as easily. We must let Logan decide."

Karen's words rang in his ears. Such a controversial decision shouldn't belong to him alone. Neither should he get pressured into choosing. If this had come up during a quiet discussion with only Karen, they could have worked it out, but six extra people had heard, each with their own ideas of how his wedding should go. They would just have to wait. First, he needed to have a chat with his fiancée.

LIGHT BLAZED in the hotel dining room. Silver trays displayed a variety of food on the tables near the large windows. Rows of chairs with people from Silver Grove, Meadow Creek, and the surrounding area filled the room. Logan stood off to the right of a runway constructed by Jake at his hardware store the day before. A curtain spanned the wall behind him, giving the women a place to change into their variety of outfits between appearances. Logan wore his suit and tie. Since his tie wasn't needed today for a baby calming tool, it stayed clean enough to complete his attire.

The baby sat on Anna's lap, true to the arrangement for her to care for Julia's little boys so she could participate in the style show. Sam cooperated fine with the plan, but Ben had already tried twice to run to the front.

Logan winked at the frowning little guy and raised his voice. "Good evening. Thank you for coming to tonight's style show, hosted by Silver Grove's teacher, Miss Karen Millerson. Miss Millerson, along with her mother, sister, and her friends, will be modeling for you the latest styles from the city. All proceeds go into the fund to help Meadow Creek build a new church. Enjoy. Let's begin."

He glanced at Tillie, not yet outfitted as a model, to start the music. She lifted the needle of the Victrola in to place and whisked behind the curtain. Reading the descriptions for Margaret's traveling suit and Karen's afternoon dress proved much easier than he thought. The show continued smoothly until Julia appeared in a coat and wide-brimmed hat.

"Mommy!" Ben's cry brought chuckles from the audience as he raced for the stage.

Logan caught him. "Go sit with Mrs. Betten."

Ben shook his head and writhed under Logan's firm grasp.

While Julia made her turns and walked the runway, Logan knelt down. "What would you like, Ben? You know you can't go to your mother right now."

"Then I wanna help you, Uncle Logan. Please don't make me sit anymore. Please?"

Logan's heart went softer than homemade ice cream in the summer sun. If being a father was even close to being an uncle to a little guy, he'd end up as the biggest push-over who ever lived. He tousled Ben's hair. "Come here, little man." With a squeal from Ben, Logan swung him up into his arms. Ben clapped and reached for the papers on the nearby podium.

"Those aren't for you, but you can hold this." Logan gave Ben the napkin left over from the snacks he'd enjoyed earlier. Ben sailed it on to Logan's shoulder and worked on making a little napkin tent.

Julia exited the stage, and Karen came next. The dress she wore must have come along with her mother because Logan hadn't seen it before. Shimmering blue material, gathered and tapered in all the right places, accentuated her figure to perfection. Words came to mind, but they didn't match the description on the page before him. The one he'd give instead would tell the audience how utterly beautiful she was and how blessed he was to have her as his fiancée. He'd go on to tell them of his readiness to join his life with hers and of how she satisfied his every dream of grace and loveliness.

Ben patted his head. "Auntie Karen looks pretty."

The simple speech jolted him back to the moment. He focused on the words typed on the page and did his best to describe Karen's dress the way she expected. Mama followed in an afternoon dress, and then Tillie in a white tea gown. As she exited, Logan glanced up to see Chet Murray standing in the back of the room. Esther sat with the Harpers near the front. Logan guessed they weren't aware of Chet lurking in the back.

His pulse sped up. Both of them were here, in the same room. He must find a way to get them back together. His attention on the man's every move, Logan continued to announce until the style show came to a close. As people left their seats for the dessert table, Logan slipped to the back of the room. Ben insisted on a piece of cake, so Logan got one for him and settled him in a nearby chair.

"Chet, good to see you." Logan held out his hand.

The man frowned. "You're Jack's preacher friend, ain't you?"

Logan nodded. "I'm glad you came out tonight to support the rebuilding of the church."

Chet shrugged. "I needed something to do. The house gets a mite lonely without Esther in it."

"She's still living with her parents?"

"Yeah."

Logan leaned in and whispered. "Stop drinking, Chet. That's all you have to do to get her back."

Chet studied his shoes.

"Ask Jack how to do it. He quit months ago. He can help you."

"Hey, Rev!" Jack Harper called out over the crowd.

Logan returned his wave.

"Nice job announcing." Jack, Amelia, and Esther drew near enough to discover Logan wasn't alone. They paused.

Jack nodded a stiff nod. "Evening, Chet."

"Jack." Chet's response was just as stiff. The women hung back, but Chet glanced at them. "Hi, Esther."

She barely acknowledged him.

"The preacher and me are talkin'. He says you'll come back if I quit drinkin'."

"For good." Esther crossed her arms. "Prove to me you'll change, Chet Murray."

Chet's jaw worked. His decision was a weighty one. Both choices carried heavy losses. Logan watched, his heart begging the man to make the right choice. There must have been a time when he felt about Esther like Logan did about Karen, in love and ready to build a life together. Chet must recover those feelings if Esther would remain as his. Logan left the group to check on Ben, concern for the Murrays filling his heart. Love came at a high price. He just hoped Chet would be willing to pay it.

CHAPTER SEVENTEEN

*K*aren's classroom dissolved into mayhem as each day passed. Now that Mother and Julia had returned to their Chicago home, she had more energy to give to restoring order. The Kent and Sanders cousins refused to pay attention or do any of their work. The boys chucked spit wads, pulled hair, and kicked their desk mates. The two girls, Carrie Kent in sixth grade and Anna Sanders in third grade, kept up a steady stream of whispers or chatter with their desk mates, depending on the group activity Karen had assigned.

If she could just keep them settled down for the sake of the students who did want to learn. She saw the discouragement in their faces when the antics from the misbehaving students proved too distracting for proper concentration on lessons.

Daily, Evie yelled at Marty to quiet down. He only pulled her hair or flicked a spit wad in her face. Then she'd turn around, cross her arms, and sulk. Karen really should discipline Evie for yelling in class, but she struggled with the longing to do the same thing. Her nerves were nearly frazzled. The smallest act of misbehavior heightened her irritation.

Cabin fever offered itself as the perfect reason for the naughtiness, but Karen suspected otherwise. Ever since the day she voiced her opinions to Mrs. Sanders, her classroom had grown unmanageable. The woman was somehow behind the mutiny polarizing the school. Vera Kent certainly wouldn't stand in her way. Her disdain for homework coupled with Mrs. Sanders's crotchety outlook made for a toxic combination.

If Karen could send the naughty students home, she might regain a measure of order. But that would go against the requirements for public education. No teacher had the authority to ban children from learning, even if their parents worked against their development from the beginning.

Karen sighed with a deep raising and lowering of her shoulders. She'd just have to do the best she could and pray for warmer weather. Maybe more time spent outdoors would give the boys a place to exhaust their orneriness. After dismissing school, Karen followed her usual routine of walking home and venting her problems to her patient fiancé.

Thursday morning, Eldon Kent came to the school along with his passel of nieces and nephews. Karen hardly needed this man visiting her at school again. She forced a greeting. "Good morning."

The words "what are you doing here" pressed on her tongue, but she bit them off just in time.

"Good morning, Miss Millerson. You are looking beautiful, as always." His gaze made her skin crawl.

If only she was free to warn him away with the news of her engagement to Logan De Witt, he'd leave her alone.

Eldon settled lunch tins for the youngest of the Kent children on the shelf. "Evan and Vera are away on a business trip, so I am staying on the farm with the children."

Karen raised her brows. Eldon probably wouldn't cooperate with the completion of homework assignments any better than his brother and sister-in-law.

Eldon touched his hat and walked out.

Karen breathed deeply and called class to order.

Mid-morning, while Karen browsed the book shelf in search of a tome on American history, a strange tin caught her eye. She picked it up and addressed the class. "Can anyone tell me where this tin came from?"

Joe glanced up from the back of Evie's head where the tip of the pin in his hand hovered inches away from her scalp.

"Give that to me." Karen held her hand out, ready to accept the instrument of torture.

He scowled and placed it in his teacher's hand, point side down.

Karen winced at the prick. She gulped away the tears that sprang to her eyes. "Now, tell me about this tin." She put the pin in her pocket.

Joe glanced around. "It's for Wade. We've got a huntin' trip planned after school today."

"I see."

"Uncle Eldon brought it."

Karen nodded. Likely story. All of Eldon's time in the class-room this morning had been spent with her. Not only was Joe a trouble maker, but now he told tall tales too. Quite an impressive resume for a boy only months away from graduation.

Karen took the tin to her desk and put it in a drawer. She'd check in with Wade later for the real story. Not one to go along with Joe's shenanigans, Wade's word could be trusted.

She'd need a reliable story. The kind of tin good old Uncle Eldon apparently brought to school was the sort gun powder came in.

WHILE WORKING around the barn after the morning milking, Logan discovered a hammer and saw when he forked hay into a manger. He studied them. These tools didn't belong to him, but he couldn't think who else might have been working in his barn.

Roy Jones.

Of course. The kind neighbor who finished Logan's roofing project. To think of how many times Logan had been to Roy's place while Karen tutored Lacy and the man never mentioned them. Maybe Roy thought Logan could use the tools, or maybe he didn't know they were missing. Either way, the project was long completed, providing Logan with a snug place to sleep. He'd drive over to Roy's farm and return the tools to their rightful owner.

Logan went to the house to tell Mama of his plan.

She stood at the stove. "But it's nearly dinner time."

Logan glanced at the clock. "This won't take too long. I'll be back soon."

Mama looked doubtful.

Logan went to the horse barn and saddled the trusted horse that had served the family for many years. The snow had been melted away for over a week, so the sleigh was no longer necessary. He guided the horse out of the barn, hopped down, and swung the barn door shut. The March breeze tousled his hair.

He inhaled, enjoying the refreshing spring air, but it carried a hint of smoke. His muscles tensed. He turned around and scanned the horizon.

There, a quarter-mile to the south, black smoke rolled into the sky, too close to come from Clyde Hixson's place, yet far enough away that nothing on Logan's farm burned.

That left only one possible location.

The school.

Logan's heart raced, but both of his legs felt as if plaster casts weighed them down. His fingers fumbled with the reins as he lumbered onto his horse.

"Yah!" One quick swat of the reins and the horse shot down the lane.

Orange flames leaped from the school building. Karen and the older boys crowded near the doorway while children milled around on the yard, none of them wearing coats.

Logan guided the horse over to the fence, looped the reins around a post, and sprinted across the lawn. "Karen!"

She glanced up. Tears streaked the soot on her face. She pushed hair away from her forehead with the back of her hand while she ran to him.

Logan caught her and held her close. "Are you all right?"

"I am. The children escaped, but Eldon is still in there."

He held her at arms' length and looked into her eyes. "Eldon?"

Karen nodded with a sob.

Logan gathered her into his embrace once more, but she pushed against him.

"Come, we have to get him out."

His attention shifted away from Karen and onto the school. He outran her and darted into the burning building.

Smoke stung his eyes.

"Eldon?" He coughed and dropped to his knees, prepared to crawl.

He landed on a body.

Eldon lay sprawled in the aisle, his clothes on fire.

Wrapping his arms around Eldon's torso, Logan dragged him across the threshold.

"Help me!" Logan called out to the older boys.

Wade and Cal came running. They took hold of Eldon's legs. Logan grasped Eldon's middle, and held himself at a distance to avoid the flames as he worked with the boys to carry Eldon to the pump. Wade and Cal were careful, too, so that their own clothing didn't catch on fire.

Karen poured water over Eldon, dousing the flames. "I sent Tim home to get his father. Clyde should be here soon."

Logan leaned down and listened for Eldon's heartbeat. The

man still had a pulse, but his skin was badly burned. He probably suffered from smoke inhalation too.

"We need to get him to the doctor." Logan stood as wagons streamed into the yard. Fathers climbed down and searched for their offspring. Then the men gathered buckets they'd brought along and pumped them full of water. The neighbors worked at extinguishing the flames while Logan, Wade, and Cal loaded Eldon into one of the wagons.

As soon as Eldon was as comfortable as possible, Logan drove the wagon to the doctor's office in town.

KAREN TURNED her attention onto her students. She clapped her hands. "Everyone, over here. Get out of the way."

The students followed her instructions and joined her at the well.

Mary Ellen whimpered and tugged on Karen's skirt. "Teacher, I lost my doll in the fire. I brought her so I could show her to Becky at recess."

Karen knelt down. "I know. I'm sorry." She offered the girl her lace handkerchief and gave her a hug.

"My coat burned." Sarah rubbed her upper arms.

"So did my favorite sweater." Alice moaned.

Karen gave her a hug too.

The boys shuffled their feet and shoved their hands in their pockets with downcast faces.

Losing the school was hard for everyone, even Joe, Marty, and Emmett who huddled together staring at the ground. Perhaps the uncertain fate of Uncle Eldon concerned them more than the loss of a building they disliked.

Tom's daughters ran to him when he joined the group. "We've got the fire put out. Not much left of the place. Let's call a meeting at the church tonight so we can decide what to do about where to hold class. Can ya tell Logan when ya see him?"

Karen nodded.

"Seven o'clock."

"Sure."

"Can I give ya a ride home?"

"Yes. Thank you." A ride in Tom's wagon beat a walk in the chilly wind since Karen had lost her coat to the flames like her students had lost theirs.

After everyone left with their fathers, Karen accepted Tom's help into his wagon. She took one last look at the smoldering ruins of her classroom. Through storm damage and broken windows, the school had survived. Unruly children and difficult days hadn't toppled Karen's ability to endure. She'd survived right along with the building. But now the school lay completely destroyed. Her stomach sank as she traveled back to the farm. Would she endure through this tragedy, or would her career see the same fate as the demolished school?

LOGAN USHERED Karen into an overcrowded church. News of the fire had spread far and wide. More people than just the local neighbors who sent their children to the school were in attendance tonight. People from town, other school districts, and couples who lived in the area but no longer had children of school age at home filled the pews. He could believe that most of them came more out of curiosity than to help with the decision making.

Karen pressed his side as they moved down the tight aisle. How he'd love to offer her a seat in the back. But as the teacher, Karen must appear accessible, even if she wasn't a member of the school board.

Two spots remained on the front pew. Logan hadn't planned to make Karen quite that visible, but every other seat was taken.

Tom Hinkley stood behind the pulpit, banging a gavel. "Good evening. Thanks for comin' out tonight. As you all know, our school burned to the ground today."

"What happened?" A deep voice boomed from the back.

Murmurs echoing the same question rippled through the gathering.

"That ain't important right now. The school board and I will check into it as soon as possible. All we need to decide tonight is where to have school."

"But we want to know." Burt Sanders spoke up.

Someone from town chimed in. "How are we to find out how the fire started if you don't tell us here in this meeting?"

Tom banged the gavel. "Like I said, that ain't important. We got business to discuss."

"Miss Millerson would know." Elsie's testy voice scratched Logan's nerves. "She was there. She could tell us."

Karen shifted in her seat. Logan had all he could manage restraining himself from taking over the pulpit and demanding these busybodies to go home.

The room grew loud with affirmation of Elsie's comments.

Tom stepped back and glanced at Karen. "You wanna give us a brief explanation of what you saw?"

Karen crept to her feet and faced the group. "The stove exploded. The door flew off and hit Eldon. He'd come to school to deliver a lunch to his niece. Flames shot out of the stove and started the desks and the floor on fire. The children and I ran out of the school. Logan came just in time. He rescued Eldon and drove him to the doctor."

Karen sat down.

"How come the stove exploded?" A man from town asked Karen. "You got ammunition or somethin' hidden away in that school? I never seen a stove blow apart before."

She stood up again. "Only the door came off, sir. Like Mr. Hinkley said, the school board will investigate at the earliest opportunity."

Tom nodded, so Karen sat back down.

"I don't think so." Burt Sanders stood up. "It's a known fact Miss Millerson struggles to maintain order during school hours. There's nothin' to investigate. Miss Millerson could have prevented the fire and kept our children out of danger."

Karen's jaw dropped.

"Now hang on a minute, Burt." Tom held his hand up. "We don't have all the facts. Better wait with your accusations until the school board gets the chance to look around."

"We have all the facts we need." Burt clutched the pew in front of him. "Miss Millerson is the most incapable and inexperienced teacher you've hired yet, Tom."

"I didn't hire her. She was sent here." Tom's face turned red, and he spoke in short, clipped words.

But Burt didn't stop. "She assigns ridiculous amounts of homework over the holidays when she should have plenty of time during school to get the work done. She plays favorites tutoring some kids while ignoring others. And the tales the kids tell when they come home. Lunches stolen. Bruises on their legs from kicks. Steps so slippery a kid could fall and break their neck." Burt whistled. "It's a wonder they learn anything at all in the Silver Grove School."

Logan clenched his teeth. He'd heard enough.

"Is it any surprise to you, Tom Hinkley, that she'd also be the one to burn down the school?" Burt crossed his arms.

Logan shot out of the pew. Before he knew it, he stood at the pulpit like this was a Sunday morning and Tom stood around waiting to take up the offering. "You may sit down now, Burt. Thank you for expressing your opinions." He caught Karen's attention and raised his brows.

Her eyes rolled to the ceiling.

He cleared his throat. "As Tom said earlier, we've gathered here this evening to make what should be an easy and quick decision. But, since we've gotten distracted by questions concerning the cause of the fire, please allow me to make some things clear. Miss Karen Millerson is the best teacher your children could ever hope to learn from. She cares about them and wants them to learn more than just their math and letters. She wants them to develop strong character too. You should be proud to have a teacher who wishes to see your sons and daughters grow into people who are responsible and who know how to make good decisions and treat others well."

He had the attention of every last person in the room. Perspiration dampened his forehead, but he didn't care. He had a few more things to say. "I've talked these events over with Miss Millerson that you mentioned earlier, Burt. Now, if I understand correctly, your two sons and Evan's oldest boys team up and cause trouble for their teacher when they should be studying. What Miss Millerson needs isn't more of your accusations but some cooperation and support. That is, if you can scrounge up a little to offer. Are we clear?"

He got no response, so asked again.

Murmurs ran through the crowd.

Logan turned to Tom. "I see Pete in the back. Ask him if we can use the church as a classroom."

Logan tromped down the steps and claimed his seat beside Karen. Those Sanderses better not give Karen any more trouble, or he'd use more than pretty words and smooth talking to teach them a lesson.

"How about usin' the church for a school?" Tom stepped up to the pulpit. "Reverend Betten, you got a problem with that?"

"Not at all. I think it's a fine idea." Pete answered in a loud voice for all to hear.

Tom scanned the room. "Can anyone else come up with a

reason why the church won't work for a new location to hold class?"

Pews creaked, and people whispered, but no one answered.

"All right then, folks. Let's take a vote. Anyone in favor of usin' the church say 'aye.'"

A unison response echoed through the sanctuary.

"Anyone opposed, say 'nay.'" Tom looked over the crowd but received no answer.

He banged the gavel. "Unanimous. Good idea, Logan. Thanks. We'll use the church for classes starting as soon as I can get a shipment of books from the superintendent. If you have questions or more concerns, you can catch me afterward."

Tom wiped his face with a handkerchief pulled from his pocket. "This meeting is adjourned."

A hearty whack of the gavel brought people to their feet. They milled around visiting with neighbors. No one seemed in a hurry to leave.

But Logan was. He clasped Karen's elbow and guided her through the crowd.

CHAPTER EIGHTEEN

*L*ogan walked with Karen across the dark church lawn.

"Thanks for standing up for me in there," Karen said.

Logan's chest swelled, and his throat tightened.

"Tom would've had a crisis on his hands if you hadn't stepped in."

He'd had a crisis anyway, but that wasn't why Logan spoke up.

"Did you see how people stared at me as we left? I fear Burt has turned this community against me even though you did such a wonderful job supporting me." Karen rubbed her upper arms although she wore a coat.

"The truth sets free, sweetheart. It always does. Let Burt blow off some steam. In the end, you'll still have friends." Logan reached to hold her hand as they walked along.

"I hope you're right. I probably shouldn't have been so impertinent to his wife." Karen's voice held a note of regret.

"Sometimes people need to hear the truth even when it's hard to accept. You did the right thing."

"You think so, even though I called her a wet hen?" Karen looked up at him.

Logan chuckled. "Sometimes the most dramatic heart changes occur after someone dares to tell the truth to another person. Let's pray that happens to Elsie." Logan raised his gaze to the stars overhead. Thoughts of Eldon entered his mind. Logan had stayed at the doctor's office long enough to learn that Eldon's condition was very serious. A prayer rose from his heart for the man lying in much pain tonight.

"Hey, my friend." Pete intercepted their path with a hearty handshake. "Nice job in there. You're an all right preacher."

"Appreciate it." Logan could take Pete more seriously if this was actually Sunday and the crowd in the church tonight was his own congregation.

"Can the two of you stop in for a few minutes? I have something to ask you."

Logan shrugged and looked at Karen.

"We'd be happy to," she answered.

Pete led the way to his house where Anna offered cups of coffee.

Logan accepted and assisted Karen in taking a seat before claiming the one beside her at the table.

Pete pulled up a chair. "I have an idea."

"What is it?" Logan glanced at his friend.

"The water damage has been repaired in our spare room. We still need to wallpaper it and put down new flooring, but Karen, if you are willing to use the room anyway, you are welcome to move in." Pete leaned forward.

Karen's eyes grew round. "I'd love to."

"Now that school will be held at the church, you might as well live nearby. The sooner the better, I think. Logan supported you so well tonight, people may start to wonder if you mean more to him than an average boarder."

"They'd be right." Logan sipped from his cup.

"Are you still sleeping in the barn?" Pete watched him.

"Of course I am." What kind of question was that? Pete should know Logan wouldn't abandon his new sleeping quarters as long as Karen occupied a room in his house.

"You could use your room again if Karen comes here."

Pete's words stated nothing new, but the meaning beneath them registered in Logan's brain. "You mean tonight? Right now?"

"Exactly." Pete smiled in a way that let Logan know he'd finally caught on.

"But I don't have a nightgown or a brush or anything." Karen frowned.

"Have Logan go to the farm and get them for you. Maybe tomorrow since you won't have any school, you can pay the De Witt family a visit and gather the rest of your things." Pete sipped from his cup.

A smile grew on Karen's face. "I like that idea."

Trembles quaked in every last muscle. Proper courtship had arrived. Logan pushed away from the table. "I'll be back soon." Tripping over his chair, he lunged for the door, nearly hitting his head on the wall. Regaining his balance, he waved to assure the others he wasn't injured and sprinted from the house. At the farm, he jumped out of the buggy and shot into the kitchen.

Mama sat at the table with her recipe card box and the glowing lamp. "Logan, dear. What is the matter? I saw you coming. Is something wrong?"

"No. Everything is fine." Absolutely wonderful, in fact. He scanned the room. A bag. That's what he needed. He must find a bag to carry Karen's belongings back to the Bettens'.

"How did the meeting turn out?"

In the pantry. Mama kept bags in there that she used to purchase flour and sugar at the mercantile. Three strides and he reached the pantry. "They're going to hold classes at the church."

A stack of pans with their handles sticking out every which

way caught his sleeve. They banged together and crashed to the floor with a terrible noise. Lids rolled at his feet, adding to the chaos. He bent down to put the pans on the shelf, but shaking in his hands made the job impossible. Maybe he should concentrate on matching the lids back up with their pans instead. He might have pulled it off, but those silly lids slipped from his grasp and clattered to the floor, wasting his precious time. He needed to be working on finding a bag for Karen's nightgown, not chasing stray pan lids all over the place.

"What is going on in here?" Mama appeared in the pantry doorway.

"I need a bag. Quick." He raced into the corner and dug through Mama's collection. The pile soon covered most of the floor. He had to find one the right size before reaching the bottom.

Mama took over cleaning up the cookware. "You say the church will be used to hold class? That should work well. What does Karen think of those arrangements? Where is she?"

These bags were way too small. A full length nightgown would never fit in there. He'd have to find something else to use instead. He darted for the stairs. "She's at Pete and Anna's."

Taking the stairs two at a time, he hit the upstairs hall. Maybe Karen kept a satchel in her room. That might work better. He threw the door open and pulled out a dresser drawer. Gloves, stockings, and various pieces of lacy clothing lay in the drawer. No satchel there. He needed help.

Logan ran into the hall and leaned over the banister. "Mama. Mama!"

A clatter of pan lids, and Mama appeared on the bottom step, lamp in hand. "What is it, dear? You made a mess of the pantry, and you're acting like the house is on fire."

Logan took a deep breath.

Tillie came out of her room. "Logan? What's going on? What are you and Mama yelling about?"

He exhaled while a grin stretched across his face. "Mama. Tillie. Karen and I are officially courting."

Mama frowned.

"What?" Tillie sounded confused.

"As of tonight, Karen is the newest member of the Betten residence. I'm free to announce our engagement now."

Tillie jogged down the hall. "You mean Karen isn't going to live here anymore?"

"No. I came home to get whatever she might need to spend the night with Pete and Anna. Tomorrow she'll come get the rest of her possessions." As he spoke, visions of his future danced in his thoughts. He could ask her to help him again on Sunday afternoons. They could share the parlor and go for buggy rides when the weather warmed. He could give her flowers and help her plan their new life together just like a real couple.

Logan wanted to twirl someone around and let out a whoop. But the hallway was too small. He'd save his celebrating for another time.

He looked at Tillie. "Could you please pack a few things for Karen to use overnight?"

Tillie nodded and entered Karen's room. She lit the lamp on the dresser and pulled open the top drawer. "What's this?"

She reached into one corner and lifted out a gold band, the diamond sparkling in the lamplight

Karen's Christmas present.

"I'll take that." Logan reached for the ring and dropped it in his shirt pocket.

Tillie looked as if she wanted to ask him more questions, but he went downstairs before she had the chance.

Mama had returned to her box of recipe cards. The pantry might need more attention. He poked his head in.

"Don't go in there. I want it to stay clean."

Logan glanced at Mama who peered at him with warning in her eye. He ran his hand through his hair and paced instead.

Tillie entered the kitchen with a satchel and handed it to him.

His shaking finally stopped on the return trip. When he reached Pete's home, Logan tethered the horse and went inside. He found Pete, Anna, and Karen seated in the parlor with refilled cups of coffee.

"Here you go. Tillie packed it." He handed the satchel to Karen and entered their conversation until Karen's cup was empty.

"Would you join me outside for a moment?" Logan led the way to the swing on Pete's porch.

The time had come to put that engagement ring where it belonged, not in the bottom of a drawer awaiting better days, but permanently on Karen's finger.

KAREN STOOD in the center of her upstairs room in the De Witt farmhouse. She sighed as she looked at the last stack of boxes awaiting Logan's next trip to the wagon parked in the lane. The bed was made. The wardrobe had been emptied of her dresses. Her books traveled in their original crates instead of stacked along the wall.

She'd miss living here. The De Witts were her family, almost more some days than Mother, Julia, and Uncle Henry and Aunt Fran in Chicago, whom she loved dearly. And yet her Silver Grove family were the ones who taught her how to let go of old hurts. Then they filled those places in with their gentle natures. Sandy with her encouragement. Logan with his love. Even Tillie. They were best friends now. Soon to be sisters. The thought cheered her a bit. Leaving the De Witt home didn't change her status as a member of their family.

She sniffed.

Logan entered the room and rested his hand on her shoulder. "Ready to go?"

"Yes."

He picked up the hat boxes and headed for the stairs. Karen followed him out to the wagon that would deliver her to a new home. A parsonage. Her life had come full circle, almost like the Lord was giving her the chance to make right all the things that had gone wrong in her earlier years.

She stole a glance at her fiancé as they drove along. No one possessed a higher integrity than Logan. Would Father have moved into a drafty barn for her mother? Would he have drained his savings to care for those he loved most?

Karen couldn't answer those questions about him, but she could about Logan. This move to the Silver Grove parsonage was the beginning of the rest of her life. Today marked a passage into new territory. A place where she could prepare to welcome into her life all the goodness and risk and reward marriage to a man like Logan would bring.

Logan drove the wagon near the front of the Bettens' home as Anna opened the door. She stepped outside and waved up at them.

Anna's waist had expanded, even overnight. Children. Another blessing Karen may have the pleasure to welcome into her future. Logan would make an excellent father. Many of those traits already came natural to him in his role as a reverend.

Karen accepted his help to the ground while a prayer rose in her heart that the Lord might provide her and Logan with a family of their very own.

"Are you wearing the ring?" Anna hovered nearby.

Pete sauntered over from the kitchen table where books of all sizes lay open. Apparently littering a kitchen table with reading material came with the job. Karen prayed another prayer, this one asking the Lord to provide the Oswell City parsonage with a large kitchen, maybe even two tables. Sandy would've gotten along much better with her bread baking if this had been available to her while Logan was laid up with his broken leg.

Karen held out her hand, showing off her ring all sparkly and glittering in the morning sunlight.

"Looks even better than it did last night in the lamp light." Pete slapped Logan on the back. "Congratulations. I knew you could do it."

Logan grinned.

"You may start unpacking." Anna led Karen to a doorway on the opposite side of the parlor.

Karen looked inside. A window let in the light. Plain white walls and a rug completed the decoration. This was a room still under construction, but it meant resolution for her need of a place to stay, and for that she was thankful.

"You'll need to share with the crib. I hope you don't mind. We kept the bed in here, but now the room is a bit crowded."

"I don't mind." A crowded room was a small price to pay for the freedom to wear the ring that dominated her left hand.

Pete and Logan worked at stacking crates and hat boxes along the parlor wall.

"I'm afraid some of your things will need to stay in storage. We don't have room in the nursery for very much." Anna scanned the room's interior. A dresser was the only other piece of furniture in the room.

"I can take my books to the church."

"You could pile your clothes in the crib." Anna moved a quilt to create more space.

"We've got a closet in the church basement. You can keep the rest of your hats and clothing in there," Pete offered.

Karen nodded. "Now that the weather is warmer, my winter clothing could get stored in that closet. I'll sort through my trunks and refill one with the dresses you may put in storage."

Pete smiled and followed Logan out to the wagon.

"You and Logan are welcome to some coffee. I'll go make it." Anna went to the kitchen as Pete and Logan returned inside with the last load of Karen's belongings.

A knock came on the door. Anna answered it.

Mr. Hinkley entered. He glanced at Karen. "I stopped at the farm, but Sandy said you were all over here. What's goin' on?"

CHAPTER NINETEEN

*K*aren's middle caved. In her impatience to make this move she'd forgotten to inform the school board chairman. "I...ah..."

"Karen is moving in with us so that Logan can court her." Pete set his load down and came over.

Mr. Hinkley's jaw dropped. His gaze passed from Karen to Logan bent over a stack of hat boxes and back to Karen. "Courtin', huh?"

"Yes, sir." Karen held her breath. Maybe she'd broken a rule and now Mr. Hinkley must enforce a consequence.

A smile pulled at Mr. Hinkley's mouth. "Well, I'm happy for ya. It never crossed my mind when you came to town last fall, but it makes sense. This probably means I'll need to find another teacher for next year."

"Most likely." Logan accepted Mr. Hinkley's hand shake.

"We oughta let folks know. I'm thinkin' of callin' another meeting. When Roy, Clyde, and I were pokin' around in the remains of the school just now, we found something. Miss Millerson, could ya come to the school with me? We need ya to answer some questions."

Karen's heart fluttered. "Yes, of course."

She buttoned her coat, one Tillie let her borrow, and followed him out the door.

At the site, Mr. Hinkley led the way to the area where the other two men squatted among the charred remains of the school. They poked at chunks of wood with sticks.

Clyde glanced up. "We found what's left of your desk."

Karen leaned in and saw the metal handles still attached to blackened drawers. Most of the desk had burned, but the drawers were still recognizable, even though they lay beneath the heap of ash and fire-damaged wood.

"We found this." Clyde held up the tin Karen had discovered on the bookshelf.

"The tin of gun powder." She clutched her throat.

"What's it doin' in your desk?" Clyde peered at her.

"I put it there after finding it on the bookshelf. When I asked the class about it, the only answer I received was from Joe. He claims Wade had a hunting trip planned in the Patterson pasture after school yesterday. I wasn't sure if I should believe him or not, so I confiscated the tin and put it in a drawer to show to Wade since he was gathering water at the time. But the school caught on fire before we had a chance to talk."

The men looked at each other for a moment. "That doesn't explain how the school burned down." Mr. Hinkley took the tin from Clyde and turned it over in his hand.

"I don't know." Karen shook her head.

"Did some of it spill?" Roy asked.

Karen tapped her chin. "Possibly. The explosion came after I swept the floor and threw the dustpan's contents into the stove."

"Didn't ya notice any gun powder in the dustpan?" Roy crossed his arms.

"It may have blended in with the other dust I sweep up every day."

A low groan came from Mr. Hinkley. "Well, boys, we don't

have the evidence from the dustpan. It burned long ago. The only thing we have to go on is this here tin."

He turned to Karen. "Miss Millerson, I'm real sorry about this, but it appears that you are responsible for the fire."

As a little girl, Karen had gone swimming and swallowed too much water. She sputtered and coughed as though she still had water in her lungs. "You...you mean... Don't you believe me?"

"Sure, I believe ya." Mr. Hinkley answered in his relaxed drawl.

The other two men echoed his words.

Karen breathed a little easier.

"But the parents may not." Mr. Hinkley shifted his weight and crossed his arms.

"Why?" If she had the confidence of the school board, surely the parents of her students would trust her too.

"Them Kents have a way of gettin' things to work out in their favor. If Joe verifies the story, you'll get everyone to believe you. If not, you run the risk of forcin' people to take sides. It ain't worked before, and I'm bettin' it won't work again." Mr. Hinkley pocketed the tin.

He waved over his head. "Come on, boys. Let's call another meeting. Invite the kids. We gotta get to the bottom of this."

Logan still sat at the table visiting with Pete and Anna when Mr. Hinkley returned her to the Bettens'. They looked at her with questions in their eyes.

Karen slumped into a chair. "Mr. Hinkley found a tin of gunpowder in one of my desk drawers. I believe it belongs to Joe Kent, but if he doesn't claim it, the parents will see me as the one responsible for the fire."

"Oh, Karen." Anna moaned.

She stared at the white table cloth. "He wants to call another meeting tomorrow night at the church."

Her stomach rolled, and her fingers turned to ice. Mr. Hinkley better find a way to make everyone hear the truth.

KAREN SAT at Logan's side in much the same place near the front as in the first meeting. This time, her students filled the pews with their parents instead of curious townspeople and strangers. She'd hardly eaten a thing all day. Even now, her stomach felt queasy. Logan reached over and held her hand. She attempted a smile, but it faded when Mr. Hinkley stood up.

He banged his gavel on the pulpit. "Good evening, folks. Thanks for makin' time for another meeting. We've got some important things to discuss tonight. Roy, Clyde, and I found this tin of gun powder at the school yesterday. We invited all you kids to this meeting so you could help us put some pieces together. Does anyone know how it got to school?"

Silence met Mr. Hinkley's question.

Siblings looked at each other. Questions mixed with guilt lingered on their faces.

"Us eighth grade boys had a hunting trip planned at my place after school on Thursday. We wanted to go lookin' for turkeys in the back pasture." Wade spoke up from two pews behind Karen.

"I wasn't aware of any hunting trip," Vern said.

"But we talked about it last week. Remember?"

"I said you could go as long as you had someone responsible supervising you. Someone like myself or one of your older brothers. Since you never asked me to go, I thought the plan fell through."

"All us eighth grade boys are responsible company. We're old enough to know what to do."

Vern shook his head. "We'll discuss this more at home."

"Did you bring the tin of gun powder to school?" Mr. Hinkley peered at Wade.

"No, sir. Why would I if the hunting trip was planned at my farm?" Wade's voice grew defensive.

Karen exhaled. At least the hunting trip part of the story was true. Wade's word could be counted on.

"Roy, your son is in eighth grade. He didn't smuggle any gun powder to the school, did he?" Mr. Hinkley turned to look at one of his comrades sharing the front of the church with him.

Roy stood. "Cal?"

The boy straightened in response to his father's yell. "It wasn't me, Pa."

Roy sat down. "Only one left."

Mr. Hinkley looked over to where the Kent family sat. "Joe, were you in on this plan? Did you bring the gunpowder to school?"

"No."

Karen's insides heated at the one haughty word. Joe had more to do with the fire than he admitted. She stood up. "When I discovered the tin at school on Thursday, I asked Joe about it. He claimed Eldon brought it to school."

Vera jumped to her feet. "Eldon would do no such thing. Do you think he would willfully contribute to a situation that ended up causing him so much suffering? Have you seen him? Evan and I never expected to come home to such a...such a...tragedy."

Evan tugged on her hand. Vera took his cue and sat down after dabbing her eyes with a handkerchief.

"Evan and Vera, we're all truly sorry about what has happened. But the fact is, our school burned to the ground, and we need to figure out why." Mr. Hinkley frowned as he scanned the group.

His attention landed on Karen. "Miss Millerson, could you please tell us what happened on Thursday?"

Karen swallowed. "I discovered the tin on the book shelf around ten in the morning. I asked the students if anyone knew where it had come from. Only Joe had an answer. He said there was a hunting trip planned and that Eldon brought it. I took it to my desk and put it in a drawer so I could ask Wade about it since he was hauling water at the time. The school burned before I had the chance to talk to him."

"Tell us about the fire." Mr. Hinkley stood behind the pulpit with his arms crossed.

"I sweep the school every day over the noon hour. I had just finished sweeping up when an explosion came from the stove. Like I said in our last meeting, the door flew off and knocked Eldon down."

"Didn't you tell me yesterday that you threw the dirt you collected from sweeping into the stove?" Mr. Hinkley asked.

"Yes."

"So not only was the gun powder at school, but it also got spilled at some point."

"That is the conclusion the school board and I have drawn." Karen breathed a sigh of relief that her voice sounded so even. This whole situation had spun out of control.

Bert Sanders stood up. "You've got your answers, Tom. Miss Millerson is the one who started the fire."

Mr. Hinkley held up his hand. "Now, Bert."

Karen gasped as if scalding water had been thrown on her. "You don't think I'm the one who owns the gun powder."

Evan stood next to his brother-in-law." Maybe not, but you could be the one who spilled it."

Karen balled her fist. "I did not! I didn't even open the tin."

"The fact that the stove exploded after you threw the powder into it gives us enough evidence. Anyone want to contest it?" One of Evan's eyebrows rose, making him look like an attorney who'd just proven a person guilty. He turned to the group

The room remained quiet. Not even the younger children fidgeted.

Evan faced Mr. Hinkley and his school board. "Looks to me, Tom, like the teacher is the one you should blame, not our children."

Mr. Hinkley's face turned red. His jaw moved a bit before he spoke. "This matter ain't settled yet. Just 'cause no one's talking doesn't mean we gotta assume the fire is the teacher's fault. Classes need to start up again, and I don't wanna waste any more time goin' in circles like we did tonight. School starts here in the church Monday morning. This meeting is adjourned!"

Mr. Hinkley banged the gavel with great gusto. Then he came to Karen. "I'm awful sorry, Miss Millerson. I'd hoped to get everything in the clear, but I only made things worse. I'm sorry."

Karen's mouth dropped open. She hardly knew what to say. Anything that came to mind wouldn't improve the situation, so she opted to shake his hand instead.

Logan took care in his skillful way of finding the right words to say. "You'll eventually uncover the truth. Don't let Evan have the last word."

Mr. Hinkley tugged at his collar. "Wish it were that easy, Logan. The truth is, each one of us owes the bank money, and no one wants to risk bein' on the wrong side. Take Roy and Clyde, for example. If you were one of them guys, where would you stand? With the man who has the power to call in all your loans, or with the teacher who's a stranger, even if she is doin' a good job with the kids?"

Karen's heart pounded. Mr. Hinkley made a good point. She'd heard the hidden message in his question. A young, idealistic school teacher was no match to the complexities ruling the lives of these families.

Logan thumped Mr. Hinkley's shoulder. He leaned in and spoke in a low voice. "Don't give up."

Karen's throat thickened. Logan's simple statement of encouragement referred to more than the disappointing developments at tonight's meeting.

Mr. Hinkley nodded. "My apologies for not getting around to

makin' the announcement about the reason for Miss Millerson's move to the Bettens'."

Logan shook his head. "You had plenty to manage tonight."

Mr. Hinkley looked relieved. "I best find Lucy."

When he moved away, Logan clasped Karen's hand. "Come on, let's go."

CHAPTER TWENTY

"*D*id Miss Millerson stay home today? I hope the conflict with the Kents doesn't affect her church attendance," Roy said as he waited on his family to hang their coats in the church's entryway on Sunday morning.

Logan's heart thumped. "No. Actually, she's here with Pete and Anna."

Roy's brow furrowed. "What for?"

"Pete suggested the move. He said the teacher might as well live with them now that the church is serving as our school." Logan glanced at Mama as she hung up her coat. Pete had said much more than that on the night he suggested Karen's move, but Roy was on the school board. He'd only care about information related to the daily operation of the school.

"Good idea." Roy nodded. Then he pointed to Tillie who sat with Andrew Carter. "It's lookin' to me like you and your mother will be the only ones left in the De Witt pew."

Roy was right. Andrew picked Tillie up more frequently and kept her to himself on Sundays. He still needed to talk with Logan as Mama had mentioned. But Logan grew more confident in his response. Watching Andrew's care for Tillie assured him they would do just fine together.

Roy slapped Logan's back as he caught up with his wife. "Have a good day."

He nodded and glanced at Mama, who was visiting with Sally Hixson. Clyde came over and asked the same questions about Karen that Roy had asked.

Logan gave the same answer since Clyde, too, was a member of the school board.

More neighbors came by, all of them noticing Karen's absence and asking about it.

How surprising that she'd attracted so much attention while living in his home. Logan gave them the same answer he'd supplied for the school board. Karen lived at the Bettens' to be closer to her classroom. It sure made sense to him. From the understanding responses of his neighbors, the explanation apparently made sense to them too.

He shrugged, pulled Mama away from a conversation, and sat down. He read a Psalm from his Bible while Lucy Hinkley pumped out a hymn from the organ.

A tap came on his shoulder. He glanced up into deep blue eyes.

"Do you have room for me?" Karen stood in the aisle wearing her burgundy-colored Sunday dress. A matching hat perched on top of golden curls. The engagement ring sparkled on her hand resting on the back of the pew near his shoulder.

"Uh, yeah. Sure." He nudged Mama, who inched closer to an older couple on her other side. A gentleman wouldn't claim the newly created space for himself. Karen already stood in the middle of a full sanctuary asking him for a seat. He might as well complete the spectacle they made and stand up to let her in. He blew out some air and stepped into the aisle.

Flashing a grateful smile, Karen slipped past him and settled in next to Mama.

The attention from the people seated in the back half of the church was on him. If he was the one standing behind the pulpit this morning, he wouldn't mind so much. But the fact that he'd already told so many that the teacher no longer lived with him would only heighten curiosity. If Logan meant nothing more to Karen than someone offering her a room, then she'd find no reason to seek him out and request to sit with him instead of Anna unless she cared about him.

Which she did. She wore his ring after all. Yep. The word was out. What Tom Hinkley had failed to include in the last community meeting Logan had just announced by offering his fiancée a seat in church.

He sat back down.

"Why are you so late?" He leaned over and whispered in her ear.

"Anna wasn't feeling well, so I cooked breakfast. Then I ran behind getting ready to come to church," Karen whispered back.

"Anna is here." Logan glanced at the front pew where Anna always sat.

"Yes. She decided at the last minute to come, but she still doesn't feel well."

"Maybe she would prefer that we don't come for dinner." Logan would miss the time spent with Karen at the Bettens' table, but Anna didn't need the extra work of entertaining.

"I cooked. Anna said she'll lie down if she needs to. It'll work out fine." Karen patted his hand.

Pete spoke to begin the service. Then they stood to sing. After praying and settling in to listen to the sermon, Logan relaxed. His friends and neighbors deserved to share in his and Karen's happiness.

A grin worked its way across his face. Just in case Karen seated with him and sharing both his hymnbook and his Bible didn't provide enough evidence of how things really were between them, Logan draped his arm around Karen. For good measure.

It worked. After the service, Logan found himself and Karen surrounded by excited people. From the congratulations he received and the admiration heaped on Karen's ring, his friends and neighbors had gotten the message loud and clear.

Logan inhaled deeply, and his gaze rose heavenward as he walked with Mama and Karen across the church lawn. How good it felt to have everything out in the open. His engagement was now public. And affirmed. And completely respectable. Oh, praise the Lord. He must do something to celebrate.

"Hey, Karen."

She turned to look at him.

"Now that you're settled in at the Bettens', how would you like to start assisting me on Sundays again?"

She quit walking and clasped her hands in front of her. "You mean it?"

"Sure I do. Starting this afternoon." He watched her, uncertain what he should expect as her answer.

But he had no need to worry. Right there, in the middle of the yard, with people streaming past them and Mama looking on, Karen clutched his neck in a tight embrace.

"Yes, Logan. Oh, yes, yes!"

His breath caught. Karen hadn't gotten this excited since, well, since the night he proposed. Mama gave him an amused look and made her way alone to Anna's front door.

Logan's heart thudded deep in his chest as the faces of the women he'd known in his past flashed through his memory. Florence had wanted him to forsake ministry and go into business. Lorraine rejected him because he might move away from her hometown. But Karen loved him for those reasons.

The church yard was nearly empty by now, so Logan cupped Karen's chin and kissed her with all the thankfulness in his heart brimming up and spilling over.

Now that was celebrating.

LATER THAT AFTERNOON, Logan walked the length of the front pews putting hymn books away. The Meadow Creek congregation was growing, even though participation in Sunday services required a five-mile drive. He was pleased for their sake. Maybe once the congregation rebuilt their church building and found a permanent preacher, they could move forward with hope and put the tragedy of last fall's storm behind them.

Karen turned from the window where she'd been watching flurries fall to the ground from low, gray clouds. "Andrew Carter is here. He's riding horseback."

Logan moved to the window in time to see Andrew dismount and enter the parsonage. "He must be looking for Pete. I hope nothing is wrong."

He returned to the pulpit to gather up his notes and Bible. Then he went to Pete's study to put on his coat.

The church door thumped.

"Hi, Karen. Is Logan still here? I've been to the farm, but Tillie said Logan hasn't come home yet." He overheard Andrew's words from the sanctuary.

"Yes, he's in Pete's study."

Logan threw his scarf around his neck and rushed out. "What is it?"

Andrew came to him. "Eldon. He's worse. He's asking for you. The doctor told me to come since I live the closest."

Eldon couldn't get much worse and still survive. Logan gulped in air as he sprinted down the aisle. "Give me a ride on your horse."

Andrew caught up with him, and in minutes they galloped to town. On Main Street, Logan leaped off Andrew's horse and hastened into the clinic.

Dr. Bolton met him and led him down a hall. He opened the door to a dim room smelling of antiseptic. The doctor set to work in the corner cutting strips of bandage while Logan approached the bed where Eldon lay.

Eldon's right leg and foot were free of bandage below the knee. The forearm on his right side also remained uncovered, but it probably could've used some bandage too. The skin on Eldon's arm looked melted. Bandages covered most of his body, even his face.

Logan held his breath. If his right side was the only part of Eldon's body in good enough health not to require bandages, what did the rest of Eldon's skin look like? He gulped in some air and claimed the chair near the bed.

The injured man stirred. He spoke with parched lips. "Logan."

"I'm here."

Eldon blinked and tried out his raspy voice once more. "You know I like to have the right answers. I hate being wrong."

Logan silently agreed.

"But I've been wrong." Eldon writhed on the bed.

"What have you been wrong about?" Maybe Eldon had miscalculated a number affecting Logan's farm sale.

"Karen."

Not what he expected to hear. This answer had nothing to do with accurate numbers. Logan waited.

"She loves you. Always has." Eldon coughed and then groaned.

Since Eldon prided himself on always having the right answer, he could certainly feel good about this statement.

"I tried to change her mind, but it didn't work. Karen never said a word about you, but I could see her feelings for you. It made me so mad." Eldon coughed again.

The doctor moved to the bed and cut the bandage away from Eldon's left leg.

"Take care of her, Logan. She deserves the best." Eldon's scratchy voice weakened.

The man needed a word of hope. "Please know that Karen and I are engaged. She's agreed to marry me."

"Then she will be taken care of. I'm glad to hear it." Eldon winced. The doctor must have reached a tender spot in preparing Eldon's leg for fresh bandages.

Eldon moaned. "I can't take this. These burns will never heal. Please help me."

Logan had heard that desperate tone before. He reached for his Bible.

Eldon's breathing grew shallow, but he still managed to croak out some words. "I've been to church off and on, but I don't know God. Not really. Tell me about Him. What do I have to do to go to Heaven?"

"Believe, Eldon. Just believe. The love you or I have for Karen is small compared to the love that Jesus felt the day He died for you. Can you believe that God loves you?"

"Yes."

"Do you believe that Jesus died for you and has the power to cleanse you of sin?"

Eldon nodded.

"He's in Heaven right now making a place ready for you when you reach the end of your life." Logan opened his Bible to the passage in John and prepared to read it to Eldon.

"It's coming soon." Eldon winced again.

Logan reached for the melted hand resting on the sheet. "Let's pray. Ask the Lord to live in your heart and forgive you."

Eldon inhaled several times. He may be too weak to complete this most important task of his life.

"Keep trying. You can do it."

After a shallow breath and a cough, Eldon prayed. "God, I'm not very good at prayer. I've thought more about money and my own importance than about You."

He fell silent.

Logan watched the faint rising and falling of Eldon's chest. The man was running out of time. If only Logan could rush in and say the words for him. But Eldon must make this crucial decision for himself.

The doctor straightened and studied Eldon's face. He moved around the end of the bed and came to stand near Logan.

Eldon coughed. "God, I know now how much I have sinned, but I believe You can forgive me. Please—"

He coughed again. Every word was costing him. "Please live in my heart. I want to be in Heaven with You."

"I'm going to call his family." Dr. Bolton left the room.

Eldon opened his eyes and focused on Logan.

"God loves you, Eldon. He won't let you go."

Eldon blinked, and then his eyes slid shut. His voice came in a whisper. "I want…do my funeral, Logan. Have Karen sing."

Eldon reached for Logan's hand and then closed his eyes. A moment later, a smile crossed his face. Not one of his cynical or manipulative smiles, but a happy and peaceful one. His chest no longer moved with the rhythm of breathing. Eldon lay still.

Logan stood. Tears blurred his vision as he looked down on the dead form of his banker, his rival, his enemy. The man was at peace and in the presence of the Lord. Eldon now had the whole of eternity to learn about real love.

The door opened. Logan turned away from the bed. Elsie and Bert, Evan and Vera, and Eldon's father entered. They gathered around Eldon. Loss etched itself on each face in different ways. Bert looked sorry. Evan's features were hard. Vera wore a stoic mask. Elsie cried. For as much trouble as the woman gave Karen, maybe she really did possess a heart under all her crusty layers.

Logan cleared his throat. "Eldon died just a few minutes before you arrived. I'm sorry. I wish you could've been here."

How unfortunate, even for a family as cantankerous as the

Kents, that their brother died in the company of a person who had never liked him instead of surrounded by the people he cared about.

The doctor entered, followed by the undertaker. Logan's time had come to leave. A clan distanced from the church, the Kents would feel more comfortable without Logan hanging around. He shook hands with the doctor.

"Evan and Elsie, let's meet sometime tomorrow. I'll share with you the requests Eldon made for his funeral." Logan left the room.

The clock in the doctor's waiting room said seven-thirty. He stepped outside. Snow was still in the air. It dusted the trees and rooftops in a quiet layer, unaware the pure whiteness glowed in sharp contrast to the dark tragedy that had interrupted their lives this week. Oh, to be as light and carefree as the flurries swirling from Heaven and landing wherever they fell.

Logan went down the street and asked Andrew for a ride to Pete's house. He had to see the one person who could understand the pain that pierced him.

She was the one who answered the door and let him in. Pete and Anna were seated in the parlor, but they left for the kitchen, giving Logan a chance to be alone with her. Logan took her into his arms and held on. For such a trim figure, Karen possessed a large amount of strength. He allowed it to soak into him.

"What happened?" Karen asked in a low voice after several moments of silence passed.

"Eldon died."

Karen gasped. "Oh, no."

Logan released his hold on her and looked into her eyes. "He asked me to come so that he could find peace with God."

Karen's eyes filled with tears.

"He also asked me to take care of you. He admitted to being in the wrong trying to court you. He was happy to hear you are engaged to me."

Karen closed her eyes and shook her head as though trying to rid her mind of painful memories.

Logan sat down on the sofa and Karen joined him.

"Eldon asked for me to do his funeral. He wants you to sing."

Karen's eyes widened.

"Are you comfortable with that?"

"Yes, but I'm not sure how well the rest of his family will like it."

Logan rubbed his forehead. "I have a meeting with them tomorrow. We will talk about it some more. I'll let Tom know we'll need the church building for the funeral. You may need to wait a day or two before resuming classes."

Karen nodded and then leaned her head on his shoulder. His somber heart welcomed the comfort that Karen offered so well.

Pete and Anna returned. When they asked Logan about his time in town, he shared the news of Eldon's death. Pete's mouth pulled into a grim line, and Anna cried.

Logan wanted to be sure and talk with Mama before she went to bed, so he stood up and prepared to make the walk to the farm. "I'll see you all tomorrow. I need to get home and let Mama know."

CHAPTER TWENTY-ONE

*L*ogan entered the farmhouse kitchen and removed his coat, slinging it over a chair.

"Oh, Logan. Is that you?" Mama hurried into the room with the lamp. The light from the glass chimney flickered on the walls and created shadows on her face.

"I'm home." His voice was heavy.

"Andrew stopped here this afternoon looking for you. What's wrong in town?" Mama set the lamp on the table.

"It's Eldon Kent. He died this evening after I arrived."

"Oh, my." Mama's hand fluttered to her chest. "I didn't realize his condition was so serious."

"None of us did." The words reflected the urgency he'd felt in the doctor's office to meet Eldon's spiritual needs. The end had come sooner than any of them expected. Logan shook his head as the image of Eldon's bandaged form played in his memory. How close Eldon had come to missing out on eternal bliss. He took a deep breath and moved to the table.

"Did you see Vera or Elsie? How are they taking it?"

"Pretty hard, I think. It didn't help that the accident happened while Evan and Vera were gone." Logan removed his suit coat and tie. The milking awaited him. He'd nearly forgotten about the cows in the course of the evening's tragedies.

"No, certainly not. There must be something Tillie and I can do for them." Mama tapped her chin.

"I'll know more in the morning." Logan slipped a coat over his dress clothes and then kissed Mama's cheek. "Try to get some sleep."

He went to the barn, leaving Mama behind watching him through the window.

After his own night of intermittent sleep, Logan arose to once again complete the milking. Mama and Tillie shared the breakfast table with him, asking questions he couldn't answer, at least not yet. By the end of the day, he should have the information to satisfy their inquiries.

He changed into his suit once more, saddled a horse, made a trip to the Hinkley farm for a conference with Tom, and then went to the church. Before entering, he knocked on the door of Pete's house. Anna answered.

"May I see Karen, please?"

At Anna's call, Karen came to the door. She wore a blue floral dress with long sleeves and lace at the neck. She hadn't pinned her hair up yet to start the day. It flowed over one shoulder to her waist.

This moment arrested his heart with a lesson for his tomorrows. When the Lord handed him tough assignments like the death and funeral facing him, the Lord would also provide him with the sort of home life that promised the support to help him through. The bachelor lifestyle had served its purpose. He'd faced some tragedies during those years, but starting today, he'd no longer do it alone. The thought of serving with the beautiful and courageous Karen at his side thrilled him and soothed him all at the same time.

"Logan? What is it?" Karen looked up at him.

His neck heated in spite of the wind's brisk temperature. He'd been staring at her, distracted by the blessings yet to be his.

He cleared his throat. "I have a piece of news for you. Tom wants to wait until next Monday to start school."

"That makes sense. Everyone will need some time to grieve before we continue our class schedule."

Logan nodded. "I'd like to have you at this meeting. The family will be arriving in half an hour."

Karen's eyes widened.

"Please? I thought since Eldon asked you to sing, you should be in on the plans. And, well, I'd really love to have you there with me."

She hesitated to answer but then nodded. "All right. I trust you will convince the Kents that my involvement in the funeral is a good idea."

Logan gave a half smile. "I'll have them viewing the world from my angle in no time."

Karen's eyes rolled. "I'll meet you there."

She closed the door, and Logan crossed the yard to the church.

He was sitting at Pete's desk with the door open to the study when Karen arrived wearing her burgundy dress and with her hair pinned in place under a hat. Logan barely had time to compliment her before the Kents arrived. He set up extra chairs, and everyone took a seat.

"What is she doing here?" Vera glanced at Karen and sniffed.

Logan leaned forward. "This is one of Eldon's requests he made in the last moments of his life. He became a Christian before he died. He asked for me to conduct the funeral and for Miss Millerson to sing."

The Kent family looked at each other with questions in their eyes.

Evan spoke up. "No. We won't hear of it. How could Eldon

want this, the woman responsible for his burns, singing the hymns at his own funeral? No."

Evan crossed his arms and scowled. Vera stiffened. Bert and Elsie frowned.

Logan cleared his throat. Clearly the situation called for a few persuasive skills. "In my experience, the dead man's wishes are always honored, even if they are disagreeable to some left behind to mourn his loss."

Vera shifted in her seat, but the others didn't respond.

Then their father looked at Logan. "You say Eldon became a believer?"

Logan nodded. "He did."

"Is that why you're doing the funeral instead of Peter Betten?"

"Yes."

"You led him to the Lord."

"Correct."

Mr. Kent considered that for a moment. "You say Miss Millerson was his choice, not yours."

"That's right."

"Did he tell you which songs to sing?" Mr. Kent peered at Logan.

"No. That is up to you as a family."

"Miss Millerson sings very well. I heard her at the Christmas banquet. Elsie, you always did favor *Amazing Grace*. Now is your chance to enjoy it."

Elsie hardly looked convinced by her father's words.

"Reverend De Witt has a point. This is Eldon's wish. We should go along with it." Mr. Kent settled back in his chair.

Logan studied the row of gloomy faces. No one said anything in favor or disagreement. He picked up his pen and ventured into decision making. "Are we including *Amazing Grace* in the funeral?"

After a moment of silence, Mr. Kent nodded. "Go ahead."

Logan wrote it down.

Mr. Kent continued to make plans with Logan. Evan engaged in the conversation when asked to share stories about Eldon. Bert consented to reading the obituary. Logan ended the meeting with a prayer and then shook hands with everyone as they left.

"Well, sweetheart, no one objected too loudly. I guess you are approved." Logan put some books away once he and Karen were alone. "In a few more days, everyone will have moved on and these details won't matter anymore."

"I hope you're right and that Vera's and Elsie's sullenness is due to their grief, not anger toward me." Karen sighed.

Her words lodged in Logan's heart, moving him to pray that Karen wouldn't be made to feel their wrath in the days to come.

When they arrived at the parsonage and Anna invited Logan to stay for the noon meal, he accepted. The meal would give him not only extra time with Karen but also the chance to talk over with his friend the best way to help difficult and contrary people like the Kents. He'd need all the advice Pete was willing to give.

THE MORNING of Eldon's funeral, Logan stood at the front of the church and watched the Kent family file in to the first pews. Since Karen and the rest of the congregation were busy singing about Heaven, Logan was free to allow his attention to roam over the assembly. The church was filled with businessmen and their wives, farmers and their families, and many employees from the Silver Grove State Bank. Mama occupied a pew on the right with Tillie and the Carters. Pete and Anna sat in the back. Members of the school board, along with their wives and children, were scattered throughout the sanctuary.

Sorrow still hung on the faces of the family taking seats in front. How Logan wished for them to truly know the goodness and love of God. He trembled to think how a family like the

Kents faced a day like today with no faith to carry them through. Their abyss of hopelessness must run deep indeed.

Logan stepped to Karen's side as she finished the song. She offered a sad smile and sat down. His chest ached as he faced the room. He hardly knew where to begin to comfort so many on this occasion made necessary through tragedy.

Someone cleared their throat. A white lace handkerchief fluttered to wipe away tears. Logan's gaze shifted to the front. Evan's features resembled stone in both its appearance and its shade of color. Vera's eyes were red-rimmed and unblinking, like two holes burned into a piece of cloth. Tears streamed down the face of Eldon's father. This was the first traumatic loss he'd suffered since the death of his wife during Eldon's teen years.

Logan took a deep breath and started in the only place that made any sense. "Good morning. We gather today to celebrate the life of Eldon Kent. He accepted Christ into his heart the night he died. We come with joy in the midst of our sorrow because we know Eldon is in the presence of the Lord today."

After clearing his throat, Logan continued the funeral with the encouragements and phrases of Scripture he always relied on to bring peace to those who mourn. His vision blurred as he read from the Bible. How close he'd come to never having the chance to share the truth with Eldon. The thought of Eldon's near miss with Heaven made Logan's voice tremble. He could've ended up trying to manufacture hope in a place where there was none. But the assurance of Eldon's testimony of faith spoke for itself. Logan shared the conversation from the sickroom with everyone.

Except for the discussion about Karen. He'd keep that to himself. But Eldon's willingness to believe carried the sermon.

Logan spoke while prayer burned in his heart that others in the family would understand Eldon's courageous decision and make it for themselves.

At the end of his brief sermon, Logan prayed out loud and then invited Karen to his side to sing another hymn. He raised his arms to pronounce a blessing and then held Karen's hand as they followed the group outdoors to the waiting hole in the graveyard where Eldon's coffin would rest until the end of time.

THAT AFTERNOON, Logan looked for tasks to complete in the barn. He needed to be alone. Not even a conversation with Karen would lift his heavy heart. Solitude and the accompanying silence gave him the most solace. After the simple jobs in the barn were finished, he still craved the quiet.

The sun had poked through the early spring clouds, and a calm wind blew mild air, making for a pleasant afternoon. Logan fastened his chore coat and left the barn. A stroll through the pasture would do him good. He wandered along the path where the dairy herd fed on the hay Logan provided them through the winter months. With the March grass not yet green and growing, the cows still relied on Logan to feed them.

His chest swelled at the sight of the sleek, spotted hides. His cows were well taken care of. For a boy who chose a career in town over staying on the farm, he'd remembered quickly how to tend to a dairy herd.

A smile crossed his face but soon receded. The date was set with the bank for the farm sale. Logan would miss those cows. He really would. They were an extension of his flock, if cows could be thought of in sheep terms.

The actual members of his flock right now were the people from Meadow Creek. They needed care, too, in the form of a regular feeding from the Word of God and a looking after to keep them healthy.

The sale of those cows meant Logan would no longer be the one to offer them care. His mind ran through the list of local farmers who might show interest in adding Logan's herd to their own. If he didn't know for a fact Oswell City wanted him to return, he just might give into the temptation to stay here and farm. The cows meant that much to him.

But Karen would never want that. Without the promise of his waiting ministry in Oswell City, he'd have to choose between Karen and farming. He loved both, but in the end, the decision was an easy one.

Logan slapped the rump of one of the Holsteins grazing on hay. Another flock waited for him to resume his care for them. He must do what a return to ministry required of him.

He moved on to the creek and ambled along the bank. The songs of early spring birds formed a chorus overhead. Squirrels scurried around the trees in search of last year's nuts. Water flowed free from ice and snow. Dad had loved the water. He'd told Logan once that if he'd ever settled in Michigan like some of Mama's relatives, he would've lived along the shores of the expansive Great Lakes. Logan understood what Dad meant when he went to seminary and visited Lake Michigan with Pete one afternoon shortly after a new semester of learning had begun.

The day came racing back to him. He could feel the warm sun on his shoulders and hear the rhythmic lapping of the waves. Off in the distance a sailboat navigated an invisible path. Logan closed his eyes and allowed the memory to bring peace to his heart. How he'd love to go back.

But for now, he'd find comfort in his own trickling stream. The afternoon passed as Logan walked and prayed. The Lord met him in those quiet hours. Love and grace filled Logan's heart, easing some of the heaviness from his grief. He returned to the path where the cows grazed. The time had arrived for the evening milking.

CHAPTER TWENTY-TWO

A stiff north wind cut through Karen as she crossed the lawn to the church. The blustery morning matched her mood. Low clouds rolling to the horizon blocked early spring sunshine in the same way the heavy grief hanging around her heart suffocated her cheer. When she'd assisted Logan on Sunday, tears welled in her eyes on every hymn. Eldon's death shouldn't affect her with such strength. He'd been an irritation to her, and now he was someone she couldn't get off her mind. Why did he have to die so tragically? She couldn't imagine anything more painful than burns over large areas of a person's body. No one should have to suffer that much, not even demanding and heartless people like Eldon.

She entered the sanctuary and shut the door on the raw day. If only she could make as definite of an end to her sorrow. It weighed her down, robbing her energy as she organized her books and waited for her students to arrive. The first to come were Cal and Lacy. They lived the closest, so their walk was the shortest. The Pattersons, Hixsons, and Hinkleys filed in and took Karen's suggestions on seating. Challenges awaited since the church provided no desk space. The children must sit in the pews and use hymn books for hard surfaces to support their writing papers.

Karen explained this while watching for the Kent and Sanders children to arrive. They might decide not to come. Only four days had passed since Eldon's funeral. They might need more time before they felt ready to concentrate on schoolwork. Try as she might at her own attempt to concentrate, her mind kept wandering from the lessons she'd prepared and onto the day of the funeral, or Logan's description of the last moments of Eldon's life, or why the Kent and Sanders children hadn't come yet. The hands of the clock on the wall crept up to ten o'clock before Karen finally admitted to having only half of her class-room present.

She dismissed everyone for recess and sat in the front pew for a moment, soaking up the silence. The children had been quite well-behaved without the influence of troublemakers. But she still felt drained. She called the class back to order, unsure where she would find the stamina to keep going.

At the end of the school day, she returned to the parsonage, exhausted yet thankful for Anna who fussed over her and always had something delicious cooking in her kitchen. Hunger and fatigue followed Karen, but she couldn't get ahead. No matter how hard she tried to choke down Anna's good food, her stomach churned. Karen could sleep for hours at a time, and still exhaustion overtook her in the morning.

Her struggle continued through the week. The Kent and Sanders children never came to class, but Karen dragged her weary self to the parsonage at the end of each day as if she'd spent hours and hours disciplining them.

Thursday night, Logan came to call. "Are you feeling well?" he asked when she answered his knock. His concerned gaze searched her face. The dark circles under her eyes would attract his notice. "You look so pale," he whispered following Karen to the table where he joined her, Anna, and Pete for the evening meal.

Karen made her best attempt to eat, but tonight was no different than the previous ones. Her stomach tightened until she gave up on forcing any more food into it. She refused dessert and went to the parlor to wait for Logan.

He and Pete laughed over a joke, and Anna joined in the conversation that followed. The dining room quieted when Pete and Anna took dishes to the kitchen.

Logan claimed the spot next to her on the love seat. The same concerned expression flooded his gaze. His compassion melted her. The dark grief and her struggle with it surged in her heart. Tears streamed from her eyes, and sobs erupted in her throat.

Karen covered her face and wept. She wept for the tragedy that had brought about so much loss. Silver Grove no longer had a school. Evan and Elsie no longer had a brother. Their father no longer had a son. Their children no longer had an uncle. The world in Silver Grove had changed. Everyone was affected in some way by this fire. Her heart wrenched tighter and tighter as each person surfaced in her memory.

"Come here," Logan said, his voice low. He wrapped one of his arms around her and covered the side of her face with his other hand.

"What happened to Eldon was so terrible." Karen leaned on him and wept.

Logan rubbed her arm.

"He shouldn't have had to suffer like he did. I can hardly eat or sleep from this heavy feeling I carry around inside all the time."

"I feel the same way."

She cried until her eyes ran out of tears. Hours must have passed. Still, Logan held her. She didn't want to leave his embrace.

The past few days had taught her how deeply she missed him. She missed sharing every meal with him. She missed knowing that he waited for her at home when she returned at the end of the day.

Her world had changed too. Maybe some of her grief was about her own loss. She'd lost her home and her close connection with her fiancé. If this new arrangement was truly what engagement was all about, it couldn't pass fast enough.

Wilting against him, Karen brought her breathing back to normal and wiped her eyes with the handkerchief Logan gave her. She straightened and blew her nose.

"Feeling better?" he asked.

She nodded. "I needed that, but let's talk of something else now. I want to enjoy our time together."

"I was thinking about our wedding."

A smile forced its way across her lips. "That's a good topic."

"I need to write Paul Ellenbroek in Oswell City and supply him with a date for my return. I'll be staying in Silver Grove long enough to help Mama with her move to town after Tillie gets married. What would you like to do, set our wedding date for a day prior to my first Sunday back in Oswell City or wait until later in the summer? I could travel here or to Chicago anytime you wish."

Karen's gloom lifted, allowing for a crack of light to shine through and rekindle her cheer. "If I come to Oswell City, you won't need to travel at all. Just leave Silver Grove whenever you feel is right, and then I will come to you."

"You still want a wedding in Oswell City." Logan bit his lip.

"I do."

He shook his head. "I'm not sure how to keep the affair small and simple."

"We may not be able to."

"I know, and that concerns me."

"Why?"

Logan puffed out his cheeks. "For a man who must stand in

front of so many as the center of their attention for a full hour every week, I really don't enjoy being in the spotlight. That's exactly what will happen if my beautiful fiancée arrives in Oswell City to marry me at my own church. Everyone will make such a big deal. I'm not sure I want that to happen to you either."

"You make a good point." Karen leaned back and studied her nails.

"But the plan is much simpler than having the wedding anywhere else."

Karen straightened and glanced at him. This was the closest he'd come to agreeing with her request.

"What about your mother? She wants your wedding in Chicago."

"Maybe Aunt Fran could host a reception for us later. She enjoys throwing parties and entertaining guests."

Logan chewed on his lip as he considered the possibility. "How about we make a trade?"

"A trade?"

"Yeah. If I let you make plans for an Oswell City wedding, then may I make plans for a Chicago honeymoon?" A grin tugged at a corner of his mouth.

Karen held her breath. "You want to stay with my family for our honeymoon trip?" This scheme was worse than sleeping in a drafty barn in January.

Logan shook his head. "No, sweetheart. I thought we could spend time with your family and their friends after the wedding, but then we'd go on to find some nice little cottage or getaway on the shore of Lake Michigan. It's beautiful in the summer."

"That's a wonderful idea. Uncle Henry would have connections to help us find a lovely spot somewhere outside the city."

"Sounds like it's official. An Oswell City wedding and a Great Lakes honeymoon." Logan wrapped his arm around her again.

"Shall we plan on getting married in July? That will give

Mother and me a month to make final preparations." Karen glanced at him, awaiting his answer.

"July is fine. But don't let your mother keep you too busy because I'll be sitting around in Oswell City, a lonely old man counting every day that passes," he teased.

She couldn't imagine Logan idle as he passed his time with nothing to do except watching the calendar. But the thought of him going on ahead to the place where they would begin their life together and waiting for her lifted her spirits, driving thoughts of tragedy and loss far away.

LOGAN JOINED Mama and Tillie in the kitchen. Today was Tillie's eighteenth birthday, so this evening's meal included a celebration. A frosted cake with a pink icing *18* adorned the dining room table set with Mama's china and awaiting their guests.

Tillie ran to the door when they arrived. Nora Carter and her husband, Ed, each took turns hugging Tillie. Andrew entered a moment later, followed by Karen whom they'd picked up on their way out from town.

She was the guest Logan had been waiting for. Karen maneuvered around the happy cluster and came to him. They moved into the dining room for their own private conversation about Karen's concerns. The Kent and Sanders children still had not come to school.

Mama bustled in, pointing at the table. "Tillie, you and Andrew sit down there." She went on with suggestions for seating arrangements. Logan followed her instructions and settled into a chair next to the one he pulled out for Karen.

With Nora's help, Mama brought the delicious smelling food to the table. Roast beef, mashed potatoes, gravy, corn, and fresh rolls completed the menu. She took her seat and looked to Logan to pray.

"Have ya heard what the bank's gonna do to replace Eldon?" Ed leaned back in his chair and crossed his thick arms over a well-fed middle as the meal started.

Logan shook his head. "I have not."

"They're givin' the job to his brother Evan."

This was news. Evan was a farmer, not a banker. "Who will do the farming?"

"Bert will keep it goin' through the spring, but they're figurin' on Joe joinin' the operation when he graduates eighth grade."

Karen glanced away from the food on her plate. "Joe is just a boy. He has a lot of growing up to do."

"Yeah, but he knows how to handle horses and harvest a crop. That'll keep things goin' enough to help Evan out until Joe really can take over more of runnin' the farm."

Logan felt Karen's concern. With only two months left of the school year, Joe could decide to drop out now that the weather was warming and his family needed him instead of staying in school and completing the much needed education.

"Maybe if I don't assign him any homework, I can convince him to finish," Karen murmured to herself.

He nodded as he sipped his coffee. Karen would have her hands full when school started up again. The news caused Logan his own level of concern about Joe's father. Evan possessed such a difficult and contrary personality, he made his little brother look like a pansy. Logan clenched his teeth at the idea of planning a farm sale with the unfavorable Evan Kent.

Mama served cake while everyone sang to Tillie. She beamed at the attention. Logan prayed that his little sister remained free from any more sorrow so she could greet her future with the love and excitement he saw written on her face tonight.

"Logan, I know this is overdue. I should've spoken with you a long time ago. If Sandy and I hadn't already reached an agreement, I would've talked to you sooner. But I need to ask for your blessing since Tillie's father is no longer living. I've been planning to ask you tonight since it's kind of a special occasion." Andrew laid his fork down and pushed back from the table. "I want to marry your sister, so I'd like to ask for your permission."

Logan set his cup down. "At first, when Mama told me of your intentions, I thought Tillie was too young. I didn't feel comfortable with her marrying and leaving my care so soon after Dad died. But now that Mama and I are selling the farm, I don't want to ask Tillie to move away so that I can continue to keep her with me. That's not fair. I can see how much you love each other and how well you will provide for her. You have my permission and my blessing to marry Tillie."

Andrew's parents and Mama applauded. Karen smiled. Logan's chest tingled. He'd done the right thing not to refuse Andrew. But Tillie's marriage meant another loss. First Dad and then Eldon. Now he and Mama were making plans to sell the farm. Then Tillie would marry and move to town.

He could start to get downright melancholy about it all. But then the work God was doing in his own life came to mind. A ministry waited for him. He was engaged. Through all his losses, God remained the same. He would never leave Logan. And He'd brought Karen into Logan's life as living proof of His constant care and love. He looked over at her. Tears shimmered in her eyes as a response to the joyful moment. He settled back in his chair and enjoyed the merriment his answer to Andrew's question had created. Their lives were changing, but sometimes changes were good. He began in that moment to do the work in his heart of releasing Tillie to the Lord's care and to Andrew's.

CHAPTER TWENTY-THREE

*K*aren sat on a blanket stretched out on the Meadow Creek church grounds in the late morning sun. She wore a sweater to guard against the chill in the light breeze, but the warm sunshine promised spring's arrival. Covered bowls of food occupied a nearby table ready for the noon meal. Karen glanced at the cake she'd brought as her contribution, made with the assistance of Sandy's trusted recipe. She'd practiced earlier in the week in Anna's kitchen and, meeting with success, chose to make the cake again to share with the congregants of Meadow Creek.

"Tell me all about fourth grade." Karen grasped the shoulder of the dear little girl, Agnes Harper, whom she and Logan had labored through the night last fall to save from pneumonia.

Agnes smiled. "It's great."

"Tell Miss Millerson how many students are in your grade." Agnes's mother prompted.

"Five."

"And what is your favorite subject?" Mrs. Harper prompted again.

"History."

"I loved history in school," Karen said.

"Then maybe I can grow up and be a teacher like you." Agnes gazed up at Karen.

She nodded. "Yes, maybe you can." She studied Agnes in search of the symptoms of illness. "Have you been staying well?"

"Yes. I only missed two days of school, and that was from a sore throat." Agnes held up two of her fingers as if to say the number of absent days could get counted on one hand.

"I'm glad you haven't had the measles. Some of my students missed school because of them."

"We heard about the measles in Silver Grove. Amazing no one has been sick with them yet in Meadow Creek." Mrs. Harper reached to hand one of her small sons a wooden train from the pile of toys on the blanket. He took the train and ran to join a cluster of other little boys.

"And how about your father? I see him at church with you often. Has he, I mean, is he…" Karen glanced over to where Mr. Harper worked alongside the other men digging around the stone foundation of the church, the only piece of the structure that had survived last summer's storm. She failed to find the right words to ask if he was staying away from liquor.

"He's sober." Mrs. Harper answered as if reading Karen's thoughts. "He's bringin' home all his pay from the mill now. We've even been able to do some repair on our house and buy new shoes for Agnes to wear to school."

The little girl poked her feet straight out in front of her to reveal a pair of smart, black boots. She wiggled her feet to show off her new shoes.

"Very nice, Agnes." Karen stroked one of the shoes.

"We've been hearin' about your school. Did it really burn down?" Mrs. Harper leaned forward.

"It did." Karen nodded.

"I'm sorry. Such a loss for your community."

"It is, but we are having classes at the church. We've done that for a week already, and the arrangement seems to be working out."

"Are there plans to rebuild?"

"I'm sure Silver Grove will rebuild their school eventually, but right now we're still trying to agree on the cause of the fire."

Mrs. Harper nodded as though she understood the tensions hidden behind Karen's answer. "I'm sorry to hear of the young man who died. What a tragedy for his family."

Karen nodded.

"Did you know him?"

"Yes. He wanted to court me at one time."

Mrs. Harper's eyes grew wide.

"I went with him to some special events during the holidays." Karen's eyes filled with tears. Sadness weighted her heart again. She really shouldn't allow the sorrow to drag her down in light of all the wonderful happenings in her life. Karen swallowed.

"If it had turned out differently." The thought found words and left Karen's mouth too fast for her to stop it. Yes, if Eldon hadn't been so persistent, Karen may have learned to care for him. And if he'd survived the fire, he might have still wanted her affection.

Karen shuddered. An attachment between her and Eldon never stood a chance. Not even from the beginning. But now Eldon didn't have a chance to form an attachment to anyone. She shivered and pulled her sweater tighter around her. Some topics were just too morbid to dwell on.

Logan had said at the funeral that Eldon was now in the presence of the Lord. She should think of that instead and trust that God knew all about Eldon. Since his life had been cut short, then God must have something else better in store for him.

Mrs. Harper patted Karen's knee. "I'm sorry. Losses like those are hard to understand and even harder to accept. Sometimes we can't do anything except move on the best we know how."

"Yes." Karen whispered. The approaching end of the school year and planning for her wedding would help with the moving on.

Both of Agnes's brothers returned and demanded their mother's attention while Agnes went to join a hopscotch game. Karen rose to her feet. Enough time remained before the noon hour for her to enjoy a little walk. She sauntered among the other blankets spread on the ground, waving to women she recognized from Sunday afternoon services.

The men dug at the nearest corner of the stone foundation. Logan had mentioned that an uprooted tree had caused crumbling, so the congregation wanted to fix it before beginning to build. Karen glimpsed Logan now, surrounded by men leaning on shovels and looking at a black metal box in his hands.

Karen moved closer.

"Open it," one man said.

"We don't have a key," Mr. Harper replied.

"Bust it open," another suggested.

"We can't do that. First we must find out who this belongs to." Logan addressed the group.

"Look at the rust. That box has been in the ground for ages." A tall man leaning on a shovel handle pointed at the box.

"Yeah, the owner may not even be around anymore," The man standing next to Logan said with a shrug.

Karen paused on the outer fringes of the group, her pulse accelerating.

Logan smiled at her before offering a reply. "Let me take it and put it at the Silver Grove Church for safe keeping. Maybe if word gets out that we found this box today, someone will come forward who can give us more information."

The men voiced their agreement and then moved in the direction of their families.

Logan caught up to her.

"What do you think is in there?" Karen pointed at the box.

"It looks like a cash box."

Karen sucked in a quick breath. "You don't suppose it contains money."

"I can't imagine why anyone would hide money at the church. And the men are right. It looks like it hasn't seen daylight for years. We may never find answers."

"Then what happens?" Karen looked up at him.

Logan shrugged.

Karen's insides quivered. "Returning that box to its hiding place might be the best for everyone."

Logan stopped walking. "What do you mean?"

Karen faced him. "What if there really is money in that box? If you take it back to Silver Grove with you, how do you know you won't get accused of stealing it? Or what if word gets out that a box of unclaimed money is waiting for an owner? Then you'll have all kinds of people showing up with fake stories. I don't like it. Not one bit." Karen hugged herself against a sudden chill.

"But Meadow Creek doesn't have a bank." Logan gestured to the group forming a line at the food table. Voices and laughter floated on the air. "The next safest place would be their church building. But as you can see, it is hardly ready to store valuables."

Karen's gaze landed on the stone slab behind them. Shovels and spades stuck in the ground nearby like posts in a rickety fence. "I still think you should put it back where you found it. No one ever needs to know what happened to it."

Logan's honest gaze shifted from her face to the black box he carried. He sighed and then spoke in a quiet voice. "I wish I could do that, sweetheart. Everything would go much smoother if I just buried the problem and denied its existence."

He looked into her eyes again, apology written in the wrinkle of his brow. "But I can't do that. You and I both know I must get involved and help these people discover the truth."

"Reverend De Witt!" A younger woman jogged across the yard holding her hat with one hand and her skirt with the other. "We need ya to come and pray so the men and kids can start eating."

Logan nodded to her. She turned around and left them alone once again.

He brushed Karen's cheek with his thumb and then walked away in silence.

Karen pulled her sweater tight against the wind. Oh, how Logan's accuracy at being right so much of the time rankled her insides. Why did he have to be so good at his job? Surely he could let down once in a while and not have to care about everything and everyone every minute of every day.

She resumed her walk. That same old pain pricked her heart. Father had never been good with money. Years had passed. Now she was engaged to a pastor who had proven himself honest and responsible over and over again. But the fear still lurked. Logan, left alone with a stash of unclaimed money, might decide to use it for himself. Secretly. And then get in all sorts of trouble.

She'd be the last to know, unable to escape the scandal. Those scenes from childhood rushed over her. Oh, if Logan would just leave that box behind in Meadow Creek, her past could stay where it belonged. In the past.

Logan's "amen" at the end of his prayer reached Karen's ears. He pivoted as though searching for something. From the smile that broke out on his face when their eyes met, that something was her.

Karen picked up her pace and went to meet him. An afternoon of work stretched before them, but at the end of it, Karen would somehow need to make peace with a mystery intruder that her fiancé was determined to drag home.

"I WAS glad to see Mr. Harper here with his family today," Karen said as she collected sheet music from the pulpit.

Logan smiled. "Yeah. He's been coming almost every week. Looks like he's winning his battle."

"I hope so." Karen returned a hymnbook to the front pew as Logan disappeared into Pete's study. A prayer for the Harper family formed in Karen's heart. Mrs. Harper and her children would suffer if Mr. Harper ever experienced a setback. He seemed to be doing so well. He must continue working and fighting and winning for the sake of his family. For the sake of his new faith.

Karen paced the aisle, deep in thought as she waited for Logan. Just then four men, still dressed in their Sunday suits, entered the church. They'd passed through the line only moments ago, shaking hands with Logan. Instead of leaving with their families for the return trip to Meadow Creek, they must have a concern that required a chat with the preacher.

Karen cleared her throat. "May I help you with something?"

One of the men looked her in the eye. "Is Reverend De Witt still around?"

"Right here." Logan emerged from the small room on one side of the sanctuary. "What can I do for you?"

"We want to see what's in that box we dug up yesterday," said a tall man, the one who had also been a part of the conversation the day before.

Karen's insides withered. If that box contained money, then it was better left shut tight for the rest of time.

"Les brought along some tools to pick the lock and pry it open." Another man in the group pointed to a third man carrying a bag which he held up at the mention of the tools.

Les. That name stuck with her. The only Les Karen could recall from Meadow Creek was Lester Brinks. She knew this name because it was the signature that filled the space at the bottom of the checks Logan received every month from Meadow Creek.

These payments usually lay on the kitchen table at the farmhouse awaiting Logan's visit to the bank. They only came from the chairman of the church board who must be Lester Brinks, which meant that these other men with him were members of the church board. They made decisions and handled the money.

The fact should've relaxed her, but Karen only tensed more. She was nothing more than the pastor's fiancée and the teacher for a district that wasn't Meadow Creek. She possessed no power to stop them in this dangerous mission.

Logan held up his hand. "Wait. Are you sure you want to do that? Don't you remember our decision from yesterday to see if we can't find the owner first?"

The men looked at each other for a moment. Les spoke up. "We decided last night that we can't really ask around to find an owner until we know what it is they're missin'. We figure if we break into that box to see what it holds, we have a better chance of findin' out who it belongs to."

Logan crossed his arms, his brow furrowed. Finally he broke the silence. "All right. That sounds fair." He turned and led the group downstairs to the little closet where Karen stored some of her clothing. He retrieved the box and laid it on a nearby table.

Les dug around in his bag and brought out a long, thin tool.

Karen wrestled with her desire to march over and knock it out of his hand. Maybe she should just go on home to the Bettens' so she wouldn't need to learn the truth and let Logan deal with this situation alone. He obviously had it under control.

But she had to know if her suspicions were right. She held her breath as Les poked at the box.

After a few tries, the tall man spoke up. "Ain't workin'. The lock's probably rusted. You'll have to pry it open."

Les reached in his bag for another tool. He banged on the

corner of the box and then slipped one end of the tool under the lid. The metal bent until the rusty latch finally gave way.

Karen closed her eyes.

One man sucked in some air. Another gasped. Logan's murmured, "oh, boy," alerted Karen to the trouble she feared lurked around that box. She opened her eyes in time to see him run his hand through his hair and puff his cheeks with air.

He beckoned her. "Karen, come see this."

Her knees weak, Karen ventured to Logan's side. Sure enough. Money. Stacks and stacks of it overflowed the box.

Les whistled long and low. "Never figured on findin' all this."

"What should we do with it?" The tall man's gaze went to Logan.

He shook his head. The look of pure wonder mixed with apprehension blossomed on his face. Her farm boy fiancé had probably never seen this much wealth hoarded in one place before now.

"I...I guess...we should put...put it in the bank."

Karen's heart thumped at Logan's stutter. This situation clearly upset him.

"Good idea." Les put his tools away. Then he turned to the group. "Who wants to open the account?"

"Reverend De Witt should do it," The tall man said. "He's not from Meadow Creek, so he can act as sort of a neutral party. That way none of us has to handle any of this money. We've only seen it, never touched it."

The words held wisdom, and yet Karen's heart ached for Logan. He wouldn't want the job. Their conflict from yesterday seared Karen's mind. "*I must get involved and help these people discover the truth,*" Logan had said. Now look where those words had gotten him.

Karen frowned.

"Makes sense. I'll check into it tomorrow." Logan leveled a

serious gaze at the men. "But tell no one. If your wives know why you stayed after the service this afternoon, then make sure they don't say anything either. This money will have to sit around overnight, and I don't want to run the risk of it falling into the wrong hands. Even after it gets deposited at the bank, we should keep quiet until we learn more. Got it?"

The men nodded. Then each of them shook hands with Logan. Karen stayed at his side as they followed the group upstairs. They stood together in the church's open doorway, Logan's gaze intent on the men's actions as they climbed into a shared buggy. His attention never wavered until the horizon cleared.

"I'm sorry," Karen whispered.

His attention shifted to her. Apprehension still lingered in the depths of his blue eyes. "So am I. Finding a stash like that should be good news, but it might just cause trouble."

Karen knew the truth behind that statement all too well. The Silver Grove church might stand way out in the country and the group from Meadow Creek might contain upstanding folks, but those conclusions didn't stop the tremors in Karen's legs. Nothing good came from storing money in a church building. She pressed Logan's arm. "You can't leave it here tonight. Something will happen to it, or to you." Gangsters didn't prowl around these Iowa prairies, but men with guns could be found anywhere.

"I'm not. That box is going back to the farm with me. It'll get smuggled up the stairs and stowed under my pillow until morning." Logan backed away and closed the door.

Karen followed, her muscles tensing again. She wouldn't rest until that money was deposited safe and sound, removing Logan from danger.

CHAPTER TWENTY-FOUR

*L*ogan entered the Silver Grove State Bank, making his best attempt to appear as normal as if he carried rusty tin boxes to the bank every day containing thousands of dollars in cash. He should probably walk on tip-toe to avoid making a sound, and stashing the tin inside his coat to prevent anyone from noticing it was a good idea. He'd never used such caution in the past. The intentional effort to hide might back fire, making him look like a criminal.

Clearing his throat, he approached the teller. He'd better just hang onto his calm the best he could and get this business over with. The tin clunked onto the counter. "I'd like to open an account, please." He might have overcome his desire to sneak the money into the bank, but the wish to conceal sensational information stayed with him, keeping his voice low.

The teller's brow furrowed as he reached for the tin and worked to pop it open. He exhaled a gasp of air as bundles of money sprang from the box. "Don't you want to apply this to your farm account? You could live a whole new life if you did."

The stash would certainly work wonders on Logan's financial standing if it belonged to him. "This money isn't mine. We found it buried in the ground. It needs to get put safely on deposit."

The teller snapped out of his amazement and began to write. He passed the slip of paper and a pen to Logan asking for a signature. Picking up the first bundle, he began to count.

Logan waited as the man worked his way through the money, counting and writing down figures. After much time had passed, the teller totaled his numbers. "It looks like you have ten thousand, five hundred dollars. Does that sound correct?"

"It does." The teller's number matched the one that resulted from Logan's careful counting in his own room after dark last night.

"I'll move the money to the safe. Here is your account number and your empty tin." The teller slid the rusted box and a small card across the counter.

Logan thanked him and left the building.

"Reverend!" A voice shouted from behind.

Logan whirled around in time to see Chet Murray jogging in his direction. Panting from the run, Chet caught up to him. "I've got good news."

"What is it?"

"I've decided to quit drinking. I want Esther to come back so we can have a family. Jack has kids. I've seen him with his wife and family at the store and around town. He's changed. I want to change too."

Logan stared at Chet, wishing for words, any words, to come out of his mouth. He hardly knew what to say to this man who appeared so desperate to live a life that mattered. "Good for you. That is a big decision and one you might struggle to keep without the proper support. How would you like to join Jack and me in our Saturday meetings? With the warmer spring weather, Jack has chosen to meet me here at the Silver Grove church. You are welcome to come."

Chet nodded and walked away, leaving Logan uncertain if he'd come. He headed to the post office. In addition to the tin of money, he'd carried another valuable item to town with him, the letter announcing the date of his return to Oswell City. June 1 seemed to him a reasonable date to give to Paul. Since Dan could cover for him until the end of May, Logan had plenty of time to travel and resume his duties on the first Sunday in June. That gave him a whole month to prepare for welcoming a wife into his life.

A grin stretched across his face as he dropped the envelope addressed to Paul Ellenbroek into the slot designated for out of town mail.

He moved on to the hardware store. With the sale nearing, Logan wanted to make a few repairs to the house and barn. As soon as he stepped into the store, he entered a zone of unrest. His life contained a short list of events that had broken his heart, like the day last summer when he'd received the news of Dad's death or the time when Lorraine informed him of her engagement to Brandt Koelman.

A scowling crowd gathered around the cash register and watched as Jake poked a pen at a piece of paper. Chills broke out on Logan's arms. Something about this scene alerted him his heart was about to be broken once more. He ventured down the aisle.

Jake cleared his throat and whipped the paper behind the counter. "It's Logan."

The crowd shuffled away from Jake and avoided eye contact as Logan neared.

"What's going on?" His voice trembled.

Jake retrieved a rag from his apron and dusted the counter.

The activity was a ruse. The hardware store's check-out counter stayed too busy with the frequent purchases that crossed over it to ever accumulate any dust.

Logan leaned against it as the men turned away and shifted

their attention to the merchandise filling Jake's shelves. Apparently no one wished to divulge the big secret.

"What's on that paper?" Logan pointed behind the counter.

Jake turned red. "Oh, I uh, we were just…"

Logan rounded the end of the counter and joined Jake behind the cash register. A rumpled corner of a sheet displaying a list of names peeked out between notebooks and ledgers. He tugged on it and read it. The information soaking into his brain pressed him to vomit, to punch someone out, and to run away.

At the top of the page in bold type appeared the statement: **WE, THE CITIZENS OF SILVER GROVE, DO HEREBY REQUEST THE RESIGNATION OF THE TEACHER OF SILVER GROVE SCHOOL, MISS KAREN MILLERSON.** In a long column under the heading was written the names of businessmen, people who lived in town, and even some of his neighbors. He read the document again and again, trying to believe it.

The list of names began with every adult member of the Kent and Sanders families. They were behind this somehow. Maybe they still blamed Karen for the fire, and this petition was their way of getting back at her. Or maybe they still hurt from Eldon's death and wanted to make sure to injure someone else in a twisted scheme to comfort themselves. Or maybe Karen had more hostile enemies than any of them realized.

Slapping the petition on the counter, he glared at Jake. He'd fight this. Karen was the best teacher the Silver Grove School had ever known. Logan stomped out of the store, not bothering to make a purchase. This time, he'd take his business elsewhere. At least the names of Pete, Tom, Vern, and the Carter family hadn't glared at him out of the others listed. How nice that he and Karen still had some friends in Silver Grove.

KAREN DIDN'T SLEEP WELL. Fearful thoughts rolled through her mind all night long. What if one of the men from Meadow Creek turned greedy and decided he wanted the money for himself? Someone might try to rob Logan's house. Maybe those men weren't capable of keeping secrets and the word had spread over the entire countryside that Logan De Witt had money hidden on his farm. She dragged to school unprepared to meet her skeleton class. The Kent and Sanders children had not returned to school. Two weeks had passed since Eldon's death, and still no one came. Maybe she should call on them or have Mr. Hinkley pay a visit. Even though their grief was still fresh, those children should come to school again. Any mother would want that.

But the Kents were unlike any family she'd ever met. They placed no value on education and offered her no support. Maybe a visit from the school board chairman would help them change their ways.

Waving to Anna in the kitchen and Pete seated at the table with stacks of books spread before him, Karen left the house. Her stomach twisted as she made the trek across the yard. Pete studied in Anna's kitchen because Karen occupied the church building during the day, making too much noise for him to use his desk. If only the school could get replaced. Then Pete could have his peace and quiet back.

Karen squared her shoulders. She could do nothing about the present circumstances except teach the students who chose to come to class and help them finish the school year. Eight weeks remained. Surely she could see them through to the end.

The morning began with its usual routine. Math class lasted until the mid-morning recess. She dismissed the students for the fifteen minute break right as Logan walked in. Children scurried past him until the room emptied. He approached her, his pained expression unsettling her. Something terrible had happened. She could tell just by looking at him.

"What's wrong? It's my family." A telephone call filled with bad news must have come.

Logan shook his head.

"Then it's Tillie, or your mother. Or you." Panic threaded through her heart. She looked Logan over to see if he was injured anywhere.

"Karen." He reached for her.

"The money." One of those Meadow Creek men had sneaked back to steal it and maybe harmed Logan in the process. Her worst fears were coming true.

"Come to Pete's study." Logan led the way. Once they were both inside, he shut the door.

Every muscle tensed, and she clenched her fists.

"I'm fine. The money is safely in the bank." He sat down in Pete's chair and pulled her onto his lap.

He'd never done that before. His news must have to do with the wedding. Nothing else she could think of would require such a display of care. Taking her hands in his, he looked into her eyes. "I went to the hardware store after I finished at the bank. The place was busy. Lots of people in there today. But they weren't shopping. Not when I got there. They were signing a petition. Jake has it. I saw it."

Logan's face lost all color. Only one other time had she seen him so ashen. That had been the night he told her of Eldon's death.

She closed her eyes. Whatever he said, she could take it.

"The petition is asking for your resignation."

Her eyes flew open. "What?"

"The Kents are behind it. Every one of them signed it. So did some of our neighbors."

"You mean parents of my own students want me to quit?"

Logan nodded, a solemn, apologetic motion.

"I can't believe this. And when I thought my students had come so far. What reason did they give?"

"I don't know. The form didn't say."

"They must still blame me for the fire."

"I'm going to fight this."

"How?"

"By finding out the truth. Tom Hinkley didn't sign. Neither did Vern, Pete, or Andrew's family. You have allies. They will help us."

Karen stood. Recess was almost over. Her students shouldn't come inside and find their teacher in Logan De Witt's lap, even if he was her fiancé. "Come back tonight when we can talk about this more with Pete and Anna. I'd like to hear what they have to say."

Logan went with her to call her classroom back to order. After a kiss on her temple, he left. But a sinking feeling stayed behind. Years of teacher training, a move from the city, and a willingness to teach country school shouldn't land her at a tragic end. Nothing she'd done deserved a request for her to resign. Her students counted on her, even if their parents didn't. For their sake, she'd keep teaching to the end of the year. She had to. Any other reaction to this new turn of events admitted failure, and failing was something Karen refused to do.

CHAPTER TWENTY-FIVE

$\mathcal{L}$ ogan settled behind Pete's desk with Jack occupying one of the chairs when Chet Murray walked in. "I'd like to join you."

Jack shook his hand, and Chet claimed the other chair. He fit in well with their small group and expressed a genuine interest in the topics of discussion. Later that weekend, on Sunday afternoon, a sober Chet attended the service. Logan went home encouraged by the man's honest effort to turn his life around.

The following week, Logan and Jack were deep into discussion during their Saturday morning meeting when the door opened and Chet stumbled in. The smell of whiskey reached Logan's nostrils immediately. Chet's new record of sobriety had been broken.

"Sorry I'm late," Chet said, his speech a bit slurred.

Jack looked at him with disgust. "You've been drinkin' again. What's wrong with you?"

"The boys came over last night. Wish I could stay away from 'em like you can. But what's a fella to do when they take over your own house?" Chet slumped.

"Did this happen when Esther still lived at home?" Logan asked.

"Yeah."

"How did she feel about it?"

Chet gave Logan a shameful glance. "She hated it. My late-night parties are what made her decide to leave me."

"Who would you rather have?" Jack peered at him.

"I was afraid it would come down to this. I'd rather have Esther." Chet heaved a heavy breath.

"Then tell those other guys to quit comin' over. I stopped hanging out with them. You can too." Jack's voice held a mix of impatience and sincere concern.

At that moment, the door burst open, and Esther Murray stormed into the room. "What are you doing here?" She glared at her husband.

"I'm wondering the same thing about you," Chet shot back.

"Need to talk to Reverend De Witt. Went out to his farm to look for him but his ma said I'd find him here."

Jack stood. "Come on, Chet. Let's you and me go outside and talk. We'll come back later." The men left Logan to face down a seething, wind-blown young woman.

"What can I help you with?" he asked.

"My money is gone." Esther settled her hands on her hips.

"Your money?"

"Yeah. I keep it buried on the church grounds. Now I can't find it. If that Chet Murray is the one who got a hold of it, I'll wring his neck."

Logan's heart skipped a beat. The tin of wealth belonged to Esther! And now she stood in his presence ready to injure the man who'd taken it. Good thing the entire sum rested in the safe at the bank. Logan might have ended up as Esther's victim if he hadn't acted so quickly.

"Let me get this straight. You kept money hidden underground at the church in Meadow Creek?" He leaned back in his chair, highly curious how Esther would answer.

"It's my inheritance from my grandpa. Didn't want Chet to know about it or he'd spend it all on whiskey. Or steal it."

"Why not put it in the bank?"

She leaned forward, her eyes sparking with malice. "Chet's only been showing you his good side, hasn't he? My husband is the outlaw in Meadow Creek. He gets himself drunk and then he gets out his guns and goes shooting them off around town. He's broken into the general store more times than the sheriff has caught him. He's held up the bank too. You think I want my money in a place where a menace like him can get to it? No way."

Esther straightened and crossed her arms. "I'm finished with the likes of Chet Murray. My sister in California has been after me to come out there and start over. She's told me to use my money to make the trip and set myself up for a happy life. That's what I'm gonna do, if I can find my box of cash, that is." She uncrossed her arms and stared Logan down.

He stared back with a gaze tempered by compassion, not the anger radiating from this woman. Her facts fit the pieces together for a sorry story. Esther married Chet before his drinking grew unmanageable. Now he was an embarrassment to her, roaming around town causing trouble, keeping company with others who had a poor influence on him. No wonder she wanted to escape.

"Where on the church grounds did you bury your money?" Logan asked.

"The east side. Before the storm, a door with steps up to it entered the church from the back. My tin of money was buried under the steps. Now that the church blew down, my money is out in the open. Or was, before I lost it." She glared again.

"That tin was pretty rusty. It looked like it had been underground for a long time."

"Hey, what do you know about it?"

Logan left his seat and went to stand face to face with her. "A group of men dug up a tin of money when rebuilding began on the church. They gave the tin to me, and I put it on deposit at Silver Grove's bank."

Esther's eyes rolled. "Just when I thought the church was a safer place than a bank, a whole passel of men get their hands on my money and make the decision for me about where it should go."

"We didn't know the money had an owner at the time. The most responsible choice we had was to put it in a bank." Logan held his hands out, palms up. The gesture would surely convince her of his innocence. "How much do you think was in the tin?"

Esther crossed her arms as if to say she didn't have time to give answers to silly questions. "Ten thousand five hundred dollars. Or at least that's what I started with. Maybe one of you tampered with it." She gave him a mistrustful glare.

The tin definitely belonged to Esther. No one else in the world he could think of except the teller at the bank knew the total amount of money Logan had put on deposit. "All of your money is safe at the bank."

"Good." She frowned and shook her finger at him. "I'm leaving for California, and no one is going to stop me."

"LOGAN DEAR, did you see this in the paper?" Mama passed the *Bridgewater Times* to him, interrupting the buttering of his dinner roll.

He hadn't read the paper yet. Preparing for the sale took all of his extra time. If Mama hadn't pointed out an article, he would've ignored this week's paper altogether. Leaning closer, he read the article Mama indicated. The news made his eyes grow wide. "This says Chet Murray bought that big house north of Meadow Creek."

"The Roberts Place," Mama said.

"Is that the farm with two houses on it?"

"I think so."

"I wonder how he could afford it."

"A large house like that one would be expensive, and require a lot of upkeep."

"Hmm." Logan scanned over other articles in the paper, but his thoughts stayed on Chet Murray. How did he manage the purchase of such a stately dwelling? An idea pricked his mind. Surely Chet didn't live up to Esther's fears and steal her inheritance in order to buy his new house. Ridiculous. Logan's name was on the account. Chet couldn't possibly tamper with it. So how did a man with Chet's struggle secure a home like that? The question stayed with him as he finished breakfast and went to the barn.

Jack Harper would know. Logan saddled a horse and rode to Meadow Creek. Amelia answered the door. "Is Jack here?" he asked.

"No, he's at Chet's new place helping him move."

Logan left and set out in search of his friends. He discovered them in a wagon backed up to the front door of Chet's new house.

"Careful!" Jack called out as he helped Chet lift a chest of drawers. The two of them heaved the furniture onto the porch.

Chet waved when he noticed Logan in the yard. "Hey, Reverend! Come to check out my new place?"

"Yeah. I'm happy for you. Must have cost a fortune."

"Not really. I put a deposit down, but Mr. Roberts is gonna let me live here in exchange for my work on the farm."

"That's a great idea, but the paper said you bought your house."

"I did if they count my down payment as covering the entire price. Anyway, the house is mine. Mr. Roberts lives in the house on the other side of the barns, so between the two of us, we'll get the work done."

Logan wanted to ask about Esther, and was nearly ready to do so when the woman herself jumped out of a buggy and marched over.

"What do you think you're doing, moving my furniture and my dishes? You probably have some of my clothes packed in here." Her hand left her hip long enough to gesture at the wagon.

"You left, but you're always welcome home again."

She sniffed. "I'm headed to California just as soon as I can."

"California?"

"My sister lives out there. She wants me to come and get a new start."

"Oh. I bought this house for you."

"You what?" Esther halted in her march across the lawn as if she'd run into a wall.

"I hoped if you saw I was serious about staying sober you'd come back home."

"And this new house is supposed to send me the message that you've quit drinking?" Esther started marching again straight to the front steps.

"The bottles didn't come with me. No whiskey anywhere. Way out here, I'm far enough from town to stay away from partying."

Esther lifted her gaze to the upper story windows where sunlight glinted on the clean glass.

"You've seen Jack with Amelia and their kids."

"Yeah, I have." Esther's voice floated soft and reflective.

"I want a family like he has." Chet stepped close to her. "I'm a changed man, Esther, believe me. Stay and make your fresh start with me."

Esther shifted her attention away from the brick façade and white trim and onto her husband's face. "I don't want my kids growing up with a drunk for a father."

Chet shook his head. "They won't. Not if they're mine. I promise."

Esther sighed and turned her head from side to side as if her focus didn't know quite where to land. "I don't know. I need to think about this."

"Will you at least come inside and let me show you around? The house has an open staircase. I remember you telling me how much you wanted an open staircase."

"With railing and a landing and everything?"

"And carpet." Chet clasped her elbow and led her inside.

Logan leaned against a porch pillar and talked with Jack until the couple returned.

"Reverend De Witt, I'd like to transfer that money you put on deposit into my name, please. Could you meet me at the Silver Grove State Bank?" Esther asked when she and Chet had finished their tour.

"Certainly, if you feel ready."

She glanced at Chet, a mixture of skepticism and softness in her eyes. "I'm ready."

KAREN FINISHED the last verse of "His Eye Is on the Sparrow" and stepped aside to give Logan space to offer the benediction. As soon as he closed the service, Lester Brinks joined them at the pulpit.

"My apologies for cutting in, but I have an announcement to make."

People shifted in the pews with a new level of interest.

Lester cleared his throat. "I'm happy to inform everyone that we have enough money to purchase materials and start building our new church."

Claps and cheers rose from the group.

"The fundraising process took longer than we expected, but

thanks to a donation from Esther Murray, groundbreaking happens this week."

Karen looked at the newcomers. Esther and her husband were in attendance today for the first time. They sat with the Harpers halfway to the back.

"And now, on behalf of the board, I have an offer to make to Reverend De Witt. He's been meeting with Chet Murray this spring, helping Chet stay sober. The Murrays are here with us this morning. Reverend De Witt's influence is working. Chet no longer takes to the streets causing trouble and robbing stores. He's settling down in a new home. Meadow Creek is very relieved and thankful. Reverend De Witt has also led us through the planning and fundraising for our new church. He's provided faithful care, and he's a good preacher. The board has decided to offer him the permanent position as our pastor in Meadow Creek."

The gathering applauded, but Karen felt more than saw Logan tense. He couldn't have been expecting this one bit. People gathered around him at the close of the service, shaking his hand and expressing their approval. Bewilderment showed on his features and interfered with his responses.

"What do you think I should do?" Logan asked after everyone left. "You're sharing my life now, or soon will be. I want to do what would make you happy." He walked with her across the yard to Pete and Anna's home.

"Isn't Oswell City expecting you?"

Logan nodded. "They are. You're more comfortable living in town. Maybe I should stick with my original plan."

"Don't make this about me and what I want."

He faced her. "The Meadow Creek congregation is too small to provide me with a salary sufficient enough to support a wife. I'd need to take a second job. Since the farm will sell, you and I would need to move to Meadow Creek. It's way out in the country. You'd have limited opportunity to be in town, worse than on the farm."

Karen swallowed. He was right. Logan's choice to stay in Meadow Creek asked much from her. Still, she couldn't stand in his way. "Test it out. Isn't that what you did about your decision to stay in Silver Grove? Maybe you need to use the same approach with your decision to leave. If Meadow Creek is where you should be instead of Oswell City, the Lord will make it clear to both of us."

A smile grew over Logan's mouth, but he continued to gaze intently into her eyes. "The Lord sure knew what He was doing to bring you here to me. Will you pray about this?"

"You know I will."

"Then I can't go wrong." He reached for her hand and resumed walking.

Karen went with him to the house.

Tom Hinkley sat at the table, visiting with Pete. The school board chairman turning up at the parsonage on a Sunday afternoon alerted Karen something was terribly wrong. She held her breath.

CHAPTER TWENTY-SIX

*a*nna invited Karen to take the chair next to her. Logan stood behind Karen and settled his hands on her shoulders. "What's going on?" he asked.

The firm set to Mr. Hinkley's mouth and the weariness in Pete's eyes deserved such a question. If someone were to announce another fire and death, Karen could fully believe the news for as somber as everyone looked.

"The petition has enough names on it to require Miss Millerson's resignation. I can't ignore it anymore." Mr. Hinkley sounded older than his years.

"You didn't sign it, did you?" Logan demanded.

"No way." Mr. Hinkley looked at him with the expression of a grade school boy who'd gotten his feelings hurt. "You won't catch me teamin' up with Evan Kent for anything."

"He is the one behind it. I thought so." Logan's voice came from somewhere above her head with enough impatience to pick a fight.

"Yeah, it's him. He threatened to call in the loans on any bank customers who won't sign."

"He wouldn't!" The thought disgusted Karen and made her stomach churn.

"Already has. Since his bank is the only one in town, he knows he won't lose customers over the petition. If folks want to stay in business, they better sign."

"What about you?" Pete asked.

"My wife and I transferred our funds over to the bank in Bridgewater Springs when Eldon died. That's where she's from. We'd kept a savings account there and now all our money is in one place."

"Smart move," Pete said.

"What about Vern? And Ed at the mercantile? I didn't see their names on the petition either," Logan said.

"Maybe they don't owe Evan for anything." Mr. Hinkley pulled a handkerchief from his pocket and wiped his brow.

"This means people are making their decision to sign based on their own fears instead of loyalty to Karen." Logan's voice held accusation.

"You got it." Mr. Hinkley replaced the handkerchief in his pocket.

"Something must be done. Evan can't be allowed to manipulate bank customers like this, or to force Karen into anything." Logan's voice took on the persuasive quality that served him well whenever he stood behind the pulpit.

"Got any ideas?" Mr. Hinkley looked up at Logan.

Pete leaned forward. "The school was on Clyde's land. What if the neighbors banded together and took it upon themselves to start rebuilding the school? Why does anyone need to know the cause of the fire first? Everyone should move ahead on their own. If the school was rebuilt, Karen could start teaching in it, releasing these families from Evan's control."

Mr. Hinkley shook his head. "Ain't that easy. I probably shouldn't be telling you this, but Clyde hit a rough patch with the bank a few years back when he didn't get a crop because of dry weather. The only thing he had to sell was land, so he gave the bank the corner the school sits on."

"The bank owns the school," Karen whispered.

"Right. That's why Evan thinks he can throw his weight around like he does. The school belongs to him."

Karen heard Logan's intake of breath. The news must sound just as bad to him as it did to her. Evan's attitudes were shared by the rest of his family. This is why Vera and her sister-in-law felt they could treat Karen with such nastiness.

But the Kents didn't value education, and yet they owned the school. What benefit did Evan and his family enjoy from its ownership? "You don't suppose they set the fire on purpose. They never have cared about education and learning. With the building gone, they could use that land however they wish."

"You think that tin of gunpowder was planted in the class-room?" Mr. Hinkley glanced at her out of the corner of his eye.

"But their own brother died in that fire," Pete said.

"That part was an accident. The Kents might not possess much heart, but they couldn't have planned on Eldon's death." Ever compassionate, Logan found the positive in everyone, even Eldon's relatives.

"I'm sure it was an accident." Mr. Hinkley leaned back in his chair. "We can trust Wade's story about the hunting trip to the back pasture. Joe and Marty probably sneaked the tin to school. With no parents at home at the time, those boys could do as they pleased. Eldon's death just happened. No one would've intended for the school to burn and for a man to lose his life. I've lived here my whole life, so I know how them Kents operate. Logan is right. They're a ruthless bunch, but they aren't murderers."

"Where do we start?" Pete asked. "Do we try to determine the cause of the fire or find a new location and start building the school?"

"We need to fight this petition," Logan said. "Evan might have strong reasons for wanting to keep control of the school, but those reasons shouldn't interfere with Karen's right to teach or the students' completion of the school year."

Mr. Hinkley stood. "You're right, Logan. Sounds like we need to call another meeting. Could you and Pete help me lead it? Roy's name is on the petition, but Vern's is not. The school board is too divided to work together on finding answers."

Logan and Pete both nodded while pain twisted through Karen's middle. Roy Jones had signed the petition. Lacy's father had turned against her, and after the tutoring and special care she gave his daughter. This fire had burned away the surface peace and goodwill of Silver Grove, exposing a deeper tangle of complexities. Karen held her chin high. She'd teach to the best of her ability for the next six weeks, and then she'd leave. No strings attached, and no looking back.

When she'd agreed to stay and teach country school, the world glittered with dreams of a career and hopes of changed lives. Instead, she'd gotten caught in the middle of tensions that had existed long before she came and would remain after she left. A discreet, quiet exit from this place at the end of May was the wisest, cleanest sort of action, if she was allowed to stay that long. But the hostilities of the Kent clan couldn't interfere with her summer. In less than two months after the end of the school year, she'd marry Logan.

As the days passed, she believed with strengthening conviction that her reason for coming to Silver Grove in the first place was to meet him. She hadn't been looking for a husband, but God knew. He'd directed her path and would continue to do so. Fires, deaths, and forced resignations couldn't change His special plans for her.

THE SMALL SANCTUARY of the Silver Grove church swarmed with indignant people. Neighbors to the De Witts, families who sent children to school, and residents from town milled about complaining to one another. Women stood with arms crossed. Men shook their heads and glared at the front pew where the new loan officer, his wife, sister, and brother-in-law, sat. Karen strained to hear bits of conversation around her. The comments brought her a measure of comfort. She wasn't the only one forced into decisions against her will. Everyone talked of the petition and Evan's demand that his bank customers sign. At least no one was choosing to take sides against her. But the fact that their fears of Evan outweighed their belief in her as the teacher pricked her heart with a sharp pain.

"Don't let this get you down," Anna said from her place at Karen's side. "Pete and Logan will get the matter sorted out and help everyone settle down."

Karen nodded. How she appreciated Anna. If she must give up her daily contact with Logan, then sharing a home with Anna was the next best option. Anna had followed through on her offer of friendship. Over cups of coffee, she listened as Karen talked about engagement to a preacher, the fire at school, Eldon's death, and now the controversy surrounding her teaching position. Anna consoled, prayed, and encouraged. Karen didn't know what she would've done without the friendship of Anna Betten.

She released the breath she held as Tom Hinkley stood behind the pulpit. He banged the gavel and the room quieted. "Good evening. Please find a seat. The meeting will begin short-ly." He waited until the gathering settled into pews.

Anna led Karen to a seat in the back. After occupying the front row at the last two school meetings, this place in the back where no one could stare at her was a relief. She sat on the end, grateful for Anna's presence between herself and the couple on Anna's other side. Knowing who was her friend or who had become an enemy grew harder and harder these days.

Tom banged the gavel again. "Let's get started. You all know

why we're here. A petition has circulated requesting the resignation of Silver Grove's school teacher, Miss Karen Millerson."

Murmurs ran through the crowd.

"One of our school board members has signed, hindering our
ability to make decisions on this matter. I was unsure how to
proceed, so I consulted Reverend Betten and Reverend De Witt.
We concluded the best course of action is to fight the petition."

Everyone talked at once.

Evan Kent jumped to his feet. "You can't do that. The petition has enough names on it to insist on the teacher's resignation.
It stands."

Tom held up one of his hands. "We can, and we will." He
stepped aside and nodded to Pete and Logan.

Karen had lost track of them in the crowded room. They
emerged now from the back and walked the aisle. Her heart
swelled as she watched Logan approach the front. His blond hair
was combed into place, and his jaw was freshly shaved. He wore
dark trousers, white shirt, and tie. He faced the group and
scanned it briefly. When his gaze landed on her, he offered a
quick smile. Authority fit him well. People looked up to him and
trusted him. He told the truth even when it hurt and yet knew
how to guard confided cares. If anyone could guide this meeting
in a positive direction, Logan could. She relaxed.

"Good evening," Logan spoke to the group. "As Tom stated
earlier, a petition calling for Miss Millerson's resignation has
circulated among us. Evan declared that the petition has enough
signatures to validate the school board firing the teacher.
Reverend Betten and I were in conversation with Tom just
yesterday, and we believe there is a better way to go about this."

Evan left his seat and went to the front. "Excuse me, Logan,
but I have the petition right here. Signed in ink. There's no
changing it. The school burned down. Clyde Hixson allowed that
piece of land to return to the bank, so I own it. In that fire, my
brother died. No cause for the fire has been found. The only

evidence we have is the tin that was found in Miss Millerson's desk drawer. She is at fault."

Murmurs ran over the room again.

Evan raised his voice. "Our family has a long list of complaints against Miss Millerson, but Tom Hinkley takes no action. The time has come for us to accomplish justice on our own. Miss Millerson is an incompetent teacher and must resign."

Mr. Hinkley stood. "But Evan, the school year ends in a little over a month. We can't find a replacement now, and our kids need to complete their grades."

Evan shook his head. "Miss Millerson's inability would eventually catch up to her. She must accept the consequence no matter what time of year it is. Fire her."

Tom's jaw worked, and his face turned red. "I refuse. We need to finish the school year."

The room erupted in support for Tom and impatience at Evan's demands.

"Quiet, everyone," Logan said, raising his hand in the air. "I have an idea. As many of you know, I'm selling my farm later this week. The school needs rebuilt, so I'd like to supply the funds for it from my sale. If the community has this outside source to help purchase building materials, we can make our own decision about the teacher independent of Evan's petition."

The talking started up again but with less intensity. Karen's insides clenched. Logan had already made so many sacrifices for her. He shouldn't commit himself like this. What if he didn't generate enough profit to satisfy the bank and the need for a school too? His generosity might create more problems than it fixed. She must talk with him about this idea, but now wasn't the time.

Roy Jones left his seat and approached the front. He whispered to Logan, who stepped aside so that Roy could speak. "Miss Millerson has done so much for Lacy. I signed the petition because Evan threatened to call in my loans if I didn't. But I didn't want to sign. I didn't see any other way to provide for my family. Logan, if you're willing to supply money for a new school, then I'm taking my name off the list." He took a pencil from behind the pulpit and marched over to Evan, where he scratched through his signature. Then he went to stand with Tom.

Vern came to the front next. He didn't stop to mark on the paper in Evan's hand. Instead, he stood with Tom and Roy as if to send the message of unity restored on the school board.

Pete looked out at the group. "Anyone else? If you join Logan and the school board, you are released from the conditions of the petition."

Five more men left their seats and crossed their signatures from the form.

Pete stepped forward and analyzed Evan's document. "It looks like the petition no longer has enough names to force Miss Millerson's resignation."

Applause broke out, but Bert stood up. Without a word, he, Elsie, and Vera stomped out of the building. Evan leveled a glare at the men standing with Logan and Tom. "I'll make sure none of my children step foot in her classroom ever again." A snarl twisting his mouth, he left with the other members of his family.

A mix of emotions swirled in Karen's middle. Worry over Logan's extravagant offer. Joy in the school board's victory securing her position. Fear of what Evan's defeat would mean for class attendance from the children in his family. She wanted all of her students to achieve success, but the Kent and Sanders children would never return to school now. They would surely drop out. But that would put each of them behind an entire grade. Evan's words had also hinted at a threat. Surely he wouldn't attempt to discredit her as a teacher. He'd already tried in Silver Grove. Maybe he could damage her reputation enough to prevent her from ever securing another teaching position. The thought made Karen's stomach quiver.

Roy stepped forward. "Miss Millerson, I saw you here

tonight, so I want to apologize and tell you I'm sorry I signed the petition. I appreciate so much the help with studies you've given to Lacy. I think I can speak on behalf of the entire school board when I say we'd be honored to have you stay as our teacher. Would you be willing to keep teaching until the end of the year?"

The room held its breath as Karen stood. "Yes. You may plan on me staying in Silver Grove until the end of the school year."

Everyone clapped. The people around her smiled. Logan wore a huge grin. He even winked when he looked her way. Evan Kent couldn't harm her career with all of this support behind her.

Mr. Hinkley picked up his gavel. "Thanks for coming. School will carry on as usual here at the church with Miss Millerson as the teacher. I'll post an announcement at Jake's to let ya know when we'll start rebuilding the school."

Logan and Pete met up with Karen and Anna, maneuvering them through the crowd. People shook her hand and thanked Logan. Karen left the building convinced enemies no longer existed among her neighbors and the families of her students. How nice to feel safe and respected once more.

Pete and Anna led the way to their house. Logan ushered Karen inside and took her coat. Anna made coffee and brought it to the parlor where the four of them talked over the happenings of the evening.

"I'm not sure I should let you make such a large sacrifice," Karen said while Logan sipped his coffee.

His eyebrows rose in a question.

"You might not make as much from your sale as you expect, and then you'll need all of your money for the bank. You won't have enough to build a school and pay your debt."

A smile tugged at Logan's mouth. "I'll manage."

"The question now is where to build the school," Pete said.

"I'd be happy to provide ground for it." Logan leaned back and let Anna refill his cup.

"Maybe your farm's new owner would be willing to work something out." Pete also accepted a refill.

After a few moments of silence, Logan retrieved an envelope from his pocket. "Here, Karen. This came in the mail today. Looks like it's from your mother." Karen set her cup down and ripped open the letter.

Dear Karen,

I write you this quick note to let you know of the teaching position I told you about when I visited you in Silver Grove. It is at a ladies college for a summer and fall term. Arthur knows the principal and highly recommended you. Please do consider. You could live at home while you teach. You would need to adjust your wedding plans, but having you back in the city again before you get married would mean so much to us.

Love,

Mother

Karen folded up the letter.

"What's it say?" Logan asked.

"Mother wrote to tell me that the teaching position she talked about while she was here is still available. Can you believe, she suggested we change our wedding date so I could return to the city for an extended stay? There's no way. I'm marrying you instead."

Logan smiled. "I hope nothing is wrong and this is your mother's way of getting you to come home."

"No, nothing is wrong. Mother just misses me. That's all." Karen stuffed the letter into her skirt pocket. If tonight's meeting had gone differently and she'd been asked to resign, she'd consider mother's offer. But her future shone bright. A job in the city was the last thing she wanted.

CHAPTER TWENTY-SEVEN

*L*ogan positioned the three-legged stool in the straw and lowered his tall frame onto it. Tonight marked his last evening milking his father's herd in his father's barn. The farm would sell tomorrow. The question of who would buy the land teased his mind. The cows might stay, but the more likely possibility was the division of the herd among area farmers. The thought of handing the care of his Holsteins over to another, maybe to many others, had stolen his appetite today. He wouldn't rest until he knew his cows landed in good homes. His last act of care for them included finding the best possible buyers.

Tears threatened to cloud his vision. Good thing he milked alone. No one wanted to see a grown man known to the world as a reverend cry. Neither did he look for chances to let the tears fall. But right now, in this historic moment, he could get by with it. He sniffed. A trickle of moisture ran over one cheek.

Maybe he could keep the cows and take them with him to Oswell City. They would really help him in sermon preparation. The quiet hours he'd spent mulling over ideas and organizing his thoughts while he milked taught him how vital his cows had become to his weekly appearance before the Meadow Creek congregation. If he could continue the practice in Oswell City, he'd preach the best sermons the people he served there had ever heard.

But the church lawn was way too small to accommodate a dairy herd. Besides, Paul Ellenbroek and the city council would never allow it. Even if his yard had space, the notion of Reverend De Witt, robe-clad and studious, bent over a milking stool in the middle of town for all to see would lead to some serious conversations during meetings with his church board. He'd tried his best to avoid tense moments of disapproval in the past, so he'd better not start now attracting spectacular attention. Getting married would give everyone more than enough reasons to keep an eye on him.

Not only sermon preparation was accomplished in the barn during milking time. Much of his grief had been processed there too. In those days following his return to the farm, the solitude of the barn had been exactly what Logan needed. He might have chosen to stay and care for Mama and Tillie, but the Lord had some care in mind for Logan too. The cows had helped him find comfort on those dark days.

He moved on to the next cow as a smile stretched his mouth. The night he'd kissed Karen for the first time flooded his memory. On the milking stool was where he thought through the whole surprising turn of events. It was also where he wrestled with the call to singleness and where he practiced what on earth to say when proposing marriage. The cows had certainly been good for him.

He stood and slapped the Holstein's rump before situating his pail and the stool near the next cow. A different matter weighed on his heart. Eldon's screams the day of the fire still tortured him. He never expected Eldon to die so tragically or so early in life. Logan should've tried harder to be a friend. He should've been more intentional about acting as pastor to Eldon too. The man may not have attended church, but that didn't mean Logan couldn't have cared about him or shared Christ with him.

But what had Logan done instead? Shown frustration over the interest payments and harbored jealousy when Eldon spent time with Karen. "O Lord, forgive me," Logan prayed under his breath. "I really missed an opportunity when Eldon was alive. I've failed You." He felt worse about that than his inability to pay off Dad's debt.

The barn door squeaked open. Logan poked his head into the aisle for a better view of his visitor.

Karen walked toward him. "Hi, Logan. Pete, Anna, and I just arrived for supper. Your mother wanted to wait to eat until you come to the house, so I thought I'd use the time to come see you."

He stood and greeted her with a kiss.

"What's wrong? You seem bothered by something." Karen searched his face.

With a quick pass over his eyes, Logan wiped his shirt sleeve across his face just in case a stray tear or two remained behind.

"You've been thinking about the sale tomorrow."

He inhaled. "Yeah. I'll miss the cows. I really will. But I've been thinking about Eldon too."

"Eldon?" Karen's brow furrowed. The name probably still brought her pain.

Logan shifted his weight to one foot. "I should've tried earlier to share the gospel with him."

"He might not have listened. Eldon was stubborn."

"That doesn't matter. I didn't treat him very well. For that I'm really sorry. He should've had the chance to hear as soon as I came to town." Logan chewed on his lip.

"He may not have been ready." Karen's voice was soft, patient. "Your interaction with him, as insensitive as it felt to you, might have been working all the time to prepare him. God has a way of covering our mistakes with His grace. The point is that Eldon became a believer. God used you."

Light dawned as he listened. "You're saying Eldon's conversion was a matter of timing instead of my negligence."

She smiled and nodded.

Logan gazed deeply into her eyes as his heart released his burden. Karen was the only one he could talk to about matters of this nature. He might lose his cows and his farm, but Karen would always be at his side. "Stay here with me."

The invitation went beyond asking her to stay in the barn until he finished milking. It requested her love and her wisdom in the delicate areas of his life. He'd never stop needing her.

LOGAN WANDERED around a barnyard filled with horses and wagons. The sun shone and a spring breeze blew through the budding tree branches above. He snacked on food Mama and Tillie served in the milk parlor. Sandwiches and pie completed the menu. Bill, the postman from Silver Grove, held a side business as an auctioneer, traveling around the area presiding over sales. He stood on Logan's hayrack talking in fast, repetitive syllables. Logan failed to interpret most of the words Bill said. The crowd gathered around must have understood, though. Hands raised one after another as Bill auctioned off Logan's collection of milk cans.

The mower and planter had already sold. Tom Hinkley bought both. Sally Hixson had purchased Mama's flock of chickens, promising to leave them here at the De Witts' until Mama moved to town. As he expected, the cows had been sold in groups to other dairy farmers. The cows were in good hands. Those men would look after Logan's cows as members of their own herds.

The land including the fields, the house, and the barn went to

Vern Patterson. His oldest son planned to move in sometime during the summer. This young man was engaged to a girl from Bridgewater Springs. Logan found peace in the sale's outcome so far. He wished the young couple all the best as they established their new home and started their family.

Evan Kent sat at a table behind the hayrack, taking payments and tucking them smugly in his black cash box. Logan should probably wander over that way and check in for an updated amount. He already had a good idea of the total sales. Bill's speedy auctioneer language may not make much sense to Logan's ears, but the dollar amounts he yelled out to the highest bidder came through loud and clear. Logan kept a mental running total as he listened.

The money would all go to the bank anyway. Evan would apply the necessary amount to the debt and then open an account for Mama. Whatever funds were left over would go to the school board to build a new school. Logan really had no reason to know exact figures. As long as Evan had enough to clear the De Witt name, nothing else mattered.

Pete drove in with his buggy, so Logan adjusted his course away from the man at the cash box and over to his friend.

"Having a good day?" Pete asked, tossing his reins to Logan.

He gave Pete a report of who was bidding and what they bought.

"You should have plenty to satisfy the bank and keep your word to the school board." Pete stayed through to the end of the sale and helped Logan put the hayrack and a few tables away after everyone left.

The setting sun told him milking time had arrived, but he had no cows to care for tonight. The spring breeze had turned gusty and blew through the empty barn just like loneliness blew through Logan's heart. He'd never been more thankful for his good friend than he was tonight. Pete's company kept his mind off the finality of the sale and encouraged him instead to look to the future.

He was getting married and returning to ministry. Tillie was also getting married, and Mama would be taken care of. He hadn't lost his father's farm. God was bringing new opportunities and new blessings into their lives, which meant the farm was no longer necessary to them. Everything Dad worked for hadn't been wasted or squandered. Logan breathed a sigh of relief over that. Instead, Dad's investments were being multiplied.

Money from John De Witt's farm would help fund a school where generations of Silver Grove children could receive an education. Mama would live in town where she could be an even greater asset to Silver Grove. Logan would be able to continue in ministry proclaiming the gospel his father and grandfather believed in so deeply.

The sale of his family's ground would multiply blessings in the lives of so many, and in his and Karen's as they married and had a family of their own. Those sacrifices John De Witt made so that Logan could leave the farm and get his education in order to preach were beginning to pay off, and in larger and more meaningful ways than any of them could've predicted.

Logan prepared for sleep that evening, humming a tune from the psalter he and Karen had used in worship on Sunday. The melody matched lyrics that were based on Psalm 1. In answer to the prayer he'd prayed last summer after the storm ruined his oat crop, he'd finally figured out prosperity's secret. Dad had a son, and someday grandchildren, out in the world who honored him, but most importantly, honored his Lord. Nothing was lost, but all had been redeemed. The time had come to move on.

CHAPTER TWENTY-EIGHT

"*H*ave some cake." Anna passed a plate filled with a thick slice of frosted cake to Logan. Pete placed a scoop of homemade ice cream on Logan's plate and moved on to do the same for Karen. Logan sank his fork into the cake and took a bite. Delicious.

"Tillie looks real happy," Sally Hixson commented to Lucy Hinkley nearby.

"Such a nice thing for her to marry Andrew Carter," Lucy replied.

"They'll do just fine together," Nellie Patterson said.

Mama and Nora Carter sat across the circle, eating cake and wearing overjoyed expressions on their faces. Tillie and Andrew occupied the seats of honor beside the table stacked high with gifts. Under Anna's leadership, the families of their congregation had come together to throw a bridal shower for his sister. Tillie loved the attention. She'd been working since Christmas on collecting articles for her new home. This evening's gifts would go far, rounding out her supply.

Andrew had bought a square, two-story house in town, down

the street and around the corner from the Carter Mercantile on Main Street. He'd filled it with furniture, and he and Tillie, along with his family, painted many of the interior walls. Curtains fresh from Mama's sewing machine already hung at the windows. Keepsakes from the De Witt attic resided in the upstairs rooms.

Tillie had also been busy sewing with Mama on her dress. It flowed from a dress form in the sewing room, hemmed and ready to go. The two of them still worked on the veil as the last finishing touch for the big day.

Anna would provide flowers from her garden and help Mama with the cake and the food on the day of the wedding. Logan would give Tillie away, and with Karen would stand up with Andrew and Tillie as their attendants. Pete planned to officiate the service. Excitement mounted for Logan with each passing day. He felt happiness for Tillie, but he also looked forward to his departure for Oswell City the very next week. He'd finally be able to start saving and preparing for his own marriage.

Karen had written her mother to let her know the wedding was planned for July in Oswell City with a Chicago wedding trip following. Margaret had replied with a favorable response. Giddiness threatened to hijack his common sense. Studying for sermons had grown impossible. He couldn't concentrate on anything except the newlywed life awaiting him.

"Give your plate to Pete. Tillie and Andrew are about to open gifts." Karen nudged him and pointed at his empty plate. She moved away to help Tillie with the opening of gifts.

Pete came by, acting as assistant to his hostess wife, and collected the dirty dishes. Guests rearranged their chairs in order to better see the gift table. Tillie reached for the first package. She opened it to discover a bowl and pitcher from the Hinkleys. Andrew took a turn with the next gift. They continued the pattern, unwrapping lamps, silverware, linens, and everything else that made for a comfortable home.

A horse and buggy pulled into the church yard as Tillie

admired the last gift. Mr. Kent climbed down and approached the group. Anna had mentioned to Logan and Karen in private that she had invited Elsie and Vera and their husbands to the shower, but they declined. Logan figured the refusal had more to do with hard feelings toward Pete and the rest of their neighbors than it did with a schedule conflict.

Mr. Kent joined the group and looked around. "Logan De Witt, are you here?"

Logan raised his hand.

Mr. Kent nodded. "I have some news from the bank you should know. The rest of you connected to the school might be interested to hear it too."

Logan leaned forward, trying to guess what had happened at the bank on a large enough scale to affect so many.

Mr. Kent took a deep breath. "Evan has been working on the De Witt account today, and it turns out that the sale didn't generate enough money to cover Logan's deficit with the bank. This means there won't be any funds for you to use to rebuild the school. I'm sorry. Truly." He lowered his gaze and turned away, climbed into his buggy, and left.

Silence reigned before everyone talked at once.

"Do ya think it's true?" Tom glanced at Vern and then at Logan.

He shouldn't have eaten that slice of cake. His stomach knotted up tight, making him sick.

Pete came over and thumped him on the shoulder. "Logan, buddy. I'm so sorry. You had a lot riding on that sale."

"What are you gonna do?" Tom studied him.

Logan shook his head. A fog had descended and clouded his vision. Dizziness settled in, making his head spin. "I...I...don't know. Sounds like Evan needs more money. I'll have to find a job." And a place to live. Maybe he should accept the Meadow Creek offer after all.

"You could find work on a farm, I'm sure. With your experience and the growing season coming on, a job like that should be easy to land." Tom's voice held enthusiasm, but Logan couldn't share in it.

Pain threaded through his chest, and heavy weight dragged on his soul. Thinking required too much work. His chin trembled as he shielded his face with his hands.

"Guess this means we'll have to start over makin' plans for a new school," Tom said.

"Yeah. We're right back to dealing with the bank." This came from Vern.

"And Evan." Roy must have joined the group. He sounded as disgusted as the others.

Logan remained where he'd always been, indebted to a Kent and without choices. The same old combination of farming and preaching for Meadow Creek on Sundays lingered as his only option. He should compose a letter to Paul as soon as possible and alert him to this abrupt change of plans. Meadow Creek awaited as his permanent home.

The failure of his farm sale meant marriage no longer fit into his future. His heart shattered. The worst had happened, and it left him with the most bitter decision he'd ever need to make in his entire life.

KAREN WATCHED LOGAN CRUMBLE. Her strong, patient fiancé received a stunning blow. Surely the bank hadn't done anything devious, and on purpose. Logan had the means to stand up to the Kent family and provide his neighbors with an escape from Evan's oppressive tactics. Maybe this maneuver was Evan's attempt at revenge. Eldon had been demanding, but he'd lacked the malicious edge of his older brother. If she had a way to get to town, Karen would march into the bank and insist on a meeting. Evan had no right to determine the course of Logan's future.

If Evan could only see how hard Logan worked, the concern he felt about replacing the school, and his desire to return to full-time ministry, maybe Evan would discover he had a heart. Karen shook her head. The man would never change. Logan must solve his own problem with no support or empathy from the one person who could help him. She left her place near the gift table where she cleaned up bits of wrapping paper and entered the cluster of men gathered around her fiancé.

"Come to the house with me. Let's talk." Karen laid her hand on his back.

He offered no immediate response. After several moments, he looked at her through red-rimmed eyes where turmoil swam. Her heart constricted. Something about the pain evident on his face unsettled her. She wanted to be steady and patient for him like he'd been for her so many times in the past. But her pulse throbbed, and her hands turned clammy.

Logan heaved out of his chair with a deep sigh. The men slapped his back, and he shook their hands as if to thank them for their simple yet sincere show of concern. He walked at her side like a man preoccupied with misery. In the house, he went straight to Anna's kitchen and leaned over the sink as if preparing to get sick.

His behavior made her shake all over. She fought for each step as she crossed the room. "What is it?" her voice trembled.

"I can't return to Oswell City. I need to stay here and find a job. Meadow Creek wants me. Guess I'll do that and find a way to keep farming to supplement my income enough so I can continue paying the bank." He turned to her. Those bloodshot eyes brought tears to her own. "I won't have enough left to support a wife."

Her stomach hardened. "What are you saying?"

Logan held her hands in his. "You deserve better than what I can give you now. I don't blame you if you want to call off our engagement."

"No!" She hurled herself into his arms and clutched his neck. Sobs choked her.

Logan held her close for a long time. "I don't want to do it either, but I don't know how to make this fair to you. I have to stay."

"I want to be with you no matter what."

Logan pulled back and looked into her eyes. "It's going to take months, maybe even years, to satisfy the bank."

"We can find our way."

"You'd have to give up everything you've ever known. I can't ask it of you." Logan turned back to the sink, looking ready to empty his stomach of Anna's yummy cake.

Karen twisted his ring around on her finger. In her heart, she'd stay engaged to him forever. He held every last bit of it. No deficits or career choices could change that. But the determination in his voice led her to believe he'd do whatever was required of him to make painful sacrifices. A lump in her throat made her feel like choking, but she had to know the extent of their new circumstances. "Are you saying we'd delay the wedding, or do you intend for us to go our separate ways?"

Anguish burned in his gaze. He rubbed the back of his neck. "I want you to be free to follow the Lord's call on your life. I thought I could give you that by becoming your husband, but now I cannot."

"What about Meadow Creek? I could continue to assist there." She studied his features, certain this suggestion would gain his approval.

Logan shook his head. "But I won't have the means or the stability now to provide you with a place to live. Even if I did, you'd be too burdened with the demands of running a farm. It would be a hard life for you, Karen. You've seen how much my mother works."

Yes, she had witnessed Sandy's unending toil raising a

garden, canning the bushels of produce, and helping out with chores. Keeping up with those jobs would leave her little time or energy to be available to him on Sunday afternoons or any other day of the week as situations arose.

"We'll get through this together." She stretched up on tip-toe and clasped the side of his face.

Logan flinched. "Karen, don't."

Ignoring his tortured whisper, she kissed his cheek while he stood still as if bracing himself against a strong current threatening to drown him.

She left the kitchen and passed through the dusky house. Her courage managed to hold her head up until she reached her room. Behind the closed door, Karen collapsed on her bed and wept.

Sunday afternoon, Karen went through the motions as she led the Meadow Creek congregation in singing. Her limbs were numb, but her heart pricked with sharp pain. Logan's love for her prompted his willingness to release her from their engagement, and yet her love for him refused to let her consider it. She must find a way to help him. Evan wouldn't. His family couldn't. The solution belonged to her. Surely she could devise a way to save her engagement. Choosing to live in the country with him wasn't the answer. Logan needed money more than she needed to adjust to life in Meadow Creek.

Ending the song, she passed Logan on his way to the pulpit. He looked like she felt, wrestling with a combination of pain and numbness that stole his enjoyment from his responsibilities. She forced a smile, but the same reserve he'd shown on the morning of Mother's arrival appeared. No indication of feeling peeked out through a twinkle in his eyes or a smile lurking around his mouth. The light had been snuffed out of his spirit, and he approached the pulpit with a face resembling stone.

Karen wanted to run back to her room and weep all over again.

Logan opened his Bible and read. Then he prayed. Then he preached. No stutters broke the flow of his words, but no expression impassioned them. If he had to stay in Meadow Creek and find work, he'd soon lose the heart for preaching. A man could only pretend for so long. Father had attempted to cover up stealing. Logan would find himself attempting to cover up heartache. Deep, raw heartache.

Maybe she could accept the teaching position Mother wrote about. She could live at Uncle Henry's to save on expenses and send her salary to Logan. He could add it to his in order to make his payments. After the church service, she shared her idea with him. "I've decided to accept the teaching position Mother mentioned. It would give me a salary I could share with you."

Logan straightened from putting a hymnbook away that had been left lying in a pew. His brow furrowed as he listened. "I appreciate your thoughtfulness, sweetheart. But I fear your teacher's salary won't make as much difference as you hope. Plus, you should use your money for yourself instead of giving it to Evan."

"But I'd be giving it to you, investing in our future." She looked up into his face, willing his intense expression to soften.

"The debt is too large." He walked away, a glimmer of pain present in his eyes.

His apparent lack of interest could not deter her. Karen continued to make plans. She wrote to Mother, asking for the date of the day the summer term would start. Mother promptly replied with the information that school would begin on June 1 with two days of teacher orientation preceding. Mother also asked for Karen to arrive by the weekend so that she might attend the anniversary dinner Aunt Fran was hosting for Arthur and Julia.

This meant Karen would need to leave Silver Grove the day of Tillie's wedding. It might work if she waited until the afternoon train departed. Then she'd be able to attend most of the reception at the farm following the ceremony.

With a determined straightening of her shoulders, Karen picked up her pen and drafted a letter to Mother announcing her arrival in Chicago the evening of May 26. Mother would be thrilled, and Karen and Logan would have their future back.

CHAPTER TWENTY-NINE

*L*ogan pounded nails into a board as he worked alongside Lester Brinks, Jack Harper, and the other men from Meadow Creek. His heart pounded almost as loudly. To think Karen would return to the city and take a teaching job she didn't want just to help him out. What a woman. They'd make a great team. That is, if he wasn't held to leftover commitments at the bank. His life had changed. As much as he wanted Karen in it, he had to let her go. She deserved her freedom, her opportunity at influence, and her comforts in a nice home on a street in town. Not eking out an existence as the wife of a man who couldn't even promise her a place to live.

"Have you decided yet about our offer to stay as our pastor?" Lester asked.

"I'm still considering it. I'm searching for a second job. If I get those details worked out, I'll let you know for sure."

"That's good news," Lester said.

"Yeah. A new building and a permanent preacher, and we'd really start moving forward." Jack pounded a nail below Logan's.

"I'm happy for you to have your church built." Logan wiped his brow.

"Should be done in a couple more weeks. The fund raising went slow, but the construction has gone fast." Jack reached for another nail and started pounding.

"Did you hear that Esther Murray ordered us a bell? It'll be coming about the same time as the stained glass," Lester said.

Logan hadn't heard. A bell would give Meadow Creek distinction.

"She and Chet are back together now. Chet's been stayin' sober, so Esther decided to take the risk and move into that big house with him. Sounds like they're startin' over. Amelia has been spendin' a lot of time out there helpin' Esther put the place in order. Chet might like a big house, but he could use some experience in the area of decorating." Jack chuckled and reached for more nails.

The time spent with Amelia was probably also helping Esther put her heart in order, giving her the courage to step back into Chet's life and make a new home for him.

"You Logan De Witt?" Someone tapped his shoulder.

Logan turned. "I am."

The man shook his hand. "I'm Esther's father. I'm going to have surgery on my leg in June, but my hay needs cut and harvested. When I was in Silver Grove earlier this week, I heard that you might be looking for a job. Since you've farmed on your own before, I'd like to hire you to work on my farm through the summer. We've got a one-room house on the other side of the barnyard. It ain't much, but you're welcome to live there. My wife would cook for ya."

The man's invitation sank in, making his mind whirl. Maybe this was his answer. If he worked on this man's farm, he could accept Meadow Creek's offer. When the work was finished at this job, he could probably find another one. He could ask around and stay employed easy enough. But deep down, hopes for a future with Karen still flickered. Saying "yes" to Esther's father seemed so final.

Everyone paused their work and watched him, waiting for his response. His tongue stiffened. Words wouldn't come. He coughed. "Thank you, sir. I appreciate your offer. I'm not sure what to say."

The man smiled. "No problem. You think it over and let me know."

Logan watched him walk away, his world spinning. The bank had been closed Saturday and Sunday. He'd needed to keep his promise to help the men this morning. This meant he'd had no chance to meet with Evan yet. As soon as he could, he'd make a trip to the bank and discover the amount of money he still owed. It might not look as bad as he'd thought. Evan might cooperate enough to help him make a decision.

When he returned to Silver Grove later that afternoon, Logan slipped into the bank and asked to speak to Evan. The surly man met him in the lobby.

"What can I do for you?" he asked. His voice reflected no intent of doing anything for Logan.

Logan gulped in some air. "Your father informed me I still owe you money. I'd like to know how much."

"Five hundred dollars."

Logan's eyes widened. "F...five...hundred dollars?" He'd grow gray preaching in Meadow Creek before he'd see that much money.

"That's right." Evan crossed his arms over his chest.

It was clear this man had no desire to help Logan create a plan. He was on his own. He reached to offer Evan a handshake and left the bank, his emotions swirling every which way. The guy sure knew how to ruin his life. It probably wasn't fair to blame Evan for his troubles. His own attempts to clear his name had failed. But the situation made his blood boil. Why was he the one expected to give up his plans? Tillie could go ahead and make her plans to get married. Mama continued to prepare to move to town. But Logan had to surrender his wishes for everything he wanted. The whole turn of events was so unfair.

At least he had the church construction in Meadow Creek to keep him occupied. Without any cows to milk, his days weren't nearly as full as they were before the sale. He didn't even need to plant the crop. Vern or one of his sons worked in the field. Logan welcomed the project underway in Meadow Creek. The time spent with the men while they assembled the walls, nailed on siding, and shingled the roof helped him deal with his new struggles. As the days passed, determination formed a shell over his heart. He'd accept what had come into his life. Meadow Creek could plan on him. He'd tell Esther's father the next time he saw him. If he could convince himself to get used to the thought of living his life without Karen in it, he might stand a chance at surviving.

MAY BROUGHT thoughtful invitations from the families of Karen's students for her to share meals with them before the school year ended. The controversies related to the fire had settled down, for which Karen was thankful. Relationships had been restored. Conversations around the supper table centered on Karen's plans for the summer.

She told them of her return to the city and tried to conceal as much of the uncertainty about her engagement as she possibly could. Her plan to send her salary to Logan had to work. No reason existed to get her friends and neighbors upset about a broken engagement. They had all attended Logan's sale and bought items from him. The deficit left behind affected everyone. She wouldn't add to their concern by sharing the details of how it changed her life too. Her time in Silver Grove should end on a positive note instead of adding to their worries.

The meal with Mr. Hinkley and his family brought the questions about the new school to the surface. A subject none of the other parents brought up with her, the school occupied Mr. Hinkley's mind. He wanted it on the land Logan had owned. That spot offered the community a good location on ground that didn't belong to the bank. Those plans were no longer possible, and he must be the one to create a new strategy. If only Karen could help him somehow. But the problem of where to build a new school and how to fund it posed too large of a challenge. She could do nothing.

Of course, the Kent relatives gave no invitation for the teacher to come to supper. She'd seen nothing of them since the evening when Evan and the rest of his family walked out of the meeting. Karen had been on alert for some sort of revenge, but surely Evan knew that a teacher backed by two preachers and a school board was someone he should leave alone.

The day of eighth grade graduation arrived with no Kents in attendance. Joe had dropped out of school. He'd stayed home to work on his father's farm just as Mr. Carter had predicted. Karen held the ceremony anyway. In honor of Wade Patterson and Cal Jones, she invited all the families to witness Mr. Hinkley present the diplomas and make a speech.

"I've decided to go on to high school in Bridgewater Springs," Cal said to Karen at the reception following the ceremony.

Karen clasped her hands in front of her. "That's wonderful! I'm so happy for you."

Cal's attention settled on Logan standing nearby. "I want to become a preacher like you. When you drove Miss Millerson to our house to tutor Lacy, you spent time with me, answering my questions about faith. I want to know the Bible like you do and maybe someday help others learn it too."

Logan smiled. It was the first one Karen had seen since the

evening Mr. Kent delivered his terrible news. "I'm proud of you, Cal."

The boy beamed and went in search of his parents.

"You were hoping he'd go to high school." Logan turned to look at her.

"I'm glad. He has so much potential." She'd discussed her hopes for each of her students with him over the past weeks. He still came to call on her at the Bettens' as if nothing had changed between them. Maybe, like herself, Logan clung to the hope that somehow they might overcome his struggles and move into the future together. She did still wear his ring after all, and Logan hadn't ever asked for it back. Karen gleaned what encouragement she could from his silence on the matter, and wore the ring as if to show the world their love would prove to be stronger than bad news or disappointments. This had become the theme of her prayers. If the Lord wanted them together, He would find a way.

After the guests left, only Sandy, Tillie, Pete, and Anna stayed. They gathered with Karen and Logan at the snack table. Sandy smiled at Karen. "Eighth grade graduation is over. Tomorrow is the last day of school. Before long, you'll have nothing to think about except wedding preparations."

Karen should share in Sandy's happiness, but her stomach twisted and her mouth went dry.

"There won't be any summer wedding, Mama. Maybe no wedding at all." Sorrow weighted Logan's voice.

Sandy's eyes grew round. "What do you mean? Surely you and Karen didn't have a disagreement."

"No." Logan paced away from the group. "I'm not sure I can marry her now that I must keep making payments to Evan. I need to stay here and find work. I won't be able to save enough to support a wife."

"You are going to take that haying job?" Sandy asked. Karen

first found out about Logan's job offer from Amelia Harper one afternoon at church.

"I'm thinking about it." Logan kept his gaze lowered and didn't look his mother in the eye.

"What is Karen going to do?" Sandy's voice held bewilderment. Logan's speech had clearly flustered her.

Logan sighed, deep and sad. "Karen is returning to Chicago to accept another teaching position. I'll be staying here and working in Meadow Creek."

"Oh, Logan." Tillie reached out and touched his arm.

He allowed the gesture but appeared to receive little comfort from it.

Sandy's attention settled on Karen for a moment before embracing her. "I'm so sorry. We love you, dear. You will always have a place in our family, even if it isn't as Logan's wife."

The tears welled in Karen's eyes. Sandy had named her heartache perfectly. She wanted to stay as a member of their family, but she wanted it as a result of marriage to Logan.

Tillie offered a hug, too, as her own tears fell. "We'll always be sisters."

The memory of both families gathered at Sandy's dining room table, sharing a meal and making plans for the style show, seared her mind. Tillie and Julia had become friends. They would both lose if Karen and Logan couldn't find a way to stay together.

Logan cleared his throat as Pete slapped his back. Anna murmured quietly to Logan and then held Karen in her embrace. The gentle touch of her good friend melted Karen's resolve. She leaned her head on Anna's shoulder and wept for precious dreams that were slipping away.

CHAPTER THIRTY

The morning of Tillie's wedding dawned warm and sunny. Logan put on his suit and went to knock on Tillie's door. Mama's muffled "come in" invited him into the room. Tillie stood before the mirror, a ray of sunshine glowing across her face as she turned to model her white gown. This kid sister he'd reacquainted himself with a year ago had grown so much. She'd worked through her grief, welcomed Karen into her life, and now stood ready to become Andrew's wife. The light on her face assured Logan the bitterness had disappeared. In its place, joy and a deeper measure of love abided. Victory belonged to her after fighting and struggling for so long.

He crossed the room and kissed her forehead. "You look beautiful. I'm so proud of you."

Her eyes watered. "Thank you, Logan. I'm so happy."

He smiled with big-brother admiration.

She leaned into him and wrapped her arms around his waist. "I love you. I'm so glad you came home last summer. I needed you."

"I'm glad I've been home too. I wouldn't have traded this

time with you and Mama for anything." His eyes felt a little misty.

Tillie reached to include Mama in their hug.

"I'm proud of you, too, dear. You and Andrew will do well together. It makes a mother thankful." Mama kissed Tillie's cheek.

"I just wish the farm sale had turned out differently for Logan. It seems unfair for me to be so happy while he and Karen must change their plans." Tillie pulled back and glanced at him with worry in her eyes.

Her words were an exact reflection of his feelings. But he must help her stay focused on the day ahead. "Don't let my misfortunes interfere with your special day. You've waited and prepared for a long time, and I don't want any part of your wedding ruined because of me." Logan graced her with a serious look.

Tillie nodded, but sadness still hung at the corners of her eyes.

Mama led the way downstairs to the breakfast table where Logan prayed a special prayer of blessing for Tillie's new marriage. When the meal was finished, they left for the church.

Karen was already there. She and Anna arranged flowers and watched for wedding guests. The blue dress she'd worn at the style show served as her bridesmaid dress. It looked every bit as beautiful on her this morning as it did the first time she wore it. Her hair was pinned up in loose curls. She smiled with her red lips as she moved about helping Anna.

Logan turned away before he rushed over to her, took her in his arms, and told her to forget the whole nonsense of his staying in Meadow Creek. He wanted to love her and cherish her. He'd never stopped. In fact, the job offer he'd received only intensified his feelings. What a mystery. He should rejoice and find peace because he had a plan. But that plan couldn't include her.

He paced the church yard. Shoving his hands in his pockets, he kept watch for Pete.

People began to arrive. Logan greeted them as they entered the church building. Music from the pump organ told him he'd better go inside and prepare to walk Tillie down the aisle.

The sanctuary filled while Mama arranged Tillie's veil. Andrew came to escort Mama to her seat. Anna handed Tillie her bouquet.

"Ready?" Logan whispered.

Tillie nodded while a nervous expression claimed her features.

Logan stepped out as everyone stood. He'd probably attended more weddings than anyone else in the room, except for Pete. The order of a wedding ceremony remained etched in his memory. He knew what Tillie should do, what she should say, and where she should stand. He guided her to the front.

Pete asked, "Who gives this woman to be married to this man?"

Logan knew the words that should get said in answer to that question, but they lodged in his throat. He coughed and his tongue went stiff. "Her...her...m...mother and I." Good grief. The only words he had to say all day, and he couldn't even spit them out. He hugged Tillie and took his place at Pete's side as a groomsman.

They'd talked as a family about Logan performing the ceremony. That would have required him to give his sister away and function as the preacher. Tillie had teased him that she got enough of his preaching already, so asked Pete instead.

Given the state of his heart today, Logan was just fine with the plan. He would've stuttered all the way through, making a disaster of Tillie's special day. All he had to do now was stand in silence. Sounded easy, but his heart made good use of the time to feel its losses, as if it had been saving up and waiting for this precise moment to torture him. It started with Karen. He did everything in his power not to look at her. If he avoided a glimpse, he wouldn't think about how beautiful she was or how he may never have the pleasure of standing with her at his own wedding.

He moved on to thinking about the loss of his Oswell City ministry. He'd written to Paul with a resignation of sorts but had heard nothing. Either they were rejoicing that he'd finally found something else to do or sad because his decision left them without any pastor. Logan was a man with no farm, no career, no money, and no wife and family of his own. He had nothing really. If he could run and hide so he might pray or bury himself in study, his heart might find something else to entertain it besides the memories of all he'd given up.

Pete prayed, snapping Logan back to the ceremony. Karen stepped forward to sing. The melody belonged to a love song that struck just the right chords to make Logan's tender heart cry even more. Karen had better finish soon, or he really would run away, a blubbering, confused mess.

The song ended, and Logan sucked in a deep breath. Pete guided Andrew and Tillie through their vows and the exchange of rings before he gave a brief message. Andrew kissed Tillie. Pete introduced the new Mr. and Mrs. Andrew Carter. Everyone clapped. Lucy played the wedding march while Andrew and Tillie walked the aisle.

His turn was next. Karen approached and gazed up at him as though she thought he looked pretty nice too. Here he was, escorting Karen down the aisle after a wedding. If he didn't need to let her go, this would be one of the happiest moments of his life. He reached for her hand and held it to the end of their walk to let her know of the grief filling his heart.

She glanced up at him with tears on her cheeks. She felt it too.

They stood together in the back of the sanctuary in a line with Andrew and Tillie, Mama, and the Carters. People filed by offering well wishes and congratulations for the newlyweds. Occasionally, someone commented to Logan on the news Mr. Kent had delivered last Friday. Questions followed. "What are you going to do?" they asked.

He didn't know. What he should do and what his heart wanted led in two very different directions. Karen stood at his side listening to the questions and wearing an expression of sympathy when he hesitated in answering. Life shouldn't include such complications. He had as much of a right as anyone to pursue the career of his choice and the woman of his dreams. If he didn't love her so much, he'd do it. But Karen had a career and dreams of her own. She needed the freedom to grow and serve unhindered by the problem forced upon him. He turned his attention to Tillie's guests the best he could and worked hard to make her day special.

AT THE FARM, Karen rushed to slip on an apron so she might assist Sandy, Anna, and Sally in dishing up food. The large, mid-day meal would get served on the lawn where tables and chairs were set up for guests. Ham, baked potatoes, beans, and rolls completed the menu. The wedding cake sat on a table in a corner of the dining room. Stacks of plates, cups, and silverware filled the kitchen table.

Celebration charged the air, but it failed to penetrate her heart. This should be one of the happiest days of her stay in Silver Grove. How she'd love to abandon herself to the joy of the marriage of her friend. But sadness shadowed every minute. Karen worked with all that was in her to stay positive and helpful.

"I'll tell Logan to direct everyone to form a line on the porch after he prays. They can come in here for table service and then go to the dining room for food. We'll cut the cake after dinner."

Sandy pointed as she spoke.

"Mrs. Betten and I will supply the food table," Sally said. "You should go outside and enjoy yourself, Sandy. Miss Miller-son, don't forget to sit with the wedding party at the designated table."

Karen nodded. The instruction meant more time spent in Logan's company. She welcomed every last minute of his atten-tion before she left on the afternoon train for Chicago, but she also dreaded eating with him. They had so much to say to each other and yet nothing to say. Logan must make new plans now. She must make hers. A new teaching position might fill her time as she grew familiar with it, but it would never fill her heart. A permanent ache had taken up residence there. She might as well get used to it. Without Logan in her life and the promise of sharing both his home and his ministry, pain was now her daily companion.

Once the food was set out, Karen took off her apron and went to the seat reserved for her. Logan gathered the group and quieted them so he could pray. He asked for the Lord's blessing on their food and their time together. He went on to ask for strength, love, and faith for Tillie and her new husband. His prayer spoke to her heart. Karen needed those things, too, if she expected to survive a life without him in it.

He gave directions to start the meal before claiming the seat next to her at the wedding party table. Andrew and Tillie and their parents went through line first, but Logan waited for the guests to get their food before he went through the line. Karen did the same, content to stay seated with him even though she could think of nothing to talk about.

He broke the silence. "Nice solo."

"Thanks." If he only knew she'd sung that song to him, not to the wedding couple.

"You must have practiced a long time to get it ready."

"Not really, I'd learned it from my voice teacher. Mother mailed me the music so I'd have it in time for the wedding."

A river's depth of silence flowed between them. Sunlight illumined the white tablecloths and Tillie's dress. A wide and cloudless sky stretched to the faraway horizon. Gentle breezes swayed the tree branches where glossy leaves began the season's growth. A gorgeous day. One Karen should revel in and store away as a lovely memory. She may have succeeded if Logan hadn't spoken again.

"Are you packed?" He stared straight ahead at the guests lining the food table.

"Yes." Her heart broke a little more, if that was even possible.

"Your train leaves in two hours."

"I know." Karen twisted the ring around on her finger. Who were they trying to fool? Logan must stay. She must go. The stark facts were that simple. The time had come to release her hold on dreams that would never come true.

She pulled the ring off her finger and set it on the table in front of him.

Logan frowned. "What did you do that for?"

"Come on, Logan. You've said it yourself that years might pass before you've paid Evan. We've always believed that the Lord wanted us together and would find a way for that to happen. But He hasn't. I guess the unexpected changes in your life are His way of letting us know marriage wasn't His plan for us." The tears stayed safely under her lids until Logan looked at her, his gaze full of love and pain.

He reached out and wiped a tear from her cheek. She could have done the same for him when a bead of moisture escaped his eye.

She swallowed. "Let's get in line before your mother hunts us down."

A smile pulled at the corner of his mouth but failed to get any farther across his face. Ever the gentleman, Logan stood and pulled her chair out from the table for her to precede him.

"Who are those people?" She pointed to a group she'd never seen before seated around a table.

"Those are Mama's relatives, my aunts and uncles, from Bridgewater Springs. I must remember to say 'hello' to them when I've finished eating."

Karen studied the group, searching for family resemblance. One of the women favored Sandy. Perhaps she was a sister. None of them looked like Logan. He must favor his father in looks. John De Witt must have been handsome as a young man. Karen's gaze landed on Sandy as she came over to the group at the table and chatted with them. What had life been like for her, marrying the young farmer, leaving her home in Bridgewater Springs, and moving out here to help him get started? She'd lost him at about the same age as Karen's own mother lost her husband.

A release from the engagement was best. Karen could make her own life independent of anyone else's wishes. No grief would ever darken her heart again. Separation wouldn't matter. She'd just be Karen out in the world, teaching and changing lives, for as long as she wanted, and wherever she wished.

But Logan would still be in the world somewhere, too, owning her heart and missing her.

She stifled a groan and attempted to eat the food she'd brought back with her. The ham had no taste, but she chewed it anyway. With a long train ride ahead of her, she would need the sustenance a full meal offered. She stole a glimpse at Logan. The food on his plate hadn't even made its way to his mouth. He pushed it around as though unaware of anything except whatever occupied his mind. Karen could guess at his thoughts. They were probably much like hers. She wanted to ask him about them but couldn't conjure up the right words.

Bill, the postman, approached their table. "Congratulations on your sister's wedding."

"Thanks," Logan said.

"I'm real sorry to hear about the outcome of your sale. It was a good sale with quality items. Too bad it didn't bring in enough to cover your loans."

Logan nodded.

Bill held out an envelope. "I'm not in the habit of delivering mail at a wedding when I'm an invited guest, but this came through with 'priority mail' stamped on it. I figured it must be mighty important, so brought it along."

Logan accepted the envelope and stuffed it in his pocket when Bill walked away. He looked over at her with a solemn gaze. "It's time."

Karen's stomach plummeted. The moment she dreaded had arrived.

"Pete agreed to drive you." Logan stood and collected both of their plates.

There would be no time for cake. But Karen didn't care. She couldn't manufacture the frame of mind to enjoy it anyway.

She went in the house for one last look at the room she'd used while living with Logan and his family. She should've squeezed more enjoyment out of those days. They'd go down as fond memories of the only time she'd share a home with him. When she descended the stairs, she discovered Logan in the kitchen with his hands in his pockets and his friend Pete nearby.

"Good-bye, sweetheart." He gathered her in an embrace.

The last time they'd said "good-bye" to each other had been the week before Christmas when Logan went to Oswell City for a friend's wedding. He'd been the one leaving, but today he was the one staying behind while she left on a journey that promised no return.

"I still love you." The whispered words brought tears to her eyes.

He deserved to hear her assurance of love for him, but it caught in her throat. She could do nothing but step outside where

Anna, Sandy, and Tillie were gathered at the gate. They took turns giving her hugs.

"We love you, dear. Don't ever forget that." Sandy held her close for a longer moment than Anna and Tillie had.

Karen would never forget. Sandy had become a mother to her. Those sorts of relationships stayed with a person. Sandy's encouragement, her tutelage in the kitchen, and her hopes for Karen's presence in her son's life had shaped Karen in a way that didn't allow her to go back to what she had been before.

The sight of the bride gathered with friends around a waiting horse and buggy drew the guests' attention. Neighbors, towns-people, and families of Karen's students clustered around, all of them waving and wishing her the best as she climbed up next to Pete.

He tapped the horse with the reins, and they were off down the farm lane. How nice if she might catch one more glimpse of Logan. But she didn't dare turn around and search the lawn for him. If she found him, she just might leap out of the buggy and run back into his arms.

After a quick stop at the parsonage to gather her trunks and crates of books and to make a quick change into her traveling suit, Pete delivered her to the depot. He made arrangements for her belongings to travel while she moved through the building and on to the platform. Other people milled about in their wait for the train's arrival.

Pete caught up to her. "Everything is loaded."

"Thank you."

He rubbed his forehead. "I'm so sorry things didn't work out between you and Logan. I'd hoped this time he'd found the kind of relationship Anna and I share."

"He did." Karen rested her hand on Pete's arm to assure him his efforts on Logan's behalf had not been in vain.

"Then I share his grief. He's giving up much to let you go."

"You and Anna have been so kind. Thank you for letting me live with you this spring." Karen stepped into Pete's embrace.

"Best wishes, Karen. May God bless you in your return to the city." Pete stepped away and after a squeeze of her shoulder, left her alone on the platform.

Tears on her cheeks once more, Karen turned to the rails. The train would arrive soon. She'd be ready. Ready to leave behind her life and all she'd loved for the past year. Her Chicago family waited for her. She must think about them now and prepare for life in the city. It would be a life lived alone, even if it did include sharing a large, comfortable home with Mother, Aunt Fran, and Uncle Henry. Squaring her shoulders and raising her chin, Karen made up her mind to meet whatever tomorrow held for her.

CHAPTER THIRTY-ONE

*L*ogan greeted his friend and helped him care for the horse after the trip to town. Karen was really gone. He took the ring from his pocket and stared at it. The single life was his once more. Maybe he should sell the ring and apply the money to his bank account. He certainly would not need an engagement ring anymore. No other woman could ever take Karen's place. If he couldn't share his life with her, then he would share his life with no one. Apostle Paul knew what he was talking about to advise the single life. But the long, dark years stretching before him proved to be more than he could stomach at the moment.

He sneaked past the group watching Andrew and Tillie cut their cake and found refuge in his room. With the door closed on the merrymaking going on down below, Logan pulled the envelope from Bill out of his pocket. Paul's address was written in the corner. He might as well see what the postman declared so important as to bring it along to the wedding.

Dear Logan,

We're sorry to receive your resignation and honestly, we're having a hard time accepting it. Can we offer you anything in the hopes of changing your mind?

The church has acquired a piece of property, donated by a relative of one of our members. We feel you are the best one to lead us in how to use it. I have some ideas which I've shared with the board, but we were waiting on your return before moving forward.

As your friend and as the chairman of the board, I'm asking you to please reconsider.

Hope to see you soon,
Paul

Logan tossed the letter aside. He'd be there today if the choice was up to him. He left his chair and punched his pillow. If only he was free to tell Paul to plan on him. Logan pulled his Bible out and read for a while, but the words might as well have been written in another language for as much as his mind comprehended them. Driven by the ache in his chest, Logan kneeled at the side of his bed and poured his heart out to the Lord.

He reminded God that he'd made a promise to Karen. In that promise, he intended to commit himself to her. He already had in so many ways. In every way really, except the ultimate union exclusively granted in marriage. He told the Lord he wanted that too. Karen did as well. Rubbing his eyes, Logan reached into his pocket and pulled out the ring. It glittered in the afternoon sunlight as he turned it and enjoyed the array of colors glinting off the diamond.

This engagement ring he'd bought for Karen and planned to meld to a wedding band was a symbol of covenant. God's covenant with Logan as his Father and sovereign provider. Logan's covenant with Karen to be her husband. They'd believed the Lord wanted them together through their faithfulness to each other, as instructed in His design for lasting love.

282

"God, Karen and I believed You would provide a way for us to be together. We've done everything we can to honor You and follow You. But now I must let her go." He didn't know if he should ask the Lord to help him do it or if he should plead for a divine turn of events. Sacrifice had become a familiar companion on his journey. He'd sacrificed his career to stay here with Mama and Tillie. He'd sacrificed his savings to provide for them. He'd even sacrificed the comforts of his upstairs room to preserve Karen's reputation. But this new assignment of releasing his hold on their relationship and completely surrendering Karen tore his heart out.

He reached for the Bible on the edge of his desk and laid it on the bed in front of him. The story of Abraham in Genesis 22 should have something to say to his situation.

The house grew quiet before he finished reading and praying. God had asked Abraham to sacrifice his son, the one God had promised him, the person he loved dearly. It sounded a lot like the quandary surrounding Logan. But what had Abraham done? He followed God's directions. He took his son to the place of worship and did as God instructed. Boy, Abraham must have felt like he'd laid his own self up on that altar, knowing he'd get sliced in pieces and burned. Logan could think of nothing that would cause a man more pain. Watching Karen walk out of the house earlier that afternoon was the hardest thing he'd ever done. He could relate to Abraham's distress. Logan rubbed his eyes before he continued reading. Abraham had assured his son that God would provide.

God would provide. Did that mean he'd provide a way for Karen to stay in Logan's life, or did that mean God would provide Logan with the strength and comfort he needed to endure the loss? The Bible didn't say. It only told Logan that Abraham continued to prepare his son for sacrifice. The patriarch of the Old Testament completed every task required for a proper offering to the Lord.

Logan's heart resisted the message, but he kept reading. Just in the nick of time, an angel called out to Abraham and told him to halt the sacrifice. God had made other arrangements by providing Abraham with a ram caught in the bushes. Abraham had passed the test of faith, so God allowed him to keep his son.

Logan straightened. Was this left-over deficit and the changes it forced upon him a test? Maybe. If it really was, then he wanted to pass it in a way that pleased the Lord. God may not provide him with a rescue like what happened with Abraham's son, but he would help Logan find the strength and the character he needed to face the days ahead. A strange and quiet peace settled over his heart. Everything would work out. Somehow, he knew God could see the end of this whole agonizing situation. This assurance infused it with meaning.

He stood and rubbed his hand over his face. He should go outside and visit with his Bridgewater Springs family before they left, if they weren't already gone. After dropping the ring on the dresser where it continued to glitter in the afternoon sun, he ran a comb through his hair, blew his nose, and went outside.

Mama's sister waved him over to her table. He joined the group of aunts, uncles, and cousins and managed to carry his end of a conversation about the happenings in Bridgewater Springs. The topic of interest turned to questions about him in their attempt to catch up on what he'd been doing since the last time they'd seen him. More time had passed than he thought. Answers to their questions included filling them in on his move to Oswell City nearly three years ago as a young preacher ready to serve his first church.

He'd just finished informing them of the mayor's plea for his return when Tom Hinkley called out to him. "Hey, Logan!"

Three strangers stood with Tom and Vern near the tree, each one dressed in dark suits, coats, and hats. Spectacles sat on the nose of one of the men. Another carried a dark case. They impressed Logan with their air of authority and expertise.

He nodded to his relatives and approached Tom. "What's going on?"

"These men have come to the farm looking for you." Tom gestured to the formal group.

"Tracking you down has been quite the challenge," the man with spectacles said.

"We'd hoped to find you in town, or at least find someone who could tell us where to locate you, but the businesses are closed today. Now we see why. Everyone is here." The man carrying the case glanced at the guests gathered on the lawn enjoying wedding cake.

"We ventured into the country in search of you, but no one was home at the church or any other farms along the way." The man with spectacles spoke up again.

Logan hid a grin. The marriage between his sister and Andrew Carter had been looked to as one of the biggest events of the year. To strangers traveling through, it would seem as though the world had shut down in order to celebrate the event.

The tallest man and the recognized leader of the group cleared his throat. "Please allow us to introduce ourselves. I am Mr. Wettig, a lawyer from Bridgewater Springs. This is Mr. Doan, a detective, and this is Mr. Hanks, a bank examiner. We paid a visit to the Silver Grove State Bank to verify our records. Evan Kent was turned in by one of his tellers for stealing. Our visit to the bank confirmed his stealing from several bank customers. One of those customers was you. He'd stolen five hundred dollars from your account. We found it in his account. Lucky for you he hadn't spent it yet. Evan is in jail awaiting trial and your money is safely on deposit. We took a look at the bank's records. Your debt has been paid with one hundred and fifty dollars left in profit. Congratulations, Mr. De Witt."

Mama may have missed her calling as a preacher, Eldon may have discovered the path to eternity, and Mr. Kent might know how to broadcast news that wrecked a guy's life, but this new piece of information outdid them all. Logan's brain threatened to burst beyond the confines of his skull. "What...what did you say?"

Tom slapped his back. "You're all paid up. That's what he said."

His tongue stiffened, but he tried his best to make it work anyway. "You mean, I...I...I'm free? No more debt?"

Mr. Wettig shook his head. "No more."

His brain took its time absorbing this marvelous news. He should laugh and shout and tell the world, but all he could do was stand there rubbing his forehead. "Tom, could you find my mother, please?"

Tom left and soon returned with Mama following him. She gazed into his face with a furrowed brow. "Aren't you feeling well? You didn't eat any cake." Her attention shifted to the visitors standing in her yard. "Who are these men? What are they doing here?"

Logan looked at Mr. Wettig. "Tell her what you told me."

The lawyer repeated his introductions and his explanation while Mama's eyes grew round and her mouth fell open. "Oh," came out as her only reply.

"Do you know what this means?" Logan asked her, his wits returning enough to begin comprehending this turn of events.

Mama clutched his arm as if to steady herself. "Tom can rebuild the school. Now you have the money for it you promised him."

Always concerned about others more than her own affairs, Mama would think of how this news affected Tom and the entire community. Logan slid his arm around her waist to assure her he shared her relief over a matter that could finally reach a resolution.

"I'd be happy to donate a corner of the pasture out there by the road," Vern said.

Logan's attention faded as his question penetrated his brain.

Did he know what this news from these visitors really meant? He could return to Oswell City. No longer would he need to adapt to an alternative plan. Meadow Creek's congregation and Esther's father had not yet received any definite answer from him. This meant as soon as he told them of his decision, he was free to go.

It also meant he could get married. His heart pounded deep within his chest. God had provided for him. These formal men with their astonishing announcement was his ram caught in the bushes, a voice calling out to him to halt the sacrifice underway. Karen was his. The future belonged to them. He'd passed the test of faith.

Tom's handshake with Vern brought his focus back to the conversation floating around him. "Let's get started as soon as possible. I wish Miss Millerson was here to hear this. Wouldn't she love to know the school finally has a place of its own?"

Energy surged in his legs. He needed to find Karen. Surely he could still catch her, if the train hadn't already come and gone, carrying her away from him.

Mama turned to him with a wild and excited look in her eyes. "Find Karen. Tell her all of this. Don't let her get away."

He grasped her hands. "I will. I'll go now. Stay right here." His feet got ahead of him in his mission to retrieve Karen from her journey, but he managed to pat Mama's hand in a display of comfort before taking off on a run.

She nodded as a smile broke out on her face.

His stride ate up the lawn, the porch, and the stairs as he sprinted to his room for the ring. After one quick glance at its sparkle, he dropped it in his pocket and flew to the barn. Cinching a saddle onto his horse, Logan shot down the lane. The party on the lawn swirled into a blur as he raced for town.

Another person who needed to hear of his freedom was Paul. What the poor man must have gone through receiving his friend's resignation and trying to figure out how to keep the congregation calm and moving forward. He should write Paul a letter this very day and tell him to plan on Logan returning as soon as possible. Better yet, he should make a phone call to George Brinks at the hotel in Oswell City and commission him to deliver an urgent message to the mayor. By this time next week, he'd be settled in. The breeze slapped his cheeks and invigorated his lungs as he breathed deeply, reveling in his restored world.

A cluster of folks standing on the sidewalk outside the bank caught his attention. Since most of Silver Grove's population gathered at the De Witts', no one else occupied the main street. He recognized the faces of Mr. Kent, Vera, Elsie, and Bert as he traveled closer.

Mr. Kent leaped into the street and waved. "Hey, Logan. Stop!"

Stopping was the last thing he wanted to do at the moment. The woman of his dreams may have left town by now. Adding minutes to his trip was a terrible idea.

But Mr. Kent remained in the street. Logan must either stop or run the man over. One Kent had already died. Another sat in jail. The father of the family should probably be spared from danger. Logan slowed his horse.

"We need to talk to you." Mr. Kent glanced up at him.

Logan came to a stop. "What's wrong?"

"Did you hear about Evan?"

"I did. The bank examiner along with a lawyer and a detective are at the farm right now." A piercing whistle announced the arrival of the afternoon train. Logan's stomach tightened. The arrival of the train meant Karen was still in town, but it also told him he didn't have much time before it departed. He cast a nervous glance at the locomotive making its slow chug into the station behind the hotel.

Mr. Kent stroked the horse's nose while he talked as if a leisurely afternoon chat topped everyone's list for entertainment. "If Evan is convicted, everything will change. We'll lose the bank. Vera is headed for hard times. We want to become believers like Eldon did. Could you help us? We're ready." Mr. Kent looked up at Logan once more.

Logan licked his lips. "I'd be honored, Mr. Kent. This is a big decision and I'm happy for you and the others in your family who are willing to change. I'm in a hurry right now, but I'd love for you to stop at the farm sometime this week so we can talk."

Mr. Kent gave a somber nod. "We'll do that. Could we come to church Sunday? Would we be welcome?"

"Of course you would. We'd love to have you." The hiss of steam from a parked locomotive reached his ears.

"See you Sunday." Mr. Kent nodded.

"Now if you will excuse me, I need to prevent a young lady from catching her train." Logan dug his heels into the sides of his horse and galloped down the street. In his mind, he imagined Karen taking a seat on a coach. He might be too late.

At the depot, he tossed his reins to an attendant and sprinted inside.

"Karen!" He scanned the interior in search of her. People crowded around, gathering bags and buying tickets.

He raced outside and called her name again. People milled around on the platform, hugging family members and searching for their coach. The congestion near one of the train cars cleared, revealing a petite blonde, wearing a dark green traveling suit and matching hat, in line at the door, her back to him. He ran to her. "Karen. Sweetheart."

His breathing became labored as if he'd run all the way to town.

She turned around. "Logan?"

He tugged on her arm, pulling her out of the line.

"What are you doing here?" She frowned in confusion.

So many words begged for expression. He hardly knew where to start. The most important thing she needed to hear from him he could say without using any words. He gathered her in his embrace and covered her mouth with his own. She melted against him for a moment before he pulled away and slid the ring back on her finger.

"What's going on?" She looked from the ring to his face.

"Evan is a crook. He stole five hundred dollars from my sale. A bank examiner, a detective, and an attorney are at the farm right now. I've paid the bank and have one hundred and fifty dollars to spare. I'll give some to Mama and some to the school board." The speech stole his breath. He heaved in more air.

"Oh, Logan!" Karen covered her mouth. "Does this mean you don't have to stay in Meadow Creek and farm?"

"That's exactly what it means. I'm headed back to Oswell City next week." A grin pulled at his mouth. "And I want you there with me."

"I'd love nothing more, but now I've committed to this teaching job." Karen's brow wrinkled.

"Keep it and live with your Uncle Henry as you planned. But save your money for us and our new marriage instead of giving it away to the bank." Logan winked.

A smile split Karen's face, but she quickly sobered. "What about the wedding date? We can't schedule it for July if I'm teaching."

"When will your term end?"

"December."

"Let's have a winter wedding instead."

Karen pondered his suggestion for a moment. Another smile lit her face. "That's a long time to wait, but the days will pass quickly. What matters is the Lord made a way for us to be together."

Logan reached for her hands and rubbed his thumb over the ring that now rested forever on Karen's finger. "Yes, He did, and nothing will come between us ever again."

Karen's eyes shone.

"Let's go back to the farm. Tom wants to tell you all about

his plans for the new school, and Mama and Tillie will be beside themselves to have you back again." Logan wrapped an arm around her.

"Could we send a telegram to Mother later today? My luggage will arrive in the city without me, and I will miss the anniversary dinner." Karen studied his face.

"Of course we can. Are you sure your mother won't mind if you are absent from the celebration?" No way did he want to let Karen go, but neither did he want to lose the approval he'd finally gained from her mother.

Karen shrugged. "Oh, she'll mind. But when she hears my explanation, she'll understand."

A grin pulled at his mouth as he reached for her hand.

"Pete and Anna will be so happy for us." Karen laughed as Logan led her from the platform.

"Remember our hopes for Vera and Elsie to have a change of heart?" Logan asked as he helped her into the saddle.

"I do."

"It's happening. Mr. Kent and the rest of the family are coming to church on Sunday." Logan swung up into the saddle behind her.

"That's wonderful. Even though I doubted they would really care, I'm so glad they are willing to take that step of faith." She leaned into him as he guided the horse down the street and out of town.

Tillie had all the young ladies lined up for a bouquet toss when Logan came up the lane. Cheers rose when everyone noticed Karen in the saddle with him. He jumped down and helped her to the ground.

Tillie came running. "Karen! I've heard all about Logan's recovered funds. I am so glad you are home again."

"For a day or two. I still plan to return to the city and teach." She returned Tillie's hug.

"The engagement is still on. Karen is going to teach in the

city until Christmas. We'll get married after the first of the year," Logan announced to the group in a loud voice.

Everyone clapped while Mama approached and took a turn smothering Karen in a hug.

Logan stepped back and turned to shake hands with Tom. "I'd still like to contribute to the rebuilding of the school."

"We'd be honored. Thanks, Logan."

"Why are Mr. Wettig and his colleagues still here?" Logan jerked his head in the direction of the men standing in the shade.

"Sandy invited them to stay and enjoy some cake." Tom waved to Roy and Vern as an invitation for them to join the conversation.

Neighbors and friends gathered around as Tillie returned to her bunch of potential brides. Deep in discussion with the members of the school board making plans for a new building, Logan noticed out of the corner of his eye a flying object, the shape and speed of it reminding him of a comet shooting through outer space. On impulse, he raised his hand to shield his face from a clobbering. The comet lodged in his grasp, and the entire group burst with laughter. Even the stiff trio visiting the farm on bank business cracked smiles.

Tillie's voice split the air. "Look! It's Logan. He caught the bouquet!"

He lowered his hand for a better look. Sure enough, the dependable predictor of future brides rested in his grasp. Well, he knew what to do with that. He handed it off to his beautiful fiancée. Applause rang around him. He joined in celebrating love, faithfulness, and happy endings that led to even better tomorrows.

ABOUT THE AUTHOR

Michelle lives in Iowa with her husband and two teenage sons. She is a graduate of Northwestern College in Orange City, Iowa, with an associate's degree in office management. She is also a graduate of Central College in Pella, Iowa, with a Bachelor's degree in Religion with a Christian Ministry emphasis and Music. Michelle is the spiritual services provider for an organization that offers services for people with physical and mental disabilities. In this role, she offers grief care, teaches Bible studies, leads retreats, and writes devotionals. Michelle is also a worship leader on Sunday mornings directing the choir, playing piano, or singing.

You can learn more about Michelle by visiting her website: MichelleDeBruin.com.

Hope for Tomorrow

When Logan De Witt learns of his father's sudden death, he returns home to the family's dairy farm. During his stay, he discovers his mother's struggle with finances and his younger sister's struggle with grief. Concern for his family presses Logan to make the difficult decision to leave his career as a pastor and stay on the farm. As a way to make some extra money, he agrees to board the teacher for their local school.

Karen Millerson arrives from Chicago ready to teach high school but her position is eliminated so she accepts the role of country school teacher. Eager to put her family's ugly past behind her, Karen begins a new career to replace the trust she lost in her own father who had been in ministry when she was a child.

Logan and Karen both sense a call from the Lord to serve him, but neither of them expected that one day they would do it together.

Can Karen learn to trust again? Will Logan lay aside his grief in exchange for God's purpose for his life?

Dreaming of Tomorrow

Love leads them to a lifetime of commitment where the dreams they have held onto for so long start to come true.

Popular and eligible, Logan De Witt must convince the women in town that he is engaged to be married. A quiet, simple ceremony is what he has in mind for his wedding day, but when the date and time of his bride's arrival is published in the newspaper, the whole town joins in the celebration proving to Logan and his new wife their sincere friendship and support. Added to the excitement of Logan's marriage is the question of what the congregation should do with the unexpected donation of an orchard.

Karen Millerson is counting the days until her long-distance engagement comes to an end and she may travel to Oswell City to marry Logan. More than anything, she wants to share in his life as a help and support, but keeping a house and finding her place in the community requires much more work than she ever expected.

Learn, laugh, and love with Karen and Logan as they start a new marriage and work together ministering to the citizens of their small town.

(Coming November 2020.)

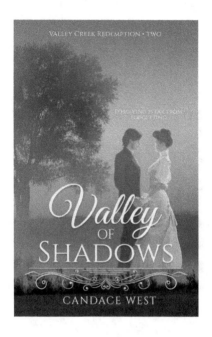

Valley of Shadows by Candace West

Valley Creek Redemption Book Two

A shattered heart.

A wounded spirit.

A community in crisis.

Lorena Steen gave up on love years ago. She forgave her long-time estranged husband, but when circumstances bring her to the Ozark town of Valley Creek, she discovers forgiving is far from forgetting.

Haunted by his past acts of betrayal, Earl Steen struggles to grow his reclaimed faith and reinstate himself as an upstanding member of

Valley Creek. He soon learns that while God's grace is amazing, that of the small-town gossips is not.

When disaster strikes, the only logical solution is for Earl and Lorena to combine their musical talents in an effort to save the community. But even if they're willing to work together, are they able to? Or will the shadows that descend upon Valley Creek reduce it to a ghost town?

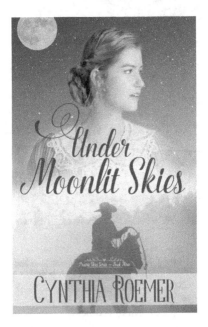

Under Moonlit Skies* by *Cynthia Roemer

Prairie Sky Series – Book Three

She had her life planned out ~ until he rode in

Illinois prairie ~ 1859

After four long years away, Esther Stanton returns to the prairie to care for her sister Charlotte's family following the birth of her second child.

The month-long stay seems much too short as Esther becomes acquainted with her brother-in-law's new ranch hand, Stewart Brant. When obligations compel her to return to Cincinnati and to the man her overbearing mother intends her to wed, she loses hope of ever knowing true happiness.

Still reeling from a hurtful relationship, Stew is reluctant to open his heart to Esther. But when he faces a life-threatening injury with Esther tending him, their bond deepens. Heartbroken when she leaves, he sets out after her and inadvertently stumbles across an illegal slave-trade operation, the knowledge of which puts him, as well as Esther and her family, in jeopardy.

Safe Refuge by Pamela S. Meyers

Newport of the West – Book One

In two days, wealthy Chicagoan, Anna Hartwell, will wed a man she

loathes. She would refuse this arranged marriage to Lyman Millard, but the Bible clearly says she is to honor her parents, and Anna would do most anything to please her father–even leaving her teaching job at a mission school and marrying a man she doesn't love.

The Great Chicago Fire erupts, and Anna and her family escape with only the clothes on their backs and the wedding postponed. Father moves the family to Lake Geneva, Wisconsin, where Anna reconnects with Rory Quinn, a handsome immigrant who worked at the mission school. Realizing she is in love with Rory, Anna prepares to break the marriage arrangement with Lyman until she learns a dark family secret that changes her life forever.

Scrivenings
PRESS
Quench your thirst for story.
www.ScriveningsPress.com

Stay up-to-date on your favorite books and authors with our free e-newsletters.

ScriveningsPress.com